Betony Lodge

Suzanne Rosenthal Shumway

ISBN: 197380395X

ISBN-13: 978-1973803959

A number of people have helped by reading early drafts of this novel, and I want to thank them here: Lizz Kepsel, Betty Rosenthal, Avis Marie Poovey, and Sheila Malleis. Their comments and questions were invaluable as I worked through revision after revision, and I am very grateful to each of them. All errors within the text, however, are my own responsibility.

…Oh! She was changed,
As by the sickness of the soul; her mind
Had wander'd from its dwelling, and her eyes,
They had not their own lustre, but the look
Which is not of the earth; she was become
The queen of a fantastic realm; her thoughts
Were combinations of disjointed things;
And forms impalpable and unperceived
Of others' sight familiar were to hers.
And this the world calls phrenzy; but the wise
Have a far deeper madness, and the glance
Of melancholy is a fearful gift;
What is it but the telescope of truth?
Which strips the distance of its fantasies,
And brings life near in utter nakedness,
Making the cold reality too real!

Lord Byron, "The Dream"

Chapter One

"That is a quiet place –
That house in the trees with the shady lawn."
"—If, child, you knew what there goes on
You would not call it a quiet place.
Why, a phantom abides there, the last of its race,
And a brain spins there till dawn."

"But I see nobody there, --
Nobody moves about the green,
Or wanders the heavy trees between."
"—Ah, that's because you do not bear
The visioning powers of souls who dare
To pierce the material screen."
--Thomas Hardy, "The House of Silence,"

I've decided that I like it here. This place is not perfect by any means, but it's got a charm all its own, and I've grown used to the trees, the plants, the shrubs, as well as the animals that prowl around the grounds. Back in the United States, as a city-dweller, I never saw much wildlife: squirrels and the ever-present pigeons are all I can remember, small animals scurrying off into the bushes as soon as a human approached. But here in Dorset, the foxes and redstarts look at me in a challenging way, with a self-satisfied sneer in their dark eyes. *We belong here,* they seem to say, *but you do not.* They saunter off at a slow, unhurried pace, into the tall brush behind the house, leaving me feeling like an intruder.

But I'm not an intruder. After more than a year in

residence, after all I've been through, it's quite clear to me at least that I belong here, in Betony Lodge.

I've grown into the landscape; I've learned to love its barely contained wilderness. Betony Lodge is not like most places I've lived, areas where the wild, unkempt fields and forests seem a last bastion of nature, a preserve slowly giving way to civilization. Rather, this place reverses the pattern: here, it is not nature that is confined or contained, but human culture and activity that are surrounded by nature. Most people think of England as an ultimately civilized country, with no areas of wilderness left—more than a thousand years of human cultivation should have pushed nature into small alcoves, as the Romans shoved the Celts into the corners of Britannia, leaving them just Scotland and Wales as a consolation prize for their defeat.

Now I know that nothing could be further from the truth. I can see how the opposite is much closer to reality. It's we humans who are pushed into small pockets of civilization, into well-guarded areas of human culture. Towns like Lyme Regis and Dorchester are deceptive, giving the impression that they are waypoints in the vast overflow of humanity that spreads like a puddle of spilled milk away from London and seeps through all the land it encounters. The truth, however, is that these towns are no different from what they have been for a thousand years at least: mere outposts of human activity.

I came to Dorset 16 months ago to study the effect of landscape on the novels of Thomas Hardy. I arrived with a brand-new husband, a grant that paid for my expenses, and a sense of security in my own identity. Now, so many months later, I've risked losing all those things—may indeed have lost some of them irretrievably, as a small child loses the contents of her pockets through an undiscovered hole, leaving a trail of treasures behind her as she walks through the park. Worse still, I'm not sure what bothers me more: the loss of these things or the fact that their absence has less effect on me than I think it should.

Before I arrived here, I had, like many Americans, certain preconceptions of life in England. I thought of it as a place only slightly different from the States, and certainly, if one doesn't stray too far from the major cities—London, Birmingham, and the like—it is remarkably similar. For me, a scholar of English literature, coming here was very much like a waking dream in which I had a strange semi-familiarity with places I had never actually seen in my life. But I felt I had seen them, had visited them, had even lived in them, from all the years of reading, and in the end, that's all that mattered. Living here has left me with a constant feeling of déjà-vu. And I suppose that kind of confusion could take a toll on a person's psyche.

Two years ago, when I first told my husband, then boyfriend, Brian, that I had received a grant to study abroad, he was dubious. "What am I supposed to do," he asked, a petulant pout on his full, red lips, "wait here for you?" But I had anticipated the question and was ready with my answer. "We'll get married," I said, offering my solution with pride. I had thought it all out ahead of time.

"You can come with me. You know, the fair-haired boy returns home."

I was joking, but there was an element of truth in my statement. Brian's father had been an executive for Ford, and he had been sent to England in the mid 1980s, when Brian was a gangly adolescent. Brian and his family had spent two years in the north of England, which was, oddly enough, one of the things that had attracted me to him when I first met him. That, and a shared affection for the early films of Alfred Hitchcock. In fact, we bonded over an answer in a trivia game at one of those bars where you punch your answers into tabletop tablets to win a free round of beer. ("What was used to simulate blood in Hitchcock's thriller *Psycho*? Brian and I both knew the answer was "chocolate syrup"; more important still was the fact that we both thought that film one of Hitchcock's worst efforts.)

Initially, Brian took no notice of my marriage proposal. "But what will I do with myself?" The pout was gone, but he was squinting, as if his eyes were focusing on some distant, unseen object. I ruffled his dark hair, smiled at him, and said, "You can write in Dorset as well as you can here in the States, Brian. All poets need to leave their country of origin. Look at Ezra Pound, T. S. Eliot, Sylvia Plath. Hell, even Robert Frost spent a few years in England. Come with me. You can find your muse in England just as easily as you can find her here."

We had a quick courthouse wedding six weeks before we left the States. Our transition to married life was completely intertwined with our transition to life in England. As we got used to our new double life, we were also trying to navigate the difficulties of finding a place to live, a car to drive, stores to shop at, and a new schedule to live by. After a month in Dorset, we had found all but the last of these things.

At first, our search for a house to live in seemed hopeless. We could find no affordable lodgings in Dorchester, the largest town in the area and the most natural place to stay while studying Hardy, and we kept on having to enlarge our acceptable commuting distance. At last, discouraged and weary of the search, we settled on a flat in a large house just west of Lyme Regis, built sometime in the early 1800s. It meant close to an hour drive to the Hardy Museum in our third-hand Vauxhall sedan for me, or a two-hour bus ride if Brian needed the car, but there seemed to be no other options. I comforted myself with the thought that I would be seeing more of the countryside during these drives, which was, after all, why I was in England in the first place: to study the landscape that had such a great an effect on the works of Thomas Hardy.

The house we settled on was charming but run-down, with old-fashioned brass doorknobs, hardwood floors, and the kind of narrow windows filled with wavy panes of glass that I associated with great age. It sat behind a low wall made from irregular stones and was covered with ivy, and it even had its own name: Betony Lodge. When we first visited the house, as we passed through the gate, I brushed my hand across the verdant growth on the wall and asked the estate agent, "Is this betony? The plant that the house gets its name from?"

He laughed. "No, not that! That's just plain ivy.

The name of the house comes from the herb patch in the back. Years ago, when this place was made over into flats, there was a huge garden full of betony. And it keeps growing, no matter what anyone has done to try to root it out."

I stood in the small car park out front and looked up at the second story, trying to imagine myself living there. Craning my neck to see through the window, I caught a glimpse of something, some movement behind the window curtain, and I turned to the agent. "I thought this property was vacant?"

"No," he said. "Not quite. Half of the ground floor flat is occupied. Nice family—mother, father, little boy and a little girl. The other half is under construction—no one lives there, and the construction has paused while the contractor gets some permits. I'm not sure what the delay is."

"But the top floor itself is empty? There are no tenants in it right now?"

"No. It's been vacant for several months."

"Come on, Kerys," said Brian. "Enough questions. Let's go in and see it for ourselves."

I glanced up at the window once more and followed Brian and the agent through the front door of the property. Although the outside of the house was staid and proper, kept in good condition, the inside had not been redone in some time—probably several decades. We passed through the front door into a small lobby. On our left was the entry to the flat of the Noudies, who lived on the ground floor; on the right, the door to the large, empty flat that was still under construction. Straight ahead, rising into the darkness, was a beautiful staircase that I later learned was made of English walnut. We climbed those stairs to reach the flat, which, luckily for us, came furnished.

I liked the house. It was quintessentially English, and that was enough to enchant me. My mail, I was told (should I get any in this age of electronic messaging) would be addressed to Betony Lodge, Stoke Camden, near Lyme Regis, and the moment I heard that, I was more or less hooked, convinced that I had entered an Agatha Christie novel. Brian was less impressed, however; he asked about drains, and wiring, and data-linkages, and after several minutes of intense conversation with the estate agent, he nodded and, eyeing me for approval, told the young man we'd like a few minutes alone to discuss the place. The agent complied, handing us the keys, and told us he was going downstairs to check on the tenants, leaving us in the flat by ourselves.

"What do you think?" I asked Brian. We were in the kitchen, gazing out on the back yard below us. I was staring at the small, enclosed garden, whose waist-high stone wall divided it from the larger area behind the house, which was overgrown with bushes and tall grass. My gaze traveled on to the tree-covered hill that rose up beyond it all. Even then, it seemed to me that the house formed a small capsule of civilization in an area that yearned to return to its natural state. I was enchanted.

I turned towards Brian, who was standing beside me by the window, and I smiled as I caught sight of the old-fashioned set of barrel keys dangling from his outstretched hand. He held them up in the streaky autumn sunlight, showing off the ornate holes that decorated the bow of each key. Together, they cast an intricate shadow on the hardwood floor, and for some reason, I laughed. "Those must be at least a hundred years old. Could they really lock anything?"

"We'll have to see," he said, smiling. "What do you think, Kerys? As long as I can get internet reception here, this place will be fine for me. It's a little far for you, though."

I shook my head. "No, not at all. I don't mind the drive." I put my hand over his and took the keys from him. Their solid heaviness surprised me. We kissed in the winter sunlight, happy with our new home. A few seconds later, we heard the agent's feet coming up the stairs. We were ready for him when he entered the flat; we agreed to lease the house, and rode back to the estate agency to sign the papers.

After three weeks, then, we had a home in England. I was happy at the time—happy to be settled, happy to begin my work, happy to experience life as an American expat in England. It seemed a good beginning for our English adventure.

Chapter Two

What she liked we let her do,
Judy was insane, we knew.
--Thomas Hardy, "Mad Judy"

We moved in, settled into our new home, and for a time things went well. Brian found it easy to write in his study, and I loved knowing that I was living right in the middle of Thomas Hardy Country. My grant was supposed to allow me to study the geography of southwestern England and its effect on Hardy's fiction in preparation for a forthcoming book on "Thomas Hardy and the Geography of Domestic Loss." Why the academic world needed yet another book on the subject is beyond my comprehension, but I had pitched the idea and somehow won a generous grant to allow me to research the topic. One requirement of the grant was that I work at the Hardy Museum, sorting and shelving and generally making lists of the items they were keeping in their collection that had never yet seen the light of day: the "deep storage" section. It was a name that thrilled me, making me think of science fiction novels in which travelers hurtled through time and space by being "stored" deep in the bowels of spaceships, floating in cryo-tanks. It would be my job to revive those travelers, I told myself. I would restore the items in deep storage to life, bringing them up out of their acid-free boxes and sharing them with the world at large.

Of course, that was before I actually went to work.

The truth is that these items were in deep storage for a good reason: no one really cared about them because they were largely inconsequential, made up of laundry lists and itemized bills for furniture, neckties, dairy records, and the like. At first I was disappointed; I saw my job at the Museum as an utter waste of time. I preferred exploring the countryside of Dorset, which was supposed to be the intent of the grant. Instead, I found myself wondering whether, in my work at the Museum, I was doing something that was so boring and dull that they could not even pay someone to do it; only a person who had become obligated by accepting a grant could be cajoled into accepting the task.

I said as much to Brian when I came home from my first day at the Museum. "Don't be such a baby," he told me, laughing. "You're not supposed to look a gift horse in the mouth, Kerys, remember? It may be dull as dishwater, but you're here, in England, and all you have to do is put your hours in at the Museum. Ten hours a week isn't much. Think of all the time you can spend on your own, gathering material for your book!"

I looked outside. We were standing in the kitchen again, drinking large glasses of red wine. It was a rainy day in February and already dark though it was just past 4 pm. If I hadn't been so excited about living in the place where Hardy spent a large part of his life, I might have been getting a little—a very little—depressed by my surroundings.

Brian didn't seem to mind; in fact, he seemed happy to be back in England. Changing the subject, I said that he certainly seemed to be feeling right at home.

"You've even developed a slight British accent," I added, before taking a sip of wine.

"What do you mean? I'm speaking just the way I always have." Brian looked at me, the blue in his eyes glinting through his glasses. I watched him as he tilted his head to the right in a movement that I had always found charming.

"I never noticed you dropping your Rs so much when we lived in the States," I said, waiting for his reaction.

He took the bait. "Are you saying that I'm putting on an English accent for show?" His eyes looked flat, bare of any expression, but the right corner of his upper lip had risen slightly, making a kind of grimace. He raised his glass to his mouth and took a sip, staring at me as he did so.

"No, not for show, Brian." I put down my glass and walked over to him, putting my arms around his neck when I got close to him. I could feel him pull away just a little before he relaxed and welcomed my embrace. "I was just thinking you must have had quite a charming English accent when you were a teenager," I said and kissed his cheek. "With long, wavy brown hair down to your shoulders." I reached my hand up to the nape of his neck and ruffled the feathery strands of hair that barely reached the top of his collar. He lifted his chin and kissed me back. Then he stood up, went over to the counter, and refilled his glass.

"You probably wouldn't have liked me anyway back then, Kerys," he said, emptying the bottle.

"Why do you say that?" I opened the refrigerator

to search for omelet ingredients. "Why on earth wouldn't I like you then if I like you now?"

"Oh, you know," Brian said. "I was such a nerd, watching all those old movies with my dad."

"Brian," I said, in the same tone I had used with my students when I gave them back their poorly written papers, "I have a Ph.D. in English literature. What do you think I was like when I was a teenager? A beauty queen? A cheerleader, maybe?"

Brian laughed, and we got to work on the omelet together. "Tell me about the Museum," he said as he began to chop onions. "Who else works there?"

"No one. Just me. At least, I only saw one other person today."

"Who was that?"

I had to wait to answer him, since Brian was pretty handy with a large knife and made a lot of noise when he diced onions. "The guy at the circulation desk is named George Marten-Douglass. He's about my age, with longish hair and glasses, and one of those beards that belong to a Victorian."

I had been struck by George's appearance as soon as I'd met him. He looked kind of like the young Dante Gabriel Rossetti, with shoulder-length brown hair and large, gentle eyes. His beard was clearly something he was proud of, trimmed to a length of three inches and a shade lighter than his hair, and his mustache was improbably curled at the ends. Before I'd met him in person, when we were corresponding by email to get my paperwork sorted to allow me access to the Museum's holdings and to set up my work schedule, I'd imagined him as a middle-aged man, heavy-set with thick black-framed glasses perched on a thick nose below a balding forehead. That explains why I was surprised into silence when I first made his acquaintance: George was roughly the same age I was. The only thing I'd gotten right was the black-framed glasses, but he wore those more as a fashion statement, I think, than to help his eyesight. He turned out to be a nice, talkative fellow who was anxious to make me feel at home.

George had taken his time showing me around the Museum that first morning, although he had to hobble around on crutches, since he'd fallen down some stairs the week before and twisted his ankle. The building was new, with shiny surfaces and a lemony smell. There were books and portraits on the walls, but my favorite exhibit contained two three-dimensional models of the thatched cottage that Hardy had been born in, as well as Max Gate, the house he had designed, built, and lived in during his years of prosperity. George took me into the archive room and showed me the boxes I would be working on cataloguing for the next few months. When we stopped for some tea, which we drank behind the admission desk, George elevating his ankle on a stack of Hardy books, I asked him how long he'd been working at the Museum.

"Ever since I left Sheffield with my degree," he said. "I studied Hardy, naturally. Wrote my thesis on his architectural work."

"Interesting," I said, though I had never thought Hardy's early years as an architect worthy of study myself.

"Not many teaching jobs out there at present, as

you know. I took this job a couple of years ago, and it turns out I really enjoy it."

"I can see why," I said. There were only a few patrons left in the Museum, and I sensed that George was just waiting for them to leave before he locked up for the day. I pointed to his name-tag. "What's the story behind that?"

"What do you mean? My badge?"

"'George Marten-Douglass' barely fits. It's quite a mouthful. Are you the descendent of aristocrats or something?"

George laughed. "Not bloody likely! Lots of people in England have these double-barreled surnames. It's kind of a thing here. It usually comes of having ancestors who ran out of money and made advantageous matches. Neither side of the family wanted their name to die out completely, so they made these kinds of arrangements. My name comes from my great-great-great-grandmother. I may be a 'great' or so off, however. I can never keep them all straight. Anyway, she was born a Marten, and the sole heir of her father. She married a Douglass, and so they hitched the names together to make it all oojah cum spiff, as P.G. Wodehouse might say. Strangely enough, I found out last summer that she actually knew Thomas Hardy. She and her husband were very involved in Victorian literary society—he was a critic for *Blackwood's Magazine*."

I set my empty cup on the counter. "I'm filled with admiration," I said. "I have no idea who my great-grand parents were, much less going back three greats ago. I like your name, too. It makes you sound like someone special," I said. "Someone awfully important."

"Well," he said, "I am. I work the front desk of the Hardy Museum."

I was still smiling when I left George and walked out to my car. England was shaping up to be all I'd hoped it would be.

Chapter Three

Our life is twofold:
Sleep hath its own world,
And a wide realm of wild reality,
And dreams in their development have breath,
And tears, and tortures, and the touch of joy;
They leave a weight upon our waking thoughts,
They take a weight from off our waking toils,
They do divide our being; they become
A portion of ourselves as of our time,
And look like heralds of eternity…
--Lord Byron, "The Dream"

I am not going to claim that moving to England was entirely painless. A month of living here had not been enough to get me used to the weather in Dorset, by which I mean nothing can adequately prepare a person for an almost total lack of sunshine. I slowly discovered that my concept of English life had been all wrong. I'd believed it was garden parties in June, rowing on placid rivers in skinny boats in July, and tromping through the Lake District in August. I had never really considered the possibility of being plopped onto the southern coast of England in the middle of winter and being told to make the most of it.

In addition, while our new flat was comfortable, I had noticed from the very first that there was something a little off about it. Maybe this was simply due to its age. Like most Americans, I had little experience living in a really old building. Betony Lodge, built in the last years of the eighteenth century, has a lovely Georgian look. This is charming, of course, but it makes for slow-heating rooms, creaking floorboards, and noisy water pipes.

Brian hadn't found anything wrong with the building during our initial walkthrough, however, or after we moved in. And in the first few weeks, he was there much more than I was. He had set up the extra bedroom as a shared writing study, but I was rarely there. Instead, I was out and about, getting used to driving on the left side of the road, and trying to locate important sites on my now wrinkled and tea-stained Thomas Hardy map. Brian was very proud of my newfound navigational and driving abilities, and the fact that he was so easily impressed by my feeble accomplishments charmed me.

But life was not as easy as I thought it would be. We were far from anyone we knew, by ourselves, in a foreign country. And don't let anyone tell you anything different: England is a foreign country to Americans, with different customs, verbal expressions, and values. George Bernard Shaw was dead right when he said, "England and America are two countries divided by a common language." Brian had less trouble adjusting than I did, having lived in the culture, even if it had been over two decades previously. But even Brian took a few false steps, like the time he asked the man at the dry cleaner for his "pants" instead of his "trousers," and received raised eyebrows in return.

On the other hand, Brian was one of the few Americans I'd ever met who understood the rules of cricket. Back in the States, at a university bar, I had once admired his sang-froid when he argued with a table full of superannuated frat-rats about the superiority of cricket over baseball. That argument did not end well, although he escaped without physical injury, but it was still enough to impress me into going on a fourth date with him. When we moved to Dorset, I actually made a valiant but futile attempt to learn about the game. It wasn't so bad when he talked about a bowler (who was like a pitcher in baseball) or a batsman (the batter), but there the resemblance to baseball ended, and although there were some similar terms, like "innings," "pitch," and "runs," there were also ridiculous expressions, like "maiden over," "night watchman," and "chinaman." This terminology short-circuited my brain each time Brian tried to teach me more about the game, and I remained in lazy, self-satisfied ignorance. He, on the other hand, was delighted that he could now watch cricket matches on television, listen to cricket on the radio, and even read about cricket scores in a paper, if he wanted to. Before we moved to England, all he could do was surf the web for cricket scores and video clips posted by a few other people as fanatical as he was.

Apparently, our downstairs neighbor was also a cricket fan. The Noudies were a small family: Gary, who was married to Leanne, and their two young children, Ethan and Gemma. Gary was some kind of white-collar worker who seemed to work long hours during the week and do little but watch sports on the weekend. We could hear him shouting at the television on Saturday afternoons. Leanne also worked, but she always brought the children home with her in the middle of the afternoon. Often Brian and I could hear her downstairs with the children, their high-pitched voices arcing back and forth below us, occasionally erupting into a squabble that ended in wailing sobs. Then they would settle down, and we could get back to work, Brian on his latest poem, and me on planning a drive deep into Hardy country.

Gary and Leanne Noudie were nice enough, and their blonde and blue-eyed children were certainly adorable, but as for friends, real friends with whom you go out to dinner, or watch movies, or debate politics, Brian and I had come up short. It's hard to meet people these days, even in this era of social media. Perhaps social media makes it even harder to strike up friendships. Yet we weren't really lonely; solitary by both nature and occupation, we put the time to good use and made progress on each of our projects. And, of course, we had each other.

Until the middle of February.

Several months before we had come to Dorset, Brian had arranged a poetry reading in London. The day arrived before either of us was ready for it, however, and when it came time to make travel arrangements, I had to beg off, because I'd forgotten all about his reading and made an appointment with the director of the Hardy Museum. We were discussing this on the Sunday afternoon before the reading.

"You don't mind too much, do you, Brian? I just feel it would look bad to cancel so close to the date." The truth was, however, I had never enjoyed Brian's readings. Either they were poorly attended and I felt sorry for him for having to read his poems to an empty house, or they were jammed full of aspiring poets, and he didn't notice whether I was there or not. I have to admit now that a large part of me was relieved at the prospect of not having to go with him to London.

Brian was very kind about it. "I get it, Kerys. This is just the first reading, anyway. There will be more. It makes sense to let me go and figure it all out while you stay here and make progress on your work. I'll look up the train schedule and find a cheap place to stay." He pulled out his phone, squinted at it, then walked over to the computer. "Damn. The internet is down."

"I was ready for a break anyway. Let's go into town and use the library there. We can go shopping, too. We're almost out of milk." I was already putting on my coat and grabbing my purse.

We drove into Lyme Regis and found the local library—I had not yet visited it since I had access to an excellent repository of Hardy materials at the Museum—across the street from some schlocky curio shops that looked like major tourist traps. Parking was a problem, as usual, and we had to find a space a few blocks away and walk through mist and cold to get to the library.

While Brian went to the computer terminals to check on the train timetables, I wandered around the library, surprised to find that although it was quite a small building, there was a basement that purported to contain rare and antique books. I asked the circulation clerk behind the desk about obtaining access to the collection.

She looked up at me from her computer screen—reluctantly, I thought—and adjusted her glasses. "That's not difficult," she said, "provided you have the proper identification forms. Are you residing here in Lyme Regis?"

"For the time being," I said. "I have a grant from the British-American Literary Association."

"Ah," she said, the corner of her mouth going up a fraction of an inch. I smiled, thinking she was familiar with the association. "You'll have to take these forms and fill them out." She picked up a heavy packet of papers. I reached for them, but she didn't let go. "And you'll need proper identification, too." Only then did she release the packet into my grasp. I felt my hands begin to perspire and wondered whether I would leave damp marks on the papers where my fingers had touched them.

"How long will it be before I can get access?" Irritated, I noticed that my voice had risen about a half octave.

"Not long," said the woman. "Several days." I started to thank her, but just then Brian caught my eye at the doorway, and I turned away, eager to flee from her apparent contempt.

We walked out of the library in silence. Brian was probably thinking about train connections and hotel reservations, while I was mulling over the woman and her reaction to my inquiry. We passed a pub with the quaint name of the "Angry Badger," and, on impulse, I grabbed Brian's elbow and pulled him towards the door.

"Stop for a quick drink?" I said, shoving the envelope into my backpack.

"Sure," said Brian. "I never turn down a drink with a lovely woman."

I pinched his cheek, and we went in. I must say that the Angry Badger, at least, met all my expectations for an English pub. There were wood-paneled walls, a smoky, well-used fireplace, a bar that was tightly wedged into one corner of the premises, with a dozen or so tables placed dangerously close to a dartboard. It seemed to come right out of a cosy mystery novel. The beer was delicious, too: neither too weak nor too hoppy, a perfect brew that had nothing to prove. In fact, it was when we were having our second round that I told Brian about the special collection and my experience with the library clerk. He slammed his glass down with some force, causing the beer to slosh against the inside of the glass like one of those miniature scientific models of a tidal wave.

"Dammit, Kerys, I can't believe that!"

"Shh, Brian." I tried to calm him, but that ship had already sailed. "Listen, this happens all the time. You know how it is."

Brian, bless him, shook his head and compressed his lips, squinting at nothing in particular. I found his outburst endearing but embarrassing, since it occurred in a public place. He sighed and took another sip from his glass, spilling a few drops onto the table when he pulled it away from his lips. "It's bad enough in the U.S.," he said, "but I thought here in England, with the grant and everything, you'd get the respect you deserve."

"Brian, it's ok. You know how used to this I am." That much was true, at least. With no jobs in my field of teaching, I'd been an adjunct instructor—a freeway flyer, moving from one part-time gig to another—for several years now. It always upset Brian, who had found the professional success that had eluded me. Maybe his latest collection of poems wasn't selling like hotcakes, but he never lacked invitations to become a poet-in-residence at colleges and universities that would never even think of offering me anything other than a stint as a visiting professor.

Initially I found Brian's reaction endearing, indicative of a tender concern for my bruised feelings, but it wasn't long before I began to see that I shouldn't have told Brian anything at all. Even after I had gotten him to calm down, I had to sit there and pump him about his plans for the week while he, still nursing a grudge on my behalf, finished his beer in a grumpy silence. By the end of our first visit to the Angry Badger, I was finding the entire situation very irritating. Here he was, trying to get me riled up about an insult that really didn't matter, since there was little, if anything, I could do about it, while he got to shed the whole thing like an itchy pair of socks the next day when he headed to London for his poetry reading. Suffice it to say that by the time we left the pub, twenty minutes later, I was more than ready to go home. We drove back in silence to Betony Lodge.

I tried to put the incident behind me; I really made an effort. But back in our flat, after he'd pulled out his suitcase and thrown some clothes into it, Brian just couldn't let the topic drop. He kept returning to it as he padded in and out of his study in his stocking feet, making copies of files on jump drives and microchips, sorting notebooks, cords, and electronics and jamming them into his briefcase. I was sitting at the dining room table, reading over my notes on Hardy's early years in Dorchester, trying to make headway on a detailed timeline of his life, when Brian would pop in with yet another abrasive comment about the state of academia. Finally, I'd had enough and told him so.

"Really?" His eyes dimmed for a moment, showing the extent of his surprise at my outburst, as well as the pain it had caused him. "I was just trying to sympathize with you, Kerys. You're always telling me to see things from your point of view, but when I try to, you bite my head off."

"Brian," I said, unable to restrain a deep sigh, "come on. It was nothing, really, but you're going on and on about it. Let it go. Please."

"Fine," he said, though it was clear that it was anything but fine. "I'm going out for a while. I have to buy another memory stick." He grabbed his coat and the car keys from the counter and stomped out of the house. I listened to his footsteps echo down the stairs and heard the front door slam, just a bit too hard.

He wouldn't find a memory stick in Lyme Regis, the closest town to us, and probably not even in Dorchester, if he drove all the way there. Not at that hour of the night. But it was just as well he went out. He needed some space; we both did. Maybe our move to England had been harder than either of us had realized. And now here was Brian having to make a trip to London, alone, to give a reading by himself, without me there to support him. It was probably stress that was making him act like a jerk. But I couldn't help resenting his ability to make this situation about him when it was really my issue, not his.

I sat there feeling sorry for myself, listening to Brian drive away. Then I stood up and walked to the dining room window, looking out into the darkness. A few raindrops splashed across the pane, adding to the general atmosphere of despair. I'd never been subject to depression—long years of graduate school had inured me to its effects—but I'll admit that I was pretty low that night. Something about the entire situation seemed to call for a stiff drink. I was sure that was where Brian was off to—getting a nip at some pub like the Angry Badger or one further afield.

At the time, I wasn't in the habit of drinking hard stuff by myself. Usually I limited my drinking to beer and wine. But tonight, I was on my own, and we had neither beer nor wine in the house, so I dropped two ice cubes into an oversized teacup and splashed some Scotch over it all without too much care. I took a sip. It tasted good, almost sweet, and its smell reminded me of brand-new leather boots. I liked the way it burned my throat as it made its way down, too. Up until that point, I'd never been much of a Scotch drinker, but I began my education that evening.

By the time Brian came home, it was well after ten. I was betting that he must have had more than a few drinks himself. As for me, I'd had three teacup scotches and was working my way through the fourth one—with no dinner to boot—when I heard a car engine in the distance. I peeked out the window, saw the sheen of headlights, and, like the coward I was, slipped into the bathroom with my half-full cup. I hurried to start the bath water, turning the spigots on full blast.

Within five minutes, which was just long enough for Brian to pull into the courtyard, lock up the car, enter

Betony Lodge's front door and make it up the stairs to our flat, I had succeeded in filling the small bathroom with heavy clouds of steam. I'd also thrown off my clothes and plunged into the tub, wincing at the hot water on my skin, and pulled the plastic shower curtain around the tub.

"Kerys?" I could hear Brian's footsteps above the noise of the water as he walked across our flat towards the bathroom. "Kerys? You'll never guess what happened at the pub. It was trivia night, and—"

He was at the door of the bathroom. Through the steam, I saw him begin to push it open, the door moving slowly. The steam had not only filled the small room, but had condensed on the clear plastic shower curtain as well. I closed my eyes, listening to him approach the tub, and just before he pulled the shower curtain open, I slipped head and shoulders beneath the water.

"Kerys! Kerys!" He was shouting at me now; I could hear the panic in his voice even from under the water. "What on earth are you doing? Are you crazy?" He pulled me up to a sitting position, wetting his sleeves in the bathwater. His anguished voice rolled around inside my head for a second before I decided to open my eyes. When I did, I saw a very worried man—I might even say a frightened man—peering at me with wide eyes squinting from behind steamed-up glasses. "What is it, Kerys? Are you ill?"

I shook my head. I didn't say anything at first, and we just stared at each other, my hair dripping in my eyes, his eyes peering through the fog. Finally I found my voice. "No," I said, "not ill. Just taking a bath. Can I finish?"

Brian leaned back on his heels, and I saw him blink. Then his nose wrinkled just a little. He released his grip on my bare shoulders and I sank back into the tub, the water lapping at my neck. I could see the muscles on his neck grow taut; at the same time his eyes seemed to lose their focus on me. Then he blinked again and shook some of the water from his sleeves. He stood up, backing away toward the door, his eyes still on mine.

"Have you eaten anything tonight?"

"I'm fine," I said, avoiding his question. Then, not knowing what else to do, I sank below the water again and held my breath. I could hear nothing for a second or two, then, from below the water, I heard the bathroom door slam like a muffled gunshot. When I re-emerged, water dripping into my eyes and my lungs ready for a breath, I was alone again.

Believe it or not, that was the first time Brian and I went to bed angry with each other. When I was younger, before I ever married or had a boyfriend, I used to admire those older couples who said they never went to bed angry. Nowadays, I believe that anyone who maintains that they can patch up a serious argument within a few hours is either lying to themselves, to their partner, or to the person they're talking to.

The truth was that I was genuinely angry with Brian, but I really couldn't say why. His overzealous reaction to the rude reminder of my status as an independent scholar was certainly irritating in one way, but also very sweet and empathetic in another one. I just couldn't see that side of it back then, I guess. All I saw was a man who had everything—prestige, respect, a steady if modest paycheck from book sales—scattering a bit of convenient pity in my direction. It was demeaning and infuriating at the same time, and although Brian didn't deserve it, I held a grudge against him.

There were, however, a few moments during that night when my anger ebbed. I even felt sorry for him, in a way, and ashamed of my own anger. He was sound asleep by the time I got into bed, or at least he appeared to be. As I rolled into my side of the bed, the room spinning unpleasantly, I told myself that if Brian only made one small move, one slight attempt at rapprochement, I'd be able to fall into his arms, we'd both apologize, and after some passionate love-making, things would be all better. But of course, Brian had no way of knowing that I was on the verge of forgiving him for an offense he didn't even realize he'd committed, and I certainly wasn't going to tell him. Even if I did, I argued, it would probably not result in him rushing to apologize. The result of all this deliberation on my part was that we each slept on the edge of our queen-sized bed, cautious not to touch each other, not even accidentally.

It would have been a long, sleepless night if not for the scotch I'd drunk, which put me out in short order. So I can't say whether Brian tossed and turned, whether he, too, was tormented by a guilty conscience, or whether he felt sorry for me or even guessed at what had bothered me so much, because, wrapped in my flannel nightgown, snuggled like a wayward mummy under the heavy comforter with my wet hair still wrapped in a towel, I was asleep within seconds after laying my head on the pillow.

I had a series of strange dreams that night, but only retain a clear memory of one of them. Usually I don't put a great deal of stock in dreams; rather than important clues to the past, or indications of the future, I believe that dreams are simply the residue of thoughts and half-thoughts that flicker through our minds throughout the previous day. But my time at Betony Lodge has been marked by vivid dreams, and I suppose that because this was the one of the first of many dreams, I remember it well.

I was a spectator, looking upon a scene that seemed to be taking place before me. Five women in Victorian-era clothes were in a parlor: one was just entering the room; two of them were seated on the sofa in the center of the room, engaged in conversation; one sat by herself, staring through the front window as the rain streamed down it; and another sat in a small nook, listening to the two women speaking, following their words with mute attention. A slight movement near the latecomer brought my attention to a sixth woman, older than the rest, dressed in black, and with a rough and imperious manner.

That was all I remember of the dream, but I woke in the night thinking about it, puzzling through it, and finally, my head still dizzy from the scotch, falling back to sleep without having figured out what such a dream meant.

Soon after sunrise, I heard Brian's alarm and knew he would soon be leaving for the train station, but I didn't get up. Nor did I get up when I heard him rummaging around in our closet, or when he dialed his cell phone for a taxi. In fact, I didn't budge until I heard the taxi drive up beneath our window. Only then did I sit up in bed, listening to the door to the flat close and Brian's heavy footsteps shuffle down the stairs. And only when I heard the car door slam shut and the taxi drive off did I get out of bed, put my robe on, and make my way to the kitchen.

Brian had made a pot of tea, as usual, and it was still sitting on the counter where he'd left it. He'd put a tea cozy around the pot, which, if I'd been in the mood to be analytical, or even charitable, I could have taken as a peace offering of sorts. But, although painfully sober that morning, as evidenced by my pounding head, I was still angry and sullen, which is why I rejected the tea Brian had made and instead took the time to prepare coffee in our little French press.

And that's when I first heard a strange sigh that sounded like the moan of a person in pain. I thought at first it was the press itself, emitting a resentful squeak as I pushed the boiled water through the filter screen. Then, when I stopped to listen, I decided it must be a peacock crying, even though I knew there were none in our neighborhood and that it was the wrong time of day for peacocks. The noise was drawn out, like a muffled howl of some sort, but still all too human. Tired and hung-over, I was hunched over my cup of coffee, breathing in its bitter aroma, regretting the fact that I hadn't remembered, after all, to buy milk the day before and wondering how I would spend my day, when I heard another sigh, this one so sad and plaintive it made me forget my own misery. I sat up and looked around, thinking Brian must still be home, after all.

"Brian?" I took a sip of the coffee, clenched my teeth against its unaccustomed bitterness, and swallowed. "Is that you?" There was no answer, so I stood up and walked to our tiny bathroom, pulling my robe tight around my shoulders. Flannel nightgowns alone, I had already learned, are not enough to keep out the chill of a wintry morning in England, especially in a very old building, even if it was converted into modern flats.

"Are you still here?" I glanced in the bathroom, took a quick peek into the study, and, cradling my cup in my hand, walked back to the kitchen. "I guess not," I said aloud. At that time, I was just beginning to indulge in the habit of talking to myself, and I was not yet worried about it.

I sat back down at the table, put my coffee mug down, and rubbed my pounding temples. What was that noise? Probably heating pipes or something like that. Back in the States, I'd lived in a variety of places that made sounds: shifting foundations, stiff winds, even small earthquakes could account for a lot of normal creaking household noises. England, too, must have its causes for these things, especially when one considered that everything here was close to a thousand years older than in the United States.

Let's face it, I told myself: there's no chance at all that this beautiful old building is situated on top of a Native American burial ground, so just forget about it. I nodded, as if I'd said the words aloud, as if someone else had said them to me and I was agreeing with them, and lifted my cup to my lips. Drinking deep, I now welcomed the scalding bitterness of the coffee. It was real, unlike the sound that had set me on edge. It was something that appealed to the senses, something you could count on, something predictable and knowable. I took another sip, thinking that milk would have made the coffee taste better, but somehow less real. Sometimes, I said aloud, my voice echoing in the empty flat, bitterness was just what you needed to get you going.

I drank my coffee as the sun came up through heavy, somber clouds, shedding a brittle winter light that wormed its way through the windows and into the flat. Moving my chair out of the brightness, I huddled in the shadows, because the glare of the washed-out sunlight made my head hurt even more, and already each breath I took ended with a pulse of pain throbbing behind my left eye. After I drained what would be the first of several cups of coffee, I made my way into the bathroom and took the towel off my head. I hung it up and, as I turned around to head back to the kitchen to refill my cup, I caught sight of my reflection in the mirror.

Had it been another time, another morning, I might have laughed at my ridiculous image: my shoulder-length brown hair was sticking up at odd angles, my dark eyes seemed to bulge from their sockets, highlighted by the dark circles beneath them, and my nightgown, visible through my open robe, was buttoned all wrong. I looked like a four year old who had dressed herself and then helped herself to her mother's make-up and pinking shears. Instead of laughing, however, I stared at the mirror until I saw my lips begin to tremble and the tears well up in my eyes. Fascinated, I watched as the large, lazy drops overflowed and trickled like a trail of heavy glycerin down my cheeks. Switching off the light, I made my way back to the dining room table, swept my papers out of the way, put my head down on my forearms, and sobbed in the cold, harsh daylight.

Crying is not something I did very often, and to be honest, I was never much good at it. I hate the way the sobs tear at you, pulling your breath out of your lungs with a rude jolt, making you gasp for air, choking you on your own tears. I know that a good cry is supposed to make you feel better, but it never seems to do me any good. I just end up with swollen, bloodshot eyes, a pounding head, clogged sinuses, and a nagging sense that I've just indulged in a fruitless activity.

But that morning, I cried. A lot. Yet I couldn't say why. This wasn't the first fight I'd had with Brian, and it wasn't even a major one. I just felt saddened, as if life itself was too heavy for me to bear, as if the weight of the world's sorrows had just settled on my too-narrow shoulders. The whole experience was strange and alien.

It took me most of an hour to pull myself together, but at last I stopped crying and made another strong cup of coffee. I forced it down, wincing at its bitterness, and then ate a slice of buttered toast and a soft-boiled egg, my preferred form of comfort food. I ate it even though I didn't feel like eating at all. But I knew I had missed dinner last night and wouldn't start to feel better until the alcohol was out of my system. Food, I thought, would help the process.

Lunchtime had come and gone before I was dressed and ready to leave the flat. I was still somewhat queasy, but the weather was good—surprisingly sunny and clear after the rain the night before—and I decided I would drive over to the Hardy Museum, even though I wasn't scheduled to work in the archive room that day. I was hungry for someone to recognize me, to acknowledge my status as a scholar, which explains, I suppose, why I was willing to drive some two hours round trip without having any real reason for doing so. I was pulling on my jacket when I thought I heard, for the third time that day, the sound that had set me on edge. It was something between a sigh and a sob, and I was now certain that it came not from an errant peacock but from a human being, and one close by—that much was obvious to me. No wayward steam pipe could create a sound with such palpable anguish; no creaking floorboard could emit such a long, drawn-out, and wistful moan.

I picked up my cell phone, thinking to call our neighbors below, but I realized that I didn't have Leanne's number. I grabbed my keys and my backpack and ran down the stairs to the door to their flat and knocked hard on their door. Impatient, I was about to knock once more when I heard footsteps approaching from the other side of the door, and so I waited.

Leanne pulled the door open and looked at me, her eyebrows raised. She was about my height, a bit heavier than I—after all, she'd obviously had two children in quick succession—with longish blonde hair and light blue eyes. She blinked, looked at my raised hand, which was still poised to knock, and smiled without conviction.

"Hullo! You're the upstairs flat, aren't you?"

"Yes," I said. "My name's Kerys Markham. Did you hear anything just now? Are you all right down here?"

"Of course I'm all right," she said, leaning against the threshold and staring at me. "Except for a couple of little ones who won't settle down for a nap. What do you mean, 'did I hear anything just now'?"

"I know it's silly, Mrs.—." I paused, realizing that I didn't know her name.

"Noudie. Leanne Noudie."

And just like that, quite suddenly, I felt very foolish standing there. The woman had obviously heard nothing. I made the best of a bad situation and changed gears at once. "Actually, I'm off to the shops this afternoon, and I wondered whether you might need anything."

"Oh, how nice, Mrs. Markham!" She smiled at me, and for a moment I felt like I'd just gone back in time, and that Leanne Noudie and I were housewives from the 1950s just getting to know each other. I fought to dispel that feeling, saying, "No, please, call me Kerys."

"Interesting—you're American, aren't you? But your name…"

"Yes, it's unusual, I know. My mother's family was Welsh. I spell it with a 'K,' not the normal 'C.' My mother changed the spelling so that people back home could say it correctly."

"Lovely," said Leanne. She looked at me for a moment, as if sizing me up, and added, "If you really are going to the shops, I could do with a bit of milk and some butter, but only if it's no trouble."

"None at all, Mrs. Noudie—" She stopped me, smiling, her hand on my forearm.

"It's Leanne to you, Kerys. After all, we're neighbors, aren't we?"

I nodded. "How much milk, and what kind?"

"None of that skimmed stuff for me or the kids," Leanne said, laughing. "Full fat, four-pint jug, and a block of unsalted butter. Let me give you a fiver—"

"There's time for that later," I said. "I should be back by six. Is that okay for you?"

"Lovely. And thanks for asking." Leanne smiled again, a broad smile that showed her large, white teeth, and she closed the door. I turned and walked through the foyer to the front door of Betony Lodge, pulling it open with some effort. Out on the front steps of the house, however, remembering the sound I'd heard, I paused, turned around, and looked back at the window of my flat. But there was no sound now, other than the small chuff of leaves waving in a light breeze above me. I shrugged my shoulders and got into my car. The mystery of the moaning man, or woman, if there was one, would have to wait until I got back that evening.

Chapter Four

Yet at midnight if here walking,
When the moon sheets wall and tree,
I see forms of old time talking,
Who smile on me.
--Thomas Hardy, "The House of Hospitalities"

At first, as I set off for Dorchester, I thought I'd take a nice, leisurely drive across the coastline to town, but when I finally got behind the wheel of the car and started the engine, I realized it was half past one, and I'd have to hurry if I were to have any time at all in the Museum, since I now had to go to the store for Leanne. So I put all notions of sightseeing out of my head, and instead pushed on to Dorchester. Even so, I had to slow down a number of times; still new to driving on the left, I was too afraid to pass on two-lane roads, so I meandered along behind older drivers and overloaded tractors, muttering under my breath. To make it even worse, the weather rapidly changed. Clouds had come in from the sea, and the afternoon grew dark beneath their gray and heavy presence. Rather than rejoice in nature, which was the original point of the drive, I now longed to get to safety, into the bowels of the Museum.

When I pulled into the car park, I checked my cell phone to see if I had missed any calls. Of course, I was hoping Brian had called me. There was one text message, sent at 2 pm, just a few minutes earlier: "Sorry. Call me tonight. Love you." Okay, so it wasn't flowers or chocolates, but it was a move in the right direction. If I waited for a proper apology, I'd be waiting forever. Brian wasn't the kind of guy to go overboard on emotional appeals. Besides, even I wasn't sure who was in the wrong anymore: I was beginning to think I'd made a royal hash out of everything. So, smiling, I texted back: "Love you, too. Talk to you tonight." Then I turned off my phone and slipped it into my purse.

On my way into the Archive Room, I stopped at the front desk to greet George.

"Good morning," I said.

"Not half," George said, pulling his eyes away from his computer screen and staring at me with one eyebrow raised.

"I beg your pardon?"

"It's well after two, Kerys," he said, breaking into a grin. "Good afternoon, you mean."

I tried a smile, even though my head was throbbing. "Anyway…."

"Yes, you can go on into the archives. But the Museum closes early today, remember."

"Thank God," I muttered, as I made my way behind his desk and through the door to the archive room. It was a relief to get into that room; tedious though the work was, it was predictable and dependable. Although I had complained to Brian, I was beginning to find that sometimes I rather enjoyed that kind of mindless work. Making notes in pencil on acid-free paper made me feel official in a way that teaching first-year composition to reluctant students never had.

Once in the archive room, I felt the tension leave my body, and my head gradually stopped its pounding. I could relax in such a room, surrounded by old manuscripts and books, amid their musty but welcome smell in the dim light. Somehow, I found it easy to breathe freely there; I felt as if I belonged. I pulled out the archive box I'd begun to work on my first day at the Museum, although I didn't expect to get much done that afternoon. I removed the lid and pulled out the sheets of paper I had left on top of the letters and small books that were stored within the box.

The next half hour was spent trying to remember where I had been in my cataloguing efforts before the weekend. I then sorted through a pile of papers with careful and gentle fingers. Two-thirds down the box, however, I lit upon a little book that caught my eye, something I'd passed over the first time I'd seen it. It was about six inches by four inches, and it had one of those swirly, marbled patterns on the cover, making it look very old and brittle despite its dark, gold-edged binding. I tallied the number on the tag hanging from its spine with the list from the box and discovered that it was the journal or logbook of one Arthur Bellemeade, a physician from Lyme Regis.

I opened it very carefully, the way the archivists had demonstrated in my online orientation, with just my thumb and forefinger. On the flyleaf of the book, in two different color inks, were the words "January 1844 through October 1850," written in a small, tight script. This had to be a personal journal, I told myself, not an official or medical one, not if it covered six full years. No medical logbook would have lasted that long; this book was small, and it would have been filled up with descriptions of patients and treatments within a few months. I turned the pages, looking only at the dates of the entries, not at the entries themselves, and discovered that there were large gaps between them, sometimes as much as a year apart.

Although I'd been studying Hardy in a serious way for several years, I had never heard of any Arthur Bellemeade. So I looked again at my master index, scanning the small print for more information:

> *Arthur Bellemeade, 1801[?] – 1865[?].*
> *Dorset physician and alienist. One of two*
> *alienists who worked at Warrinder House, a*
> *private asylum near Lyme Regis. Moved to*
> *Dorchester in 1845 and became physician in*
> *attendance at Mr. Last's Academy for Young*
> *Gentlemen in Dorchester, which TH attended*
> *from 1849 to 1856. Mentions TH three times*
> *in this journal.*

There were page numbers, followed by "O" or "V" to indicate on which side of the page these references to Thomas Hardy could be located. Of course, I looked each one of them up at once.

The first reference was entry dated 1850, and was quite brief. Hardy's name and age (10 years) was listed among five boys whom Bellemeade had visited at the Dorchester School on February 15, in order to treat a chest infection. There were no notes or comments—only a short line explaining the purpose of the physician's visit and the patients seen.

The second entry was only a little more interesting. Dated April, 1852, it described an outbreak of measles at the school and listed the boys affected: William Dewy, Tranter Reuben, Peter Ledlow, John Frederick, Thomas Hardy, and Timothy Tankens. Treatment details were given: bed rest in darkened rooms, beef tea, diminished diet. During this period, Dr. Bellemeade apparently visited Mr. Last's School three times in three weeks, at four- and five-day intervals. The last few words of the entry indicated that the outbreak was contained to the doctor's satisfaction: *"No complications— all cured."*

I had to turn towards the end of the little book for the last appearance of Thomas Hardy as Bellemeade's patient. Hardy got this entry all to himself:

May, 1856: Visited at Mr. Last's establishment, saw young Mr. Hardy, who complained of ear pain. Poor boy in great discomfort. Diagnosis: wisdom teeth.

That was it—no mention either of treatment or resolution of the problem. This was another reason why I decided the book couldn't be a medical logbook; there simply wasn't enough information in it. Having looked at what were supposed to be the interesting and relevant passages, I was unimpressed. This book was clearly of little importance to Hardy scholars. Why and how it had made its way into the archive was a mystery, but of course, many of the archival boxes were filled with miscellaneous items that were only slightly related to

Thomas Hardy. I paged through it again, just to be sure that I hadn't missed anything, although I knew I hadn't. That's when I saw the sketch on the third page of the book and stopped short.

It was a picture of Betony Lodge: I was sure of it. A few things had changed—some trees were gone, and some bushes added, but the wall surrounding the house, and the house itself, all looked exactly the same. I stared at the picture for a while, perplexed. Beneath the sketch, which was presumably done by Dr. Bellemeade himself, were the words "Warrinder House." This made no sense to me, since I was sure that the structure, whatever Bellemeade labeled it as, had to be Betony Lodge. I made a few notes on my own pad, and then thumbed through Dr. Bellemeade's journal again, looking for any kind of clues.

Then I put the journal back into the box, put the lid on the box, and put it back on the shelf. I made my way out of the archive room and found George clearing up his desk, making small piles of papers beside his keyboard. He looked up and smiled at me.

"That's all for today?"

I nodded. "Yes," I said, "but I'll be back tomorrow. Hopefully a little earlier in the day."

I picked up my backpack, already thinking of driving to the Tesco store on the way home.

"Kerys?"

I turned around, my keys in my hand. "Yes, George?" I wondered why he had stopped me.

"You do realize we're closing down for a week come Wednesday, don't you?"

"What?" I set my backpack down on the floor and stared at him. "But what about my appointment with Dr. Chatto?"

"That's not until the 18th, Kerys. I have it marked here, on the calendar."

I looked over his shoulder at his computer, which showed the appointment clearly on February 18th. I had gotten the date wrong. I could have gone to London with Brian, after all. But it was too late now.

George must have noticed the way I sagged, because he made a valiant effort to cheer me up. "Could have happened to anyone," he said, smiling. "We're closing for our usual mid-term break. Didn't anyone tell you about this?"

"No," I managed to get out, thinking what terrible timing it was for me. As soon as I get settled in England, the museum I've come to work in closes down. "But you're open tomorrow for the usual hours?"

George nodded, his dark hair swinging just above his shoulders. "Yes. And half the day on Wednesday, too."

"Well," I said, picking up my backpack again, "thanks for telling me. I guess I'll have to plan accordingly. Good night, George."

"Good night, Kerys." A few minutes later, I was out in the darkling car park, watching what sunlight there was fade from the sky as I began to make my way home.

It was 6:30 by the time I made it back to Betony Lodge and stopped in at Leanne's flat to deliver her milk and butter. She invited me in for a drink. Normally, I would have declined—I tend to be on the shy side—but because Brian wasn't home, and I was just the slightest bit lonely, I took her up on her offer.

"What would you like to drink, Kerys? Anything in particular?" I had seated myself on her couch, trying not to notice the images of obnoxious puppets that the television was casting in my direction, while Leanne stood in front of a cabinet that contained a variety of liquors.

"Whatever you're having," I said, unsure of the protocol involved in these afternoon happy hours at home. She turned back to the cabinet and poured liquid into two glasses, then brought me mine and sat down on the chair across from me, cradling her glass in her hand. She seemed to have no problem at all ignoring the television. I don't even know why it was on in the first place, since Ethan and Gemma were nowhere in evidence. I assumed they were still napping in their bedroom, although Ethan seemed a bit old to me for naps.

"Thanks for picking up the provisions," said Leanne, and added, almost as an afterthought, "Chin, chin!" I raised my glass to mimic her gesture and took a sip. Scotch—again. It was the second time in less than twenty-four hours I was drinking scotch, which must have set a record in my personal drinking habits. I forced it down.

"Hope you don't mind it with a bit of water," Leanne said, watching me. I shook my head and tried to smile. "My father's Scottish, so I drink it as he does, with a wee bit of water to release the flavors."

"It's good," I said, clearing my throat a little. We

exchanged pleasantries then, trading information about ourselves and our families. Leanne and Gary had been married ten years; Gary was a mid-level manager in a hotel chain, which is why they were living in Lyme Regis, a tourist mecca, at least in the summer time. Leanne worked at the local preschool, which her children also attended.

"Lots of people think I'm daft for working as I do," she told me. We were halfway through our drinks, and I had already told her about Brian and me and how we had ended up in England. "But the truth is that if I stayed home with Ethan and Gemma, they wouldn't learn a thing. Look at this," she said, pointing at the television, which showed an orange and green animated hedgehog dancing through a shopping mall. "They'd be watching this rubbish non-stop, and here I'd be, smashed to the gills. It's better for us to have the structure of the nursery school. I make just enough to pay for some extras, and we have our schedule. It's lovely, really."

I nodded. I could see Leanne's point. When time stretches out in front of you, as it had for me since I'd won the grant, it's hard to push yourself into accomplishing things on a daily basis. I took another sip of my drink.

She smiled. "So," she said, "Thomas Hardy, is it? I thought you looked the bookish type when I first saw you. That's what I told Gary—they're students or professors or some such thing. He'll be happy to know I was right!"

We both heard the car drive up. "That must be him now," I said. "I'd better get going."

"Wait," said Leanne. "Let me pay you for the milk and butter, Kerys."

I waited while she got her purse, feeling rather uncomfortable. I have always hated exchanging money in this way. As it turned out, Leanne didn't have a note smaller than a £10, which I refused to take. "It's okay," I said. "What's a few pounds between neighbors? You can pay me another time." I moved to the door, listening to Gary's heavy steps trudge up the gravel walkway to the front door. Then I remembered that I'd wanted to ask Leanne about the name of the house we lived in, so I stopped in front of the door of her flat. "Leanne, do you know if this house has always been called 'Betony Lodge'?"

"As far as I know it has been. But let's ask Gary— he'll know. He knows everything about this town. It's part of his job."

"What's part of my job?" I turned to look at Leanne's husband, a slightly plump fellow with bad taste in ties. He was wearing a yellow one that looked like it had been bought at a dollar store, with green blotches that might have been part of its design or simply the result of a sloppy lunch. But his hazel eyes were bright and active, and his smile was genuine. "Hullo, who's this? We have a visitor, Leanne? Have I met you?" He hung up his coat by the door and turned to face me.

"Not in person," I said. "You might know me by my footsteps, though."

"Eh? What's that?" He looked confused. Just then, Ethan and Gemma came tumbling out of the hallway leading to the bedrooms, where they must have been playing all along, and attacked Gary's legs with cries of excitement. He patted them on the head and walked by me to the couch, sitting down and letting them crawl into to his lap. Leanne handed him a drink. I stood with my hand on the doorknob, ready to leave, but Gary stopped me, raising the drink in his hand as if it were a crossing guard's sign.

"What's this about knowing you by your footsteps? Are you a dancer?"

Leanne and I both laughed. "No," I said. "I'm your upstairs neighbor."

Gary took a sip of his drink. "I see." The children were wiggling across his lap, and I could see it was time to make my exit. The scotch wasn't sitting well with my stomach, or my head, for that matter, and I was ready to be in my own house. I picked up my own sack of groceries and walked to the door.

"Thanks for the drink, Leanne. It was great getting to know you."

"Wait, Kerys! Don't you want to ask Gary your question?"

"Oh, right," I said, remembering. "Gary, has this house always been called 'Betony Lodge'?"

"Getting into the local history of the place, eh?" Gary looked amused. "You Americans always do that when you come to England. Can't help it, I suppose. Comes from living in a place without history." He took a sip of his drink and swallowed. "It's been Betony Lodge for most of this and the last century," he said. "Before that, it was vacant. It was used as a home for unwed mothers just before the Great War, I think, the, some years later, it was made into these flats. But it's most famous for what it was before all that, back in the early

1800s: an insane asylum."

I took a step away from the door, back into the living room, and looked at Leanne and then across to Gary. "Really?" My voice sounded as shaky as my head felt, and I fought the urge to clear my throat.

"That's right," said Gary, pleased at my reaction. "A private loony bin. Nothing big—not on the scale of Bedlam or Ticehurst or anything like that. Just a modest little house filled with crazy women. Pretty interesting, eh?" He took another big gulp of his drink and nodded as the children jostled for primary position on his lap.

"And was it called 'Warrinder House,' by any chance?" I had control of my voice now.

"Could be. That's right, I think." Gary's eyebrows lifted. "How did you know that?"

"I ran into something at the Hardy Museum today." I turned back to Leanne. "Anyway, I really should leave you to your evening now. Thanks again for the drink, Leanne."

She walked me to the door this time. "Come again soon, Kerys," she said, and a few seconds later, I was in my own flat, looking at it as if for the first time. I put the groceries down on the kitchen table and took a deep breath. Usually I am neither superstitious nor squeamish, but something about this new discovery unnerved me. Perhaps I was just feeling the after-effects of drinking too much, but I was more than a little creeped out about all the coincidences that had converged to have me discover, on the day when I first began to hear eerie sounds coming from the walls of my own home, that my flat had once housed crazy women. I looked around very slowly, taking in the view: a large, open room for sitting in, a kitchen area looking out over the back yard—which was just then, true to form, filled with the shadows of trees and bushes swaying in the night-time breeze—and the hallway leading to the bathroom and two small bedrooms. Nothing in this layout suggested an insane asylum. Whoever had renovated and remodeled the house had done a fine job. Not a single trace of lunacy lingered.

My phone buzzed just at that moment, and I jumped. I pulled it out of my purse and saw that it was Brian. I pressed "Receive."

"Hi, Brian."

There was only a slight pause at the other end, and then Brian said, "Kerys?" There was a question in his voice.

"Yes, it's me. Who else would it be?" My words came out sharper than I'd meant them to, and I hurried to buffer them. "How are you?"

Brian's voice sounded uncertain, hesitant. "I'm fine. You?"

"Doing well." A second later, we both said we were sorry at the same time, then laughed. After that, we were able to proceed with a normal conversation, in which he told me about London and his hotel room, and I told him about my recent discovery. Brian was intrigued.

"An insane asylum—really? That's pretty interesting."

"I don't know, Brian. I think it's pretty weird and unsettling."

"Yes, but think of the history! The very place we live, sleep, eat—think about what those walls would tell us if they could talk!"

"Don't say that, Brian!"

"Why not?" I could hear him laughing at the other end of the phone. I didn't want to tell him about the sound I'd heard that morning—not over the phone, anyway—so I changed the subject.

"When do you think you'll be coming home?"

"In a couple of days, if you're good with that, Kerys."

I told him I was, and we exchanged the kind of pleasant good-byes that married people do, and then hung up. I put my groceries away, started the water boiling for tea, and pulled out the ready-made sandwich I'd picked up for dinner at the store. But instead of spending the evening poring over books and articles, I opted for a television show instead. The truth was, I was a little off-kilter and preferred the noise of a ready-made show to the random thoughts and half-shaped fears of my own imagination.

Only when I got into bed did I listen for the moans I'd heard earlier that day. I heard nothing but the winter wind blowing the leaves about in the yard below, and I soon fell into a dreamless and soothing sleep.

Chapter Five

My drama and hers begins weirdly
Its dumb re-enactment,
Each scene, sigh, and circumstance passing
In spectral review.
--Thomas Hardy, "The Flirt's Tragedy"

When I woke the next morning, I realized at once that I felt much better than I had the day before. With our quarrel settled, I was now looking forward to Brian's homecoming, and I was successful in pushing all thoughts of insane asylums, mysterious sounds, and strange coincidences from my mind that morning. I had decided to be proactive and make use of my remaining time alone. But then I remembered about the Hardy Museum and its archive room closing in a day, and I fell into a mood of irritated frustration.

Instead of giving into it, though, I took action. I pulled the almost-forgotten forms from the County Library out of my coat pocket and filled them out. If I couldn't get into one set of archives, I told myself, I'd dig my way into another. With Brian gone, he wouldn't know that I had gone back to the library, that I'd lowered myself enough to submit the application, or that I was hoping that they would favor that application soon enough to get me into the basement in the next few days. As far as I was concerned, it was perfect timing.

That's how I found myself, two days later, with a brand-new identification card for the Lyme Regis Library,

one with a special stamp that allowed me to descend a set
of industrial-looking stairs into a darkened hallway, and
emerge in a cramped and musty basement, the opposite end
of the spectrum from the climate-controlled, state-of-the-art
archive room of the Hardy Museum. The Lyme Regis town
archive collection was small and dusty, and it lacked the
atmosphere of scholarly enterprise that wafted about the
Hardy archives. I sniffed when I got to the basement,
waiting for my eyes to adjust to the dim and outdated
lighting, alert for the scent of old books, a fragrance I'd
always enjoyed, as any scholar does. But all I got was
mustiness, the kind of odor that greets you when you're
going through worthless old magazines that your parents
and grandparents have saved in fraying paper grocery sacks
up in their attic.

Yet it was the principle of the thing that was
motivating me, and I wasn't about to forgo my chance in
the archives just because the surroundings weren't shiny
and new. I set my backpack down on the lone metal table
and started meandering along the shelves. I picked out a
couple of boxes, similar in size to the ones I'd been ranging
through in the Hardy Museum, but more decrepit and
dusty. I carried them, stacked on top of each other, over to
the table and removed the lids.

Inspecting their contents, I discovered very little of
note: a few old brochures for hotels dating from the 1870s,
some newspaper clippings from the 1950s announcing a
new dance club opening in Lyme Regis, and a 1982 bus
schedule, among other things of even less interest. At the
bottom of the second box, however, after I'd already spent
an hour and a half in that basement, I found something

more interesting. A small book, its cloth binding barely holding its cardboard covers together, with a picture of Betony Lodge gracing the flyleaf.

I caught my breath, beginning to think there was more than coincidence at work here. What was it about the house I had chosen to live in? Everywhere I turned I seemed to find an image of it. Could there be some strange scandal in its history that I knew nothing about? Perhaps one reason the building had only rented two out of the three flats was because everyone else knew about its sordid past.

Beneath the picture on the flyleaf, the publishing company was listed: "New York: Ivison, Phinney, Blakeman & Co., 1852." It was a company I'd never heard of, and I was surprised to find a book that had been published in New York here in England. Still, the most surprising thing of all was the picture of my house, which was similar, though not identical, to Dr. Bellemeade's sketch. I turned the page and read the title, which was printed in block letters:

MY TIME AT A LUNATIC ASYLUM:
THE CRIMES AND HORRORS OF WARRINDER HOUSE,
WITH A VIEW TOWARDS
EXPOSING THE INADEQUACIES OF THE PRESENT METHOD
OF TREATING LUNACY.

BY CECILIA DAVIS

I opened the book to reveal a piece of verse, quoted as an epigram:

THE MIND CAN MAKE
SUBSTANCES, AND PEOPLE PLANETS OF ITS OWN
WITH BEINGS BRIGHTER THAN HAVE BEEN, AND GIVE
A BREATH TO FORMS WHICH CAN OUTLIVE ALL FLESH.
--BYRON

I couldn't help thinking it should have been Shelley who wrote these lines, not his earthier, more cynical rival. In addition, it was creepy to see a verse about the power of the mind to create imaginary, unreal forms quoted by a woman who had been shut up in a lunatic asylum. I looked up from the book and closed my eyes, musing over bright beings, planets, and undying forms—and, of course, about this madwoman-author who knew enough poetry to quote an obscure poem. I remember that I actually hesitated before opening the book and reading the first page. Perhaps I was just screwing up my courage; maybe I was putting off that decisive moment when I confronted this woman's strange tale. Of course, as a student of Hardy's work, I have an appreciation for fatal and momentous actions—they occur in Hardy's novels all the time—and scholars always end up imitating, to one degree or another, what they study. After a few seconds, I took a deep breath and turned the page.

I stared at the tiny print that lined up beneath the header "Advertisement":

> *At the age of 28, I was unlawfully imprisoned in a private lunatic house. Several months earlier, I had lost all the protectors given me by God and man: I, a recent widow, whose sister and parents were carried off by the same illness that took my beloved husband,*

was left alone in a world that allowed for no variations in its concept of what was expected of a lady. My husband's family, finding my presence an inconvenience, removed me to Warrinder House, near Lyme Regis, while I was still recovering from the disease that had laid my closest friends low. I take up my pen now, at the urging of Mr. John Perceval, my dear friend and secretary of the Alleged Lunatics' Friends Society, to tell my story, and to bring to the notice of a willfully ignorant public the ills that have been done to people like myself, and to those less fortunate, true lunatics, whose treatment at the hands of charlatans and scoundrels amounts to nothing less than torture for profit. I attach my own name, not a pseudonym, to this little book, because, far from being ashamed of my experiences, I wish to blazon them to the skies—if it prevents one other poor soul from experiencing what I did.

I read and re-read the paragraph, savoring the heavy language, the ornate expressions, the old-fashioned and formal feel of the prose, the way it leveled forthright and angry criticism in a powerful, muscular style of writing.

Perhaps I would have read the book anyway, knowing that its author had been locked up in the very building I was then living in. Maybe that would have been enough to have pulled me into its narrative. But now, so many weeks and months later, I believe that Cecilia Davis told her story for someone just like me, using descriptions, and even specific words and phrases, that worked together to pull me into the book, calling to me across the years that distanced us from each other. More than that: I believe that my own story—the story of my real life—began on that day, when I first began to read this woman's account about her time at Warrinder House. And I believe that day had been destined to arrive since the very moment, more than 150 years earlier, when she had first put pen to paper in order to tell about her ordeal.

This realization didn't descend on me all at once, of course. It was a slow dawn of understanding, a sense that I had discovered something missing from my own consciousness for some years, though I had never really detected its absence before. To put it another way, that day when I first held Mrs. Davis's book about Warrinder House in my hands, I didn't really know what I was touching. And yet I flipped through it, spending a good twenty minutes studying the drawing of Betony Lodge/Warrinder House on the fly-leaf, reading the first page carefully, and then re-reading it two more times.

Finally, realizing the library would be closing in the next half hour, I put the book back into the box, setting it lightly at the top of the pile. I placed the lid on the box and lifted the box up onto the shelf where I first found it, content to let it sit there until I came back for another dose of Cecilia Davis's angry prose. I wanted to pace myself— to savor the book as much as I could. I was already planning my next visit to the library. I climbed the staircase in the half-shadows, breathing in the smell of linoleum and searching for the steps in the darkness, until I pulled open the door to the main library and found myself back in the twenty-first century, blinking my eyes in the fluorescent lights.

I hesitated for a couple of seconds. And, then, driven by a strange instinct, I doubled back on my path, going through the door to the basement and running down the steps to the archive room. Without a moment's hesitation, I ignored a lifetime of playing by the rules, of being the good student-scholar and honest library patron. In one swift series of movements, I grabbed the box from the shelf, opened it, and pulled out the book. It was all too easy for me to drop it into my backpack, stuff my scarf on top of it, and return the box once more to its place on the shelf. Finally, hefting my pack to my shoulder, I climbed the staircase again, out of the nether world and into the light.

At that moment, I expected everything to change. After all, here I was, in the very act of stealing a rare book. Maybe the book wasn't really worth much anyway, and maybe I was the only one who was interested in it, who had ever even looked at it, but the point was that I was about to steal a book, to deprive a library of a one of its treasures. I mean, we've all had overdue books from the library, and maybe some of us have even had the disconcerting and embarrassing experience of discovering *A Day in the Life of Ivan Denisovich* at the bottom of our closets not months but years after its due date. But to take a book knowingly from a library for no good reason? This is serious stuff, and to me, at this distance in time, considering what happened afterwards, it certainly looks like I was under the influence of the book itself, because I had never, not once, done anything like that before—or, needless to say, since.

I felt as if a thousand eyes were on me as I made my way to the front door of the library. In the quiet reception area, my footsteps echoed like a soldier's boots, and I struggled to breathe, the straps of my backpack digging into my shoulders. Still, I walked towards the turnstile, willing myself forward, my fingers clenched into a sweaty fist. I pushed on the metal bar, waiting for something—a siren, a flashing light, a scream from one of the circulation clerks—but nothing happened.

And then I was outside, squinting against the fading light of an English winter afternoon, with contraband in my backpack. Turning up my coat collar against the cold gusts of wind, I headed to my car. I needed to get back to my flat, to find out what I had stolen, and to discover what this thing was that had taken possession of me.

Chapter Six

*I was born in 1814, to a Warwickshire
family, the third of six children. My father was a vicar,
and though we were not wealthy, we were quite
comfortable. When I was 22, I married my husband,
Frederick, who was my father's curate. He had met my
older brother John at Oxford, and taken holy orders
with him, and after John died unexpectedly, Frederick
rather took his place in our family. It seemed natural for
Frederick and me to marry after a certain time, and for
a few short years, I was quite happy with him.*

*My life was a pleasant one in the beginning,
but unfortunately, I was to pay dearly for my early
happiness. To begin with, we lost our child hours after
his birth, and I was not well for many weeks afterwards.
Six months after my confinement, my father fell ill after
visiting a sick parishioner in his cottage. My mother fell
ill some days later, and for a week they both lay in their
beds, burning with fever, the flesh on their arms and legs
turning red with a spreading rash. It was all Frederick
and I could do to tend to them, especially while
Frederick had to take my father's place in both the
parish and the pulpit. Without the help of my younger
sister Margaret, I would not have been able to manage,
for I was still weak and ill from my lying-in some months
before.*

*And then Frederick himself was felled by that
ominous fever and rash. I was beside myself with fear
and worry. In another week, my parents had lost their
battle, dying within hours of each other, but I hardly had*

time to grieve, so worried and beset was I with Frederick's own precarious state. When even Margaret grew feverish, I cursed my fate. Here was I, the sickest of our family, still weak from childbirth and grief, left to care for those who had fallen.

There is little use in drawing out the tale. My family circle collapsed to a mere nothing. Frederick died, and then Margaret, and I was left alone. It is no wonder that I myself fell ill. I waited for it, then welcomed the fever when at last it began to ravage my body. I wished to die, to join Frederick, Father, Mother, and Margaret. And for a time, it seemed I would not be disappointed. A flame seemed to rage through my brain, and my skin grew hot with fever as the rash crept up my forearms. The tragedies I had undergone, the deaths of mother, father, husband, beloved sister, infant—all these emotional ravages, combined with my weakened physical state, left me no recourse from the illness. Grief and worry had turned my head in such a way that, while ill, I could not tell waking from sleeping, for all life seemed but a hazy shadow. I heard voices, voices that we all hear from time to time, those still, small voices that tell us the right things to do, but these voices were insistent and repetitive, and they annoyed me.

I did not go to my family's funerals, nor did I witness their burials. I was alone in a house of servants, tossing in my bed while strangers attended my loved ones to their graves. And I, the weakest, the poorest of all, was left to live alone in this harsh world, left with no one to ease my journey through life. It was more than a mind could bear.

Reader, I confess that I collapsed beneath the strain. Between feverish illness and deep, abiding sorrow, my mind simply broke. I raved for a time, out of my senses. It was then that my husband's parents arrived at the house, too late to see their son, too late even to bury him, while I myself was sick and unable to make sense of their visit.

They were grieved at their loss, certainly, for who could not love Frederick's sweet and gentle spirit? I do not begrudge them their grief, yet I cannot help but think that they blamed me, the lone survivor of such devastation, for his death. For why else would they consign me to a madhouse? It is true that I raved somewhat in the early days of their visit, but I was ill, and had I not seen Father, Mother, Margaret—even dear Frederick himself—do the same? But they did not see these things, having arrived late to the scene of tragedy. They saw only its outcome, and when I first emerged from the blanketing stupor of my fever, weak and frightened, I could not converse with them. My mind was paralyzed with grief and torpor, it is true, but I was no more mad than you, Reader. I was ill, far more ill than anyone realized, but I was not deprived of my senses.

That did not matter to them, however. They had no use for me, since their son was gone. Indeed, they did not know what to do with me. Was I a relation? If so, in what way? Certainly, had my little babe lived, their duty to me would have been clearer, but as it was, they simply washed their hands of me, sending me off to Warrinder House and returning to their own lives. I

*never saw them again after that morning when they
bundled me off on a cold winter's day, placing me into a
coach with a little serving girl and directing the
coachman to Dorset. It was as if I had never been part of
their lives at all, as if I had never married poor, dear
Frederick.*

*My days at Warrinder House numbered, all
told, 756. More than two years of seclusion from
everyone I knew and loved. Truly, I do not know how I
ever survived those dark days of deprivation, how my
mind was able to heal itself and emerge once more into
the light of sanity and health and moral cleanliness. But
heal it did, and I have my brother Alfred to thank for it.
He it was who saved me from Warrinder House and its
evils. Upon returning to England from India, my
brother, newly retired from the Third Light Dragoons,
found me and took me from the asylum, against the will
and advice of Mr. Warrinder himself. It is because of
Alfred that I am able to write this today—indeed,
because of Alfred that I am alive at all.*

--Cecilia Davis, My Time in a Lunatic Asylum

I spent most of the next three days reading Mrs.
Davis's book. I jumped each time my cell phone rang,
fearing that it was the city library asking for their book
back. I neglected mealtimes, existing on cream crackers,
cheese bits, and chocolate spread, washed down by copious
amounts of tea. In fact, one day, I'm ashamed to say, I
never even changed out of my nightgown.

The only thing that distracted me from Cecilia
Davis's story was the arrival of Diggory. I had discovered

Diggory—the name I gave to an orange marmalade kitten—on one of the few days I left my flat, while exploring the grounds of Betony Lodge on the first sunny afternoon since Brian's departure for London. I had been looking for something to do, tired of going over my materials on Thomas Hardy, trying to keep from reading about the crimes and horrors of Warrinder House for the third straight day, and unwilling to take a drive through the countryside, pleasant though the views were. Instead, that day, I had decided to take a stroll behind my house, in the area that would be called the backyard if I were in the States. Of course, I was constructing a map of Warrinder House in my head as I prowled through the back field.

It was, to be honest, an overgrown mess of an area. There had been a nominal attempt to keep nature at bay at some point, but by this time the bushes were indistinct from the brambles that had invaded them, straggling stems reaching towards the all-too-scant sunlight, holding dry clods of dirt and pebbles between them. There was some sort of plant, probably betony, growing everywhere, but none in a clump together. I am no gardener myself, but I knew that flowers were supposed to grow in patches, not in a scattering of independent stands like libertarians at an election. Yet, despite its wayward growth, there was a strange kind of beauty, a lush fertility that permeated this abandoned garden plot.

I'd been walking about a small area for some twenty minutes, listening to the wind blow through tree branches that strained across the garden wall several feet behind me, watching the clouds float across a fiercely blue sky, when I tripped over something hard in the dirt, nearly falling to my knees. Looking down, I saw that some animal had been digging at a spot right by my feet, unearthing the edge of a stone some two inches below the level of the topsoil. I couldn't tell what kind of animal's handiwork it was, but I saw that there were other stones placed in a line with the exposed one, indicating that this was some kind of foundation for a building long disused.

I was curious, so I bent down and clawed at the dirt, hoping to figure out what kind of structure I'd stumbled upon. After a few minutes of unproductive digging, I heard a soft cry behind me: and there, emerging from a huge bush with wicked spines on its branches, was a tiny orange kitten, its pupils mere slits in the bright sunlight, its tail hardly more than the length of a sock needle and almost as thin. I held out my hand towards it, and it tumbled forward to greet me, mewing in a high-pitched squeal. There were no other kittens to be discovered, and apparently no mother around either. How this little kitten got himself to this particular place would remain a mystery.

But it didn't matter to me where he came from, not once I picked him up, because he began to purr, softly at first, and then so loud I could hardly believe it came from him. I turned around, convinced there must be some other cat in the area, but I was alone with the kitten, whom I lost no time in naming "Diggory."

I knew what a mistake it is to name a stray animal, how it increases the chance that you'll want to keep it as a pet, but to be honest, feeling lonely and more than a little alienated, I didn't care. I also knew that it's silly to name a cat after a character in a book, but I couldn't help it, because I thought it was fitting: in Thomas Hardy's *The*

Return of the Native, Diggory Venn is a reddleman, a seller of dye so red it stains his skin permanently. I felt that I'd found the perfect name for my new kitten.

I never did find out where he came from, but he made my life, and the troubles I was about to face, just a little bit easier to handle, and I'm glad he appeared out of nowhere. Still, Brian and I had never had a pet before, and, as busy academics trying to get ahead in our careers, we'd never really considered the possibility of acquiring one, which was why I was a little nervous about how he would take to Diggory on his return.

When I say the next few days of my life were consumed by the book I'd taken (even now I shy at the word "stolen") from the public library, I am exaggerating. I did read it during that time—to be honest, I read it through exactly three and a half times—but I did other things as well. I went to the pet store in Dorchester to buy a litter box and some food for Diggory, and I stopped on the way home to fill the car with petrol. I went for walks like the one I described above—up until the point at which I found Diggory. I ate a little, slept, and, when I remembered to, I bathed.

I will admit that my obsession about *My Time in Warrinder House* is inexplicable. For one thing, the book wasn't terribly well written. As with so many other books, it was the story it told that lured me in, not the writing. Cecilia Davis had penned a melodramatic accusation against the director of the insane asylum, Mr. Warrinder, for mistreating patients and keeping them wrongfully confined. She charged him with physical abuse as well as with what today would be termed psychological abuse, in that he restrained patients with ropes and chains, secured them in outlying buildings without access to heat or water, and mocked them for their illnesses and their actions. Anyone who found herself in Warrinder's House, she stated, would certainly become insane with such treatment, even if they arrived in a state of perfect mental health. Mrs. Davis tended to write in a dramatic vein, overdoing it every so often: "*How many more unfortunate souls faced the same fate as I?*" she declaimed. "*What other dark and villainous secrets lay hidden in the walls and beams of this dreadful house? These are the questions that plague me daily, yet there are no answers to them.*"

I can't lie: I began to be plagued by these questions myself. In no time, I had become fascinated by the book; I read and re-read it. And yet I'm not sure whether I would have been interested in it at all if it had not been describing events and actions that occurred in the very same place where I was living. Every so often, I would stop reading and look up, gazing at the room around me, trying to imagine what it had looked like with two or three madwomen, or rather, women accused of madness, sitting on a couch or lying on a bed.

I remember the afternoon I returned from the pet store, carrying a litter box and a sack of kitten food in my arms. It was dark, and for a moment, struck by the thought of a former asylum being my home, I stood on the front lawn, peering up at the second floor of Betony Lodge, looking at the window of my flat. The lamp I'd left on glowed behind the thin cotton curtain, but as I stared, my thoughts on a Warrinder House that had existed over 150 years earlier, I noticed a subtle flickering, as if a pulse or current was affecting the light. Then, in the next moment, the light went out completely, leaving the window a dark gap in the side of the building.

Was it a faulty switch? Or had Diggory knocked the lamp over? I am not ashamed to say that I had to gather my courage before going up into the darkened room, feeling my way with my one free hand splayed on the wall, like a sun-blind woman coming off the beach. When I finally managed to open the door to my flat and switch on the ceiling light, Diggory was sitting on the floor, his large green eyes blinking in the unaccustomed light. He mewed softly and toddled over to me, curling around my ankles. I put my parcels down and picked him up, hugging him to my chest, grateful for the comforting rumble of his purring. As I reached beneath the lampshade on the table and turned the switch, the light came on immediately. There was apparently nothing wrong with the lamp, and I could not explain why it had switched off abruptly a moment earlier. But I had Diggory to take care of, so I shrugged my shoulders, refusing to think about it any longer.

But of course even Diggory wasn't able to completely banish the idea of Warrinder House from my mind. It was an idea I kept with me throughout the day— and during a good part of the evening as well. Perhaps if I'd been going into the Hardy Museum regularly I'd have been able to keep more balance in my life, but it was, as George had warned me, closed during this period. At any rate, the knowledge that I was comfortably living in what was once an asylum even crept into my dreams at night. Several times in the next few days, I would wake from them in a sweat, breathing hard, the sound of my own heartbeat thudding in my ears, a sense of dread remaining from a series of troubling images.

In one particularly vivid nightmare I had, I was a visitor to Warrinder House as it was 150 years ago. With the frustrating logic that inheres in dreams, the furniture and décor were the same as that in Betony Lodge, but it was filled with mentally ill people. At first, the only way I knew they were ill was through some kind of omniscient dream-knowledge: the women, dressed in heavy Victorian garb, looked normal enough. But, as we were watching a cricket match on the television (yes, television), one woman started clucking like a chicken, and another leaned towards me to ask me if I realized that her companion was singing Handel's "Lascia Ch'io Panga" in the wrong key. I turned my head to ask someone else their opinion and found that I was restrained by silken cords, tying me to my seat. I tried to say that a mistake had been made, that I myself was perfectly sane, but found that I could not move my lips at all. I struggled, realizing that it was becoming hard for me even to draw a breath. And there was nothing I could do about it.

Panic gripped my entire body, and I could feel all my muscles tighten. My tongue pushed against my teeth, but I could not open my mouth to scream. "This is it," I told myself. "This is how I die." By a supreme effort, I opened my eyes, and at the same instant, I realized that my paralysis was caused by Diggory, who had curled up on top of my neck. I pushed him away and sat up, trembling in the early morning light, looking around my bedroom for any vestige of Victorian madwomen. It took the better part of an hour and three cups of tea for me to push the terrifying sensation of paralysis and lunacy out of my memory.

The real problem, of course, was that I had an overactive imagination: too much time and solitude on my hands, in addition to a thrilling discovery and no one to share it with. Brian, engrossed in his own work, was far away: London was, after all, a world apart from Dorset. And compounding the geographical distance was the fact that I was disappearing more and more into a world of my own, a world that bore little if any relation to the world that Brian inhabited. We were growing apart, much more quickly than I ever thought possible, and I felt like there was nothing I could do about it.

But all of that didn't bother me then. To be honest, I'm not even sure if it bothers me now, after all is said and done. Because what I experienced at Betony Lodge that winter was worth whatever it cost me, which is just a fancy way of saying that living in a re-purposed madhouse was my idea of fun.

And if that isn't crazy, I don't know what is.

Chapter Seven

When I first arrived at Warrinder House, I was weak, confused and frightened, and I feared for both my safety and my sanity. With good reason: in those first few weeks, I was dragged from my room in the early hours of the morning at least three out of seven days and taken to a room on the ground floor of the building, where I was administered a cold shower bath. Forced to disrobe (more often than not, I resisted, and so I was held down and stripped by slovenly attendants as I kicked and screamed, for I felt that I was fighting for my honor, if not for my life itself), I was shoved into a wooden chair, to which my arms and legs were clamped tightly. A bucket of cold water—none too clean, I might add—was dumped over my head. This was repeated upwards of three times each session. I believe the thought was that the shock of the water to my system would be enough to re-set my mental faculties. I need not spend too much time here, I hope, explaining it produced quite the opposite effect. I was left feeling violated, bewildered, and confused. Each time, the cold water mingled with the very tears on my face, so pitiable an object had I become.

When this treatment failed to bring about the desired improvement, I was taken to a building behind Warrinder House and thrown into a bath—this in the winter time, and after numerous other nervous patients had been treated in this way before my turn arrived. The water was unwholesome, and the atmosphere seemed specially designed to promote sickness. Fortunately, for my sake, I caught cold, and the treatments stopped for a time. I believe that if I hadn't succumbed to a minor illness, they would have continued with this treatment until I contracted pneumonia.

I will confess that I often thought that the doctors at Warrinder were determined, if they could not cure my mental sickness, to do the next best thing in their minds, and simply ensure my early death. They could hardly have done more to work towards that event. But in the end, my constitution and my youth aided me in withstanding these assaults on my health, and my full reason gradually returned.

And yet no one—not one servant, nor either of the two doctors, nor Mr. Warrinder himself—seemed to notice or acknowledge my return to health and lucidity of mind. Reader, I confess that after a time, I grew impatient. I have not described in great detail the domestic situation of Warrinder House, and I shall not delve into such detail, but imagine how it is to a poor benighted soul thrown into an asylum. One day, without warning, you are wrenched from your home, hauled into a coach, and installed like a piece of furniture in a large building that you have never seen before. You are attended by people who correct you when you address them as your servants; it seems that you are rather to serve them, low as they are, and comply with their wishes. If you fail in this regard, their wishes are quickly re-issued as orders, and if you resist those orders, you are struck, and shoved, and pulled about, until you feel you have no choice but to fight. You are then attacked with greater force, outnumbered by these surly attendants, and *rendered completely powerless.*

Is it any wonder that few patients improve under such circumstances? Is it any wonder that our mad-houses worsen the illness rather than treat it? People of England, look at the system you have created and have allowed to grow and spread among you; and remember that no one is immune to insanity, from king to peasant. Remember that it could strike you, or someone whom you love: your son, your daughter, your aged father or mother, your husband or your wife. I entreat you to remember that lunatics deserve pity as much, and perhaps more, than any other of God's afflicted creatures.

--Cecilia Davis, My Time in a Lunatic Asylum

Two days passed, and I was still engaged in my new favorite hobby: matching up locations vaguely hinted at in *My Time in a Lunatic Asylum* with real places in Betony Lodge. The layout of the asylum was pretty much impossible for me to ascertain since so many renovations and reconstructions had occurred over the years, but the grounds, the outlying buildings, the gardens—those things, I thought, might be fairly easy to identify. So, during a few days of sunny weather, when the Hardy Museum was still closed and Brian was delayed in London with business matters to do with setting up more readings, I prowled around behind the house for hours at a time, beyond the small walled garden behind it, kicking up stones, picking up colored glass shards, and pushing my way through weeds and hollowed-out stalks of dead plants, until I made my way to the area far behind Betony Lodge itself, to the very edge of the forest that abutted the property and climbed up the hill behind the house.

One afternoon, I found myself crawling on the ground, examining the remaining brickwork of the foundation I'd found the day I discovered Diggory in the grass. It looked to my unpracticed eye as if it could have been a barn. Of course, there were no walls left, just chunks of bricks or stones laying in a regular pattern in the ground. I could imagine the wooden walls of the building, however, rising up from these stones, and I thought about the horses and other animals that must have been kept inside it so many years ago.

I had never thought to play archeologist, but who can resist the mystery of the past? Don't we all dream of finding old pieces of jewelry, ancient coins that once slipped out of a pocket or saddlebag, or brass buttons dropped from liveried servants' jackets and breeches? Intrigued, I knelt on the ground and started scrabbling in the dirt like a two year old, hoping against logic that I might find something interesting.

I have to admit, I enjoyed myself. How often do adults really get to dig in the dirt for no apparent reason? I knew it was a silly thing to do, knew I was tearing up my fingernails, dirtying my slacks, probably encountering any number of germs and microbes, but I couldn't help myself. I felt that I had to keep going, not knowing what I was looking for or how I was supposed to look for it. The sun beat down on my back, warming my shoulders, and yet I kept digging. I could hear seagulls crying in the far distance, along with the calls of other birds that I couldn't identify; I listened to the light breeze rustling the leaves of the trees nearby, and still my hands kept exploring the earth, like those of a blind woman feeling her way through an almost-familiar room. My mind was empty; I resisted the urge to question my actions, to worry about what Brian was doing in London during these extra days of his trip, even to wonder how Diggory was faring back in my flat. In short, I was having a grand time playing in the dirt by myself.

I was rewarded for my childish efforts. I have no idea how much time passed while I was kneeling there, scratching in the sandy earth, when my fingertips brushed against something hard and perfectly oval in shape. I thought at first it was a stone when I pulled it up to look at it, or perhaps a fossil. Even so far from the shore as Betony Lodge, people had occasionally turned up fossils in their fields—Dorset was not called the Jurassic Coast for nothing, after all.

But it wasn't a fossil. It was a dirt-encrusted piece of jewelry. I still remember the thrill of discovery, the electric tingle that went down my spine as I turned it over in my filthy hand to get a look at it. It was like the charge of emotion you get when you're fishing and the line suddenly goes taut, then wiggles, then goes taut again, and you know that it's no false alarm, no snagged line, but rather a real, living fish on your hook. I tried to brush the dirt off, but it was caked on good and hard, so I decided to take the piece, a locket by the look of it, inside to clean it up and identify it.

Standing up, I realized that my back was aching. How long had I been there, crouched on all fours in the afternoon sunlight? Sweat was trickling past my ears, even though it was a cool day at the end of February. I lifted my shoulders and rolled them, raising one, then the other, to get the kinks out of my scholar's weak muscles, then glanced down at the shiny object I held in my palm and shoved it deep into my pocket. It seemed surprisingly heavy for its size, and I wondered if it could be gold.

When I reached the back gate of the garden, Leanne was leaning against it, watching Ethan and Gemma running around the fenced-in area like maniacs. A sunny afternoon in England, especially in the wintertime, is no joking matter, and everyone takes advantage of it if they can. I put my hand on the gate, and still looking at her children, Leanne shook her head. A moment later, she turned towards me, opening the latch to let me in.

"I can only hope they'll tire themselves out and go to bed early tonight," she said, adding "little fiends" under her breath. "Making me nutters, they are."

"Well," I said, coming through, "it looks like they're having fun now, anyway." Gemma was chasing Ethan with a stick, and since it didn't look like this scenario would end well, I hurried to make my exit into the house. Hearing Leanne discipline her children was not my favorite pastime.

"What were you doing out there, anyway, Kerys?"

I stopped in my tracks, my hand on the back door of the Lodge. I don't know why this question made me nervous—I certainly wasn't doing anything to be ashamed of—but I suddenly became aware of the weight in my pocket as I turned to face Leanne.

"What do you mean?" I turned around, making sure I looked directly at Leanne and keeping my voice level.

"You were out digging in the dirt. I saw you. Did you drop something? You were there a long time. I thought maybe you'd lost a contact lens or an earring or something. Did you find it?"

"Yes," I said, automatically. "Oh yes, I found it."

"What was it?"

I paused for a moment, not sure of what to say.

"The thing you dropped. What was it?" Leanne was persistent.

"A two-pound coin," I said, wincing at my stupidity, at my strange reluctance to share my discovery with anyone else. "They don't grow on trees, after all. Not for poor scholars like me."

Leanne laughed, and I hurried into the house. I was not surprised to find, when I had run up the staircase and reached my own flat, that my heart was racing. My fingers, too, were clammy with sweat, making a muddy mess of the object I pulled out of my pocket, which I placed on the dining room table before I went to the bathroom to clean myself up.

I'm usually pretty good at self-discipline. Years of being a graduate student meant that I often had to forego parties, movies, and other self-indulgent but normal activities (like sleep and exercise) in order to complete important academic tasks. There are whole television series that I've missed because of grad school, for example. But it seemed that all my self-control was dissipating quickly during my time alone at Betony Lodge. I had thought, as I began to soap up my hands beneath the cold water flowing from the tap, that I would take my discovery, whatever it turned out to be, to the local historical society. But by the time I had rinsed the caked dirt from my hands and dried them, I knew I would be doing no such thing.

I looked around to make sure Diggory was engaged and wouldn't bother me, and located him sleeping right on my pillow. Ordinarily, I would have moved him since I'm not fond of burying my nose in cat fur at night, but I didn't want to risk waking him and having him interrupt me, so I left him alone and tiptoed to the kitchen, filled a saucepan full of soapy water, and brought it over to the table. Just before I sat down, I dropped the object into the pot and retrieved some towels and a scouring pad.

I'm sure I did it all wrong—I'm no archeologist, after all. But apparently that didn't matter, because when I pulled the object from the sudsy water, it was obvious that it was a piece of jewelry—not a button, or a pull-tab, or a random piece of metal. I placed it on the towel and wrapped it up, as if it were a treasure, a gift I was planning to offer to someone. I held it in my hands and felt the towel dampen beneath my fingers. For a few seconds, suspended between discovery and analysis, I was not merely content, but happy.

My reverie ended abruptly, with the rude buzzing of my cell phone. Picking it up, I saw that it was Brian, and I answered it. We chatted for a few minutes, but it felt forced to me. I was itching to get back to my locket, and I got the feeling that Brian was just calling out of a sense of duty. I could have been wrong about it, of course, distracted as I was by the towel and the treasure buried inside it, but at any rate, we didn't talk long. He told me he planned to come home the next day, and I tried to sound enthusiastic about his return, but I'm not quite sure I actually managed it.

When I put the phone down, I sat for a moment in silence. Then I took a big breath and looked around the room, as if I expected an audience for this next part of my work. From beneath the table, I heard a soft mew, and I looked down to discover Diggory between my feet, blinking as if he just woke up—which, apparently, he had. On the other end of the table, *My Time at an Insane Asylum* lay, its cover dark and spotted with age. I pulled the towel to me and unfolded it as if it were a swaddled infant.

There, nestled in the blue and white terrycloth, lay a golden locket. It fit in the palm of my hand, was no bigger than a half dollar, if that, and it had a crosshatch design on the front. I flipped it over with my fingertip; the back had no design on it, and was smooth but scratched. There were still bits of dirt buried in the grooves of the design, and it wouldn't open on the first try. I pressed the top of the bail again, this time a little harder, and the locket opened, not springing open as it should, but pulling apart like a lazy curtain. Inside, the two sides reflected each other, shiny and unscratched.

There was no picture within the locket, however. I tried to repress my disappointment. Of course, that would be too much to ask, and I realized what a miracle it would be to find an intact locket, even without a miniature portrait inside. I squinted at the inside of the locket again, and that's when I noticed a few strands of hair centered in it, held in place by the framework for the missing picture. I closed the locket and turned it over in my hand again, looking at the back of it, and could see, but not read, the words etched upon it.

Rushing to the utility drawer in the kitchen, I began digging around in it, oblivious to the racket I was making, until I found what I was looking for: a magnifying glass. I took it back to the table, held it over the locket, and was able to see the words "August 23, 1841." Just below that, a name, in cursive letters that were too tight and small for me to read, even with my drugstore magnifying glass.

That was it—but it was everything to me. What I held in my hand was something from Victorian days, and while that might not have been enough to excite a native Briton, I found it thrilling. What's more, I realized that 1841 would have been right around the time Betony Lodge was Warrinder House, and that this locket could be part of the legacy from those dark days in this house's past existence. I put the locket back down in the center of the towel, which I pushed over towards the book I'd found.

Then I walked across the room to look out the front window, towards the gates that still stood in front of the house, the gates through which unfortunate and confused women had passed through, gates that had been present when this structure had housed lunatics—and, by Mrs. Davis's account at any rate, many sane people who had become burdens to their families as well. The sun was on the other side of the house, casting long, golden shadows across the hedges. It would be dark soon. But that didn't matter. I turned away from the window and surveyed my dining room table, with the locket and the book resting on it.

My newfound treasures. My empire.

Chapter Eight

From manuscripts of moving song
Inspired by scenes and dreams unknown
I'll pour out raptures that belong
To others, as they were my own.
--Thomas Hardy, "Let Me Enjoy"

The next day was rainy, which was the norm for England: one or two beautiful days, followed by several days of cold, damp, and windy weather. But I was content to stay inside with a big pot of tea, a packet of biscuits, and Diggory to play with.

Of course, I also had my book and my locket to muse over, as well. I have said the book was not particularly well written, but that didn't matter. The story it told was fascinating, and I was a motivated reader. After the diatribe she leveled at the mad-doctors ("alienists") from Warrinder House in the first few pages of the book, Mrs. Davis settled down and told her harrowing story. There was a quirky Victorian feel to the writing, and I soon grew quite fond of the style, at which I had once rolled my eyes. It was certainly good reading material for a rainy day, especially since I was sitting in the house the lady had been incarcerated in—perhaps the very room she'd been confined to. Certainly I was entranced by Cecilia Davis's words, and when my attention flagged, all I had to do was glance over at the locket, still wrapped up in its towel on my dining room table, to be reminded of the close connection I already had with this narrative. The book, the locket, and me—all three of us in the same room, at the same time. It felt as if we were all home again, for the first time in many years.

Brian was due home that afternoon, yet I had not told him about Diggory or about my recent activities. He had done well: he'd gained the attention of the English literary community, and even secured some invitations to various readings and workshops around Great Britain. He was as happy as I'd ever heard him, and he told me that he was looking forward to getting back to Dorset to do some more writing and some preparation for his upcoming readings.

I had not wanted to rock the boat by telling him about Diggory, however. I put it off, worried about his reaction. "What will we do with him when we go back to the States, Kerys? It will be impossible to keep him, you know that, don't you? Why bring this kind of responsibility and frustration on yourself? Don't you have enough to keep you busy?" I could hear the words coming out of his mouth, knew exactly what he would say even before he said it.

So, the first subject of conversation after I picked Brian up at the train station that evening was—naturally— Diggory. I mentioned that I'd found a kitten and was nursing him back to health, and then I waited for Brian's reaction, bracing myself for an argument.

But to my surprise, there was nothing. Just a quick, "Oh really? Can't wait to see the little guy!" Then Brian told me his big news: a couple, Melissa and Jack, whom Brian had met at a cocktail party, had invited him to Hay-on-Wye, in Wales, to do a reading and book signing at their own little bookstore in a few days. It didn't occur to me back then to wonder about why I was so far off on my prediction of how he would react to a new kitten in the house. It was nice to have him back for a little while, especially since he seemed quite happy to be home. Our moods didn't usually match up so seamlessly.

But that night they did. Brian and Diggory got along famously, and the dinner I'd planned and prepared turned out well; the wine was good, and the sheets were soft and welcoming when we crawled into our bed together for the first time in ten days. It was an excellent homecoming, although just before I fell asleep with Brian's arms around me, I thought I heard the sound I'd heard the day he left, only this time it sounded to me just like a woman in pain. But I was drowsy, and sated, and perhaps a little tipsy as well, and it was so easy to ignore the sound and fall into a gentle sleep as the wind rattled the bare tree branches against our bedroom window.

I hadn't allowed myself to talk about my recent discoveries with Brian on that first night home. After all, he had so much to share with me, and I—I wasn't quite ready to tell Brian that I'd deviated so far from my own work plans while he was away. But I may have paid the price for self-censorship, or perhaps it was all the wine I drank with dinner—whatever the reason, I dreamt of Warrinder House that night. I was walking up the stairway, a bag of groceries in my arms, moving ever more quickly with a powerful sense of urgency. Apparently, I had to be in a certain room at a certain time, or I would be subject to punishment. I was late, and worried, and so I started to run up the staircase, which grew longer and longer without regard to logic or physics. The house echoed with low moans and sobs, and I knew that there were people suffering from some kind of intense sadness, from fear, from a sense of neglect and isolation, in every room in this house that I knew as Betony Lodge. I began to run faster, hoping to gain my own apartment and shut the noises out.

At last I reached the top landing, but as I gathered my strength for the final sprint down the hallway, the noise, that fearful sound of people in pain, grew ever louder, like the climax of a strange and fearful aria in an opera I didn't want to see. I dropped the bags and began to run down the hallway to my own door, and the hallway grew longer and longer, just as the staircase had. I pumped my legs harder, until I could go no faster, and then I saw, as I looked towards the end of the hall, a dark figure silhouetted by the light behind it. I knew he was waiting for me, and I knew he was not my friend. So I stopped short, panting, and looked for an escape. And then every door in the house began to open in such a way that I could not see who was opening them.

I screamed, but no sound came from my lips, although I tried again and again to call for help. I was swallowed by my unnamed fear, and, as in my first dream about Warrinder House, I could neither move, nor make a sound, nor will myself awake. At last, however, I was able to make a sound, which to my sleep-numbed ears sounded deep and guttural, the sound that an old man breathing his last gasp makes. I flung my arms out before me, and then I felt myself being shaken, softly at first, but then with more and more force.

"Kerys. Kerys! Wake up!" Brian had his hands on both my shoulders, pressing them into the bed and shaking me like a rag. "You're having a nightmare." He had turned the light on and was sitting beside me, on my side of the bed.

I sat up and pushed my hair out of my eyes. "What time is it?" I asked.

"It's one a.m. We've only been asleep a couple of hours. What on earth is the matter?"

"I had a bad dream, that's all."

"And?" Brian stared at me, waiting.

"And what?" I shrugged. "Everyone has a bad dream once in a while."

"Yes, but are you okay? I've never known you to scream out in your sleep before."

"Scream out? What did I say?"

"You were yelling at someone. 'Get out, run'— that's what you said. 'I can help you get away now' –you kept on saying that." He paused and watched me for a moment. I'd gotten my breath back, and some of my presence of mind.

I tried a tentative smile. "Thank you for waking me up."

He didn't smile back at me right away. "What's frightened you, Kerys?"

"I'm not sure. Nothing, probably. Just a bad dream, that's all." I settled back into my pillow.

"Kerys," said Brian, "If there's anything that's bothering you—anything at all—don't you think you should tell me?"

It was just like Brian to try and make something crazy out of a mere nightmare. I laughed, which was precisely the wrong thing to do. His eyes narrowed, and he looked hurt. "I'm sorry, Brian. It really was just a bad dream. There's nothing Freudian about it."

He looked angry now, not just hurt. He stood up and walked around back to his side of the bed. Then he turned out the light, and for a moment we both stared up at the dark ceiling. After a moment, he asked, "What was your nightmare about, Kerys?"

"I was running through some halls, trying to get into our apartment."

"That was a nightmare? Sounds pretty innocent to me."

"I guess you had to be there," I said, and pulled his arm over me, moving closer to him. He didn't answer, and I figured we'd talk about it more in the morning. But even with Brian's arm draped over me in a protective embrace, it took me a long time to fall back asleep.

Chapter Nine

Reader, it is not enough for me to state this; I find it necessary to show you the extent of the cruelty that I myself, and others I knew, had to suffer. Surely it is a dreadful thing to revisit the old scenes, and it will not be easy even for you, settled in your own house, in your own chair with all your comforts about you, to come with me inside those forbidding walls. But screw up your courage, my friend; take my hand in yours, and we shall go together. It will be no small help to you, and no little grief to me, that I know the way so very well.

Warrinder House had, and still has today, a modest facade; it was, after all, once a family domicile. The half-moon drive led right to the front steps of a red brick house, and at the top of them, a broad front door, with a large brass door-knocker in its center. The entry way was a close and shallow hall, dimly lit, with hard flagstone on the floor. The lower level of the house was comprised of the usual rooms—a dining hall, a sitting room, and a study, in addition to the kitchen and scullery.

The servants seemed to have inordinate freedom in Warrinder House. Patients were lodged upstairs and, occasionally, in outer buildings on the estate. It was part of our treatment, apparently, to find out that our sense of self-importance was a delusion. We patients were not given any respect at Warrinder House, which was strange, since the mad-doctor and proprietor of the place made his living, and indeed a tidy fortune, off of us so-called lunatics....

--Cecilia Davis, My Time in a Lunatic Asylum

The next morning, I left Brian wrestling with the coffee machine, which I hadn't used since he'd left for London a week earlier, being mostly a tea-drinker myself, and set off for the Hardy Museum for my first shift in the archive room since it had re-opened after its midseason break. It was about eight-thirty when I closed the front door to the flat behind me and started down the staircase, haunted by a disturbing but fleeting memory of my nightmare. So it's not surprising that I was startled when I heard a small voice calling out "hi" to me as I passed by Leanne's door. I turned towards it, not knowing what to expect, and saw Ethan peeking out of his flat, the door slightly ajar. His blonde hair was tousled, as if he'd just woken up. I could see that he still had his pajamas on.

"Hi," I said, stopping and bending down to his level. "What are you doing?"

"Looking for the noise," said Ethan, opening the door a little wider.

"That's cool. How do you look for a noise?"

"You listen for it. You know that!" I felt foolish for a moment, as if Ethan was right, and I should have known how to look for a noise.

"Right. Well, what kind of noise are you looking for?"

"You know," he said, his large blue eyes squinting with impatience, exasperated by my stupidity. "You hear it, too. The noise that comes at night. The sad one."

I stared at him.

Just then, Leanne called from inside the flat. "Ethan! Oh, there you are. What on earth are you doing?" Leanne came to the door and saw me and smiled. "Hullo,

Kerys. On your way to Dorchester?"

"Yes," I said, pulling my gaze away from Ethan to look up at Leanne. She was dressed as if ready to go to work.

"Right! Have a good day," she said, and then, turning to Ethan, "You need to go get dressed, young man! I don't want us to be late again!" Ethan kept looking into my eyes as Leanne practically pulled him back inside. Then the door shut, and I went to the car park in front of the building with Ethan's odd comment still on my mind.

I suppose it was natural that I was distracted that day at work. To be honest, my discovery of Dr. Bellemeade's notes about young Hardy and his medical ailments had paled beside my discovery of the lurid past of Betony Lodge and the locket I had dug up the previous day. I kept asking myself: was Bellemeade's journal really significant? I was beginning to feel that I was being an unreasonable and illogical researcher, expecting each new box I catalogued to contain something important, some earth-shattering discovery that would change the shape of Thomas Hardy studies. I thought of all those discoveries that make the news: Richard III's body unearthed in a modern car park; James Boswell's *London Journal* found in an Irish castle centuries after it was written; the earliest version of the King James Bible discovered by an unknown junior professor at a state college in New Jersey. But do scholars really need to know when a teen-aged Hardy had the measles and how many wisdom teeth he had pulled? I didn't think so. The truth was that I had my own insignificant but fascinating discoveries waiting for me at home. I mused on them as I continued itemizing dusty pieces of paper and worked the entire day without talking to anyone except for Brian, whom I called during my lunch break, and George, whom I had greeted briefly as I entered the Museum. And throughout the day, in the back of my mind, I replayed my strange conversation with young Ethan.

How did he know that I had heard the same noises he had? I was puzzled and more than a little unnerved. I've never been all that comfortable with children, and now here was one who seemed to read my mind before I even knew myself what I was thinking. Several times that day I had to force myself to pay more attention to the boring letters, invoices, and laundry lists I was cataloguing.

I resolved to tell Brian all about it when I got home that night. I would confess everything: about the book I'd stolen, the locket I'd found, the whole shebang. He might raise his eyebrows about the book, but I was pretty sure he would find it as fascinating as I did: he was a writer, after all, awake to the possibilities of plot, character, and coincidence, and there was no danger that he would turn me in or force me to take it back or anything like that. At least I didn't think there was.

So I went home to Betony Lodge, determined to come clean. As I passed Leanne's door, I paused, remembering my unnerving conversation with Ethan that morning. But all I heard was the television blaring. I took a deep breath and climbed the stairs to my flat, ready to tell Brian all I'd been up to since he'd left for London the previous week.

He was in the kitchen making dinner, and I gave him a quick kiss to show I appreciated his efforts as I took the large glass of white wine he offered me. I could tell he'd had a good day of writing by the scanty amount of wine left in the bottle. Brian always celebrated his productivity in a liquid way. I didn't mind—it made him all the more amiable and talkative and pleasant to be around.

"What's for dinner?" I asked, standing beside him and looking at the pan. It was filled with pale chunks of meat and cubes of celery. Brian was adding green peas and splashing the mixture with the rest of the wine. I couldn't tell what he was cooking, but it seemed like he knew what he was doing.

"Chicken parmesan," he said. "Open another bottle of wine, would you, Kerys?"

"Okay. Just a second, though."

I went into the bedroom and opened my dresser drawer, where I'd put the book and the locket after I'd wrapped them both up in the terrycloth dish towel the last time I'd had them out to look at them, just before I had picked Brian up from the train station. As I put my hand in the drawer, however, I heard a low moan, barely audible, coming from behind me. I turned, thinking it might be Diggory, but he was sound asleep on the bed and had apparently heard nothing. I turned back to the drawer, and then I heard it again. It sounded, as Ethan had said, just like a sad lady crying. It seemed to waft up from the floor, so I bent down and looked beneath the bed.

Nothing. The moan came once more, louder this time, and I rose from my knees and went into the kitchen. "Did you hear that, Brian?"

"Hear what?"

"I guess you didn't. It was a weird noise, like a

woman crying."

"Probably just some peacocks down the road or something."

"Yes," I said, "but—"

"Hey, where's that new bottle of wine? Weren't you going to open it up and pour us some more? A person can't cook without a little inspiration, you know."

I had already turned around to go back into the bedroom and get my confessional objects, but something made me stop. It wasn't just Brian's request for more wine, either. There's a funny thing about marriage and relationships: you feel like you know someone really well, join your entire life to theirs, take them to have and to hold till death do you part and all that stuff—but when it comes to a simple thing, even an insignificant thing, all too often you don't trust them.

And at that moment, I didn't trust Brian. I don't mean that I was afraid he would turn me in for taking the book from the city library or anything like that; it was simply that I didn't trust him not to make fun of my discoveries, not to poke holes in my newfound mysteries— not to take my story away from me and diminish it in some way. And so I said nothing to him on that night, or on any other, about my purloined book, the eerie sounds I'd been hearing, or my newly discovered locket.

In fact, I guess you could say that it was on that particular night that I first started keeping secrets from Brian. Of course, it was difficult to hide my growing obsession for *My Time at a Lunatic Asylum*. It would have been impossible if Brian hadn't been caught up in his own work; he was producing poems at a prodigious rate in those days, and the connections he had made in London during the conference were beginning to pay off. The following week he was supposed to go on that trip to Jack and Melissa's bookstore in Wales, and to be honest, I was looking forward to the freedom his absence would afford me.

I hadn't been able to look at my book for several days, since Brian was almost always in the flat when I was. I often thought about it, remembering its form, its heft, even the smell of its thick pages. And although only a few days had passed since I'd been able to pick it up and hold it again, to lose myself in its painful story, during that time I caught myself returning to the memory of the book with something akin to pleasure. It was like remembering a person from an earlier time in my life—like my third-grade teacher. I might not remember the exact shade of her hair, or the color of her eyes, but I could remember the boiled wool jacket she wore at recess, the way she would kneel at my desk to help me when I was having trouble with the 7 times table, and the way she had smiled at me when I told her, on the last day of school, that she was my favorite teacher ever.

Even in those early days of possessing the book, I could tell it was exerting a strange effect on me. Perhaps I would have read it in normal circumstances, knowing that the author had been locked up in the very house I myself was living in. Maybe the temptation simply to correlate events in the book with actual places in Betony Lodge—the building itself, the grounds, the surrounding woods and fields—would have pulled me into the story that Cecilia Davis told. But I'll never know. My feeling is that the book's style, its descriptions, its narrative, the very words and phrases used, all of these things worked together to pull me into it, calling to me across the century and a half that distanced us. It might be crazy to admit it, but I believed then, as now, that the day I discovered *My Time at a Lunatic Asylum* was a day that had been destined to happen since that day 150 years earlier that Mrs. Davis had first put pen to paper to tell the world about her ordeal.

I drove Brian to the train station for his trip to Wales that Friday morning, after he'd been home a week. As he pulled his backpack out of the car, Brian looked at me and smiled, and I could tell he was happy about this new adventure of his and the way his career was unfolding.

"Bye, Kerys," he said, after kissing me. "I'll call you tonight, ok?"

I nodded. "Have a great time, Brian."

"You, too." Then he paused, apparently thinking about what he said, and added, "I mean, I hope your research goes well. Give old Tom Hardy hell!"

"I intend to," I said, smiling, although I had given him scarcely a thought for several days.

He pulled his pack onto his shoulder and walked through the station to get to the train tracks. I waved to him after he went through the doors, but I don't think he saw me. A few moments later, the train pulled out from the station, and I was in my car, headed towards home.

By noon I was parking the car in front of Betony Lodge and pulling a bag of groceries out from the passenger seat. I walked up to the heavy front door and pulled it open, looking at the door to Leanne and Gary's flat, expecting Ethan to be there again. He wasn't, but as I started to climb the stairs, I discovered him sitting on the third step from the top.

"Hi," I said, making sure to smile at him. "What are you doing, Ethan?"

"You know." He didn't smile, just said those two words, which sent a chill down my spine.

"Does your mom know you're out here on the landing?"

"No."

"Do you think she should know where you are?"

He stood up and nodded, but said nothing. I held out my hand and he took it to go down the stairs. We said nothing as we went down. But, putting his hand on the doorknob of his flat, he turned back towards me and said, "I heard her again last night. Did you?"

I shook my head. "You know, Ethan, it's probably just the pipes or something."

He shook his head. "It's not. You've heard her. You know it's not."

I opened my mouth to reply, but I couldn't think of anything to say. Just then, Leanne opened the door. "There you are, Ethan! What are you doing out here? I've got your lunch ready, you little imp!" She looked over at me, and I saw the question in her eyes.

"I just got home," I said. "He was here on the landing when I got in." She stared at me. I shrugged and tilted my head, as if to say, "I don't know what's going on," and then turned to climb the stairs to my flat. I swear I could feel Leanne staring after me in suspicious disbelief every step of the way.

Upstairs in my own flat, I started putting my groceries away. The weather was changing yet again, turning from sunny blue skies to a low, cloud-covered drizzle that seemed to soak into one's soul and dampen the very fibers of one's being. Maybe I was just belatedly sad at Brian's departure. At the train station, he was so clearly excited at his new adventure that I hadn't felt it was right to seem lovelorn or clingy.

I made up a pot of vegetable soup that I thought would last at least a couple of days. After that, I straightened up the flat, cleaned up Diggory's litter box, and swept the floors. I watched some television—a very depressing documentary on Richard and Karen Carpenter, of all things. British television is not always what it's cracked up to be.

About six o'clock Brian called to let me know that he had arrived safely in Hay-on-Wye. I could hear people laughing in the background, and I knew he was having fun with his new friends, whom I had yet to meet. I remember thinking how strange it was that he hadn't told me much about Melissa and Jack, and that it was even stranger that I hadn't asked about them. I really knew nothing about them. I said as much to Brian on the phone.

He laughed. "No problem, Kerys. Next time you'll come out with me. It's beautiful here. You'll love it, I promise."

"Next time? I didn't know you were planning regular visits."

Brian laughed again. "Kerys, come out of your books once in a while and live in the real world. This place is really charming, with bookstores everywhere, and I know you'll love Melissa and Jack." He paused, and I could tell he was trying to think of a way to get back to his friends.

"Have a wonderful reading, Brian," I said. "I know it will be just great. Bye! Love you!"

"Love you, too, Ker. Talk to you soon."

He sounded pleasant enough, but he hadn't even hung up the phone before I heard him laughing and asking for another drink. Suddenly I was feeling lonely and out of sorts.

I sat down with a cup of tea and tried to plan out the next few days, including time for plenty of activity and interaction with others. But it seemed that Brian had sealed my fate when he told me to come out of my books for a change; perversely, the first thing I did was to reach for my new favorite book, place it in my lap, and let it fall open to a random page. For just a few seconds I sat with the book on my knees and looked through my window, watching and listening to the rain falling in the gloom. I breathed in the rich, salty smell of wet earth wafting through the air as it mixed with the scent of old printed pages, and I savored the moment as I entered the world of Cecilia Davis.

Just as I became fully engaged in my reading, disappearing into the pages as if I was part of the story myself, I heard it. A low, mournful sound that seemed familiar enough to have come from my own lips. I felt my pulse quicken and looked over at Diggory, who, curled up by my side in a tight and compact ball, seemed not to have heard anything. I wondered if it was an animal outside, perhaps an owl. I looked up at the ceiling, closed my eyes, and forced myself to listen to the silence.

The sound came again in a few seconds, and I opened my eyes with a start, looking around the room. This time there could be no mistake—I had heard something. And there was no mistake, either, about Ethan's description of the sound. I had to admit now that this was no owl sitting outside my window, no more than it was some superheated water surging through aged pipes.

No. I knew now, without a doubt, that Ethan and I had been hearing the same sound, and that it was the melancholy sound of a woman crying.

I have to admit that I was surprised by my reaction. I didn't scream, or drop the book, or grab Diggory and run out into the hallway. I just sat there for another moment, listening to the noise, hearing it for the first time as a human sound, not as a mechanical or an imaginary sound. It was a long and loud moan, with a clear beginning and end, and it overflowed with pain, frustration, and sadness. It was like nothing I'd ever heard, but sitting there with my eyes closed, I found nothing to fear in it but the pain and the heartache it expressed.

Chapter Ten

When I flew to Blackmoor Vale,
Whence the green-gowned faeries hail,
Roosting near them I could hear them
Speak of queenly Nature's ways,
Means, and moods, --well known to fays.
--Thomas Hardy, "The Bullfinches"

The next morning was sunny, and I woke up
determined not to stay inside reading all day, listening for
every little noise, waiting for an apparition of some kind to
materialize and scare me out of my skin. I decided that I
would go for a long walk outside after breakfast. That
would get me some fresh air as well as a little exercise, and
it would have the added benefit of helping me gain
perspective on my situation.

I put my plan into action, taking the time to feed
Diggory and give him some attention. This done, I grabbed
my trash, thinking to deposit it in the rubbish bin
downstairs, and headed off. As I rounded the landing past
the Noudies' apartment, I hesitated only slightly. But then
it opened suddenly to reveal Ethan's worried little face, and
I jumped back, startled. Behind him a vacuum cleaner
roared, interspersed with bumps and knocks. Apparently
Leanne was none too careful with the furniture when she
did housework. Catching sight of me, Ethan smiled, his
blue eyes shining, and said, "I heard her again last night.
The sad lady. Did you hear her, too?"

I stared at him for a second, thinking about what I
should say. I didn't want to lie, but I didn't want to
encourage him, either. I had just opened my mouth to reply

with a safe, neutral answer when the vacuum switched off and Leanne appeared behind Ethan. "There you are again, sneaking out onto the landing! Come back inside now, Ethan—you've not even finished your breakfast yet." She took him by the shoulders and pulled him from the doorway, then slammed the door. I felt somewhat rebuffed, even hurt, by her actions. I was beginning to think she didn't like me, or that she thought I was a bad influence on her son. But what could I do? I shrugged my shoulders and headed to the back door, dropped off my trash in the bin, and made my way out into the garden.

Outside, on a bright day, it was difficult to believe in the existence of ghosts, or spirits, or whatever the noises were that Ethan and I had heard. I looked around at the trees and shrubs reaching up towards midwinter sunlight, noting the early buds and the way earth, flora, and sunlight worked together to create a harmonious effect, and I felt surprised that the house behind me could ever have been a lunatic asylum. Yet, according to Mrs. Davis, these very grounds had once been a garden for those poor souls back when it was Warrinder House.

I left the small play yard, going out through the gate that separated it from the grounds, and started prowling around the old foundations, where I'd found the locket that was still wrapped up and hidden in my sock drawer. But this time, I decided I'd go further afield, and so I walked up an overgrown path towards the stand of tall trees that covered the hill behind the house. From the top of the hill, I thought, it might be possible to see the sea, if enough trees had dropped their leaves. I was somewhat out of breath when I reached the edge of the forest, and I decided to take a rest before I walked on. Looking back at Betony Lodge, I could just make out Diggory's tiny outline in my kitchen window. I walked to the nearest tree and sat down in front of it, intending to use it as a backrest.

It was chilly but pleasant out, and the morning sun was casting long shadows in front of me. I looked up through the branches, heavy with new sap, and watched thick, puffy clouds racing across a pale blue sky. It was good to be outside. Sometimes the heavy atmosphere of Betony Lodge colored my thoughts and moods, and being out in the sunshine, weak and wintry though it was, had the effect of improving my outlook. I closed my eyes and sighed, relaxing, expelling the tension that had been building up inside me since the previous night.

I think I must have dozed for a moment, because the next thing I heard made my heart race. Someone was nearby—I could hear rustling in the brush near me. I opened my eyes, my limbs frozen. Did ghosts appear outside, in broad daylight?

But it was no ghost. Suddenly, a man's face loomed before me, his green eyes peering into mine. He was squatting in front of me. He reached out towards his right side and picked up a long, thin object. I remember thinking, "this is it. This is how I die: a crazed hunter blows me away with a shotgun." And then another thought flew into my beleaguered brain: "How ironic that I've lived all my life in urban areas, only to die a violent death in a pastoral setting like Dorset."

I smiled at the thought, even though I believed I had only seconds to live; the irony appealed to my wayward sense of humor.

"Good to see that you're alive, after all. I thought you might be a corpse! But tell me, what's so funny?" The man cocked his head at me, with a half-smile on his wide mouth. It was then that I saw he had been reaching not for a gun, but for one of those metal hunting contraptions.

Relieved and genuinely amused by the situation, I couldn't help laughing out loud. The man stood up and backed away. "It's ok, miss," he said. "No need to get excited. I'll move off if you're bothered."

"I thought you were going to kill me," I said, standing up, "with your contraption there."

"This?" he held up his machine. "This wouldn't kill anything. It's a metal detector." The man looked shocked and offended.

"Yes, I see that now. I'm sorry—overactive imagination."

"Ah. American?"

"Yes. Here for research."

He nodded, and then, a second later, he said, "Thomas Hardy." Actually, we both said it at the same time, and laughed. He seemed to be middle-aged, judging from his thinning hair and the lines around his eyes when he smiled. He was only a little taller than I, with a slight paunch around his mid-section, making it clear that he preferred to spend his afternoons at the pub rather than at the gym. He wore a kind of flak jacket, like a soldier's, with all kinds of tools and magnifying glasses hanging off of its loops and clips.

"Do you come up here often?" His voice was soft, with a trace of the Dorset burr and rounded "r's" that seemed to insert themselves even into words that didn't have them.

I pointed towards Betony Lodge. "I live there."

"Oh." It was a long, drawn-out syllable, and I couldn't tell whether it indicated interest, puzzlement, or just politeness. But his next question was more to the point. "You know it was once a loony bin?"

I didn't think he meant to be insensitive or politically incorrect on purpose; it was just the way he spoke, part of his vernacular. "Yes," I said. "I've just found that out. It's interesting but a bit creepy at the same time. Is that why you do your metal detecting here?"

"Partly," he said. "Since it's a rental, it's easier to gain access to the land to do my sweeps. None of the tenants ever seem to come back this way, and the estate agents don't care if I come through the grounds. In fact, you're the first person I've met out here since I started doing this patch—about two years ago now."

For a moment—a split second—I thought of telling him about the locket I'd found the week before. But I didn't. I wasn't ready to share my find with anyone yet, much less a complete stranger. Instead, I said, "I'm really interested in the history of this place. Do you have any idea how the asylum was laid out? I think I might have found some old foundations over there." I pointed at the bottom of the hill.

"Oh, yes," he said. "I've been working on that very thing. And I think I have it all mapped out, actually. On a big sheet of paper. Not with me, of course, but if you're interested—"

"I am," I interrupted. "Would you let me see it some time?"

"Look-see," he said, scratching his head. He was leaning against his detector as if it were a cane. "We could meet down at the pub in town later this afternoon, if you like. I'll bring my map with me and show it you, and you can buy me a pint for my troubles."

I hesitated only a moment before I nodded. Obviously, I wasn't in the habit of meeting strangers and buying them drinks at their suggestion, but this was too big of a chance to pass up. "What time?"

"Four-thirty—that's my regular time." He straightened up, shouldered his metal detector, and turned to head back through the forest. "I'll look for you, then— what did you say your name was?"

"Kerys," I said. "And yours is?"

"Don't laugh," he said, his thick brown eyebrows contracting into a sheepish scowl.

"I would never laugh at anyone's name," I said, somewhat scandalized that a stranger would peg me as such a person.

"Well, then," he said. "It's Tom. Tom Hardie. With an '-ie,' not a 'y.'"

He turned and walked into the forest, and by a supreme effort, I was able to keep from laughing until I was sure he couldn't hear me.

I continued to prowl about the outer grounds for another hour or so. Then the sun disappeared behind a layer of high clouds and the wind picked up. It felt like rain was coming once again, so I went inside and curled up with my book. But after an hour or so, I shut the book and put it aside. It was taking up too much of my day, and I wanted to do a load of wash before I met my new acquaintance at the pub that afternoon. I took the basket of clothes into the kitchen and set the washer going.

Doing wash is an adventure in England. The machines abroad are not like those in the States—at least the one we had in Betony Lodge wasn't. It took a long time to do the wash, and it actually dried the clothes as well, or at least it implied it could. In reality, the dryer didn't work, and we had taken to laying out our damp clothes on pieces of furniture and hanging them from hooks and hangers throughout the flat to get them dry. Besides that, the wash cycle took a very long time. I had been warned in the early weeks of living in our flat, by both the estate agent and Leanne, never to leave the flat when the washer was going for fear of malfunctions and ensuing floods, so after I straightened up the living room, I sat down, knowing that I would have to stay put for the next hour or so. I fought with temptation for a couple of minutes, then gave into it and reached for *My Time at a Lunatic Asylum*.

I was getting addicted, like a kid with a video game. I couldn't leave the damn book alone. Part of me was worried about my new obsession, but part of me wanted to shrug my shoulders and say, what's the harm in it, anyway? It's not like smoking, or alcoholism, or drug abuse. I wrestled with myself for a few minutes, told myself I would just look at the table of contents and at the frontispiece, that enticing picture of Warrinder House/Betony Lodge.

While I was staring at the drawing of my house, I heard Ethan's sad lady once again

At first I thought it was the washing machine, going

through its cycles and cranking its gears while draining the soapy water from its drum. I didn't want to admit to myself that it was Ethan's sad woman again. Then, as the washer juddered to the last orbit of the spin cycle and wheezed itself into silence, the moan came again, this time louder and more pitiful against the heavy silence.

I felt the hair on my neck prickle and looked over at Diggory, who was curled up on the couch, sound asleep. I took a deep breath and spoke out loud.

"Okay. I can tell you're unhappy. You've made it clear. So what is it that you want?"

I waited, but nothing happened. It was like going out in your backyard to silence a pair of loud, chittering squirrels only to have them freeze as you show up on your deck, making you feel foolish and reactive. I wasn't going to back down, however.

"What's the point of it all, anyway?" I flung the words out, feeling them fall into empty space, and I held the book up in the air. "I'm already reading your book," I added. "What more do you want from me?"

Again I waited, and this time, I felt as if a reply was coming. The air tingled with expectation. Something, I was sure, was about to happen.

When, a second later, my cell phone chimed, I jumped so violently that I dropped the book on the floor and sent Diggory careening off into the bedroom, his claws scratching at the floorboards as he scurried away. I stared at my phone; it was shaking the coffee table as it vibrated. Taking a deep breath, I picked it up, looked at the caller ID, and pressed "Receive."

"Hello, Brian," I said. "How's it going?"

"Hey, Kerys! You sound like you're out of breath—did I catch you at a bad time?"

"No, not really." There was a long pause, and I could tell he felt as uncomfortable as I did. "How are you doing, Brian? How's Wales?"

"Great. Really good. How are you doing, Kerys?"

"I'm doing fine." I could hear laughing and conversation in the background. "Sounds like you're having fun."

"I am." He paused, then added, "Melissa invited some friends from the university in Aberystwyth down for a few days. Literary types, you know—writers and scholars and such. She and Jack have been just great, helping me make connections like that. And most of them are staying for the reading tomorrow night, so that's going to be awesome."

"Oh, fantastic," I said, and felt awful for faking my own enthusiasm in order to match Brian's. Another silence divided us, and then Brian asked, "How's your research going?" But he didn't wait to hear my answer; instead, he added, "And how's Diggory doing? Keeping you good company?"

"He's fine," I said. "We're both doing fine." I started to tell him about meeting Tom Hardie, but decided against it. There was too much noise in the background, and I felt like Brian wanted to get back to his newfound friends. "You're still coming home on Wednesday?"

"Yes, well, that's what I was calling about, Kerys. Mel and Jack asked me if I wanted to do a short walking tour with them. I told them I had to check with you first, though. I don't have to go if you want me to come home."

"No," I said, quickly. "That's okay. If you want to go, that's fine. I can use the time to write and read. This book won't get done by itself, you know."

His laughter sounded genuine; he was clearly happy. I was glad I'd said the right thing. "Well, I'll be home by next Sunday, anyway, Kerys. I'll call you tomorrow night after the reading, okay? Take care of yourself. Don't work too hard, now!"

"I won't," I said, and then, after a half a second, added "good-bye." But he'd already hung up.

Chapter Eleven

Meanwhile the winds, and rains,
And Earth's old glooms and pains
Are still the same, and Life and Death are
neighbours nigh.
--Thomas Hardy, "Nature's Questioning"

An hour later, in Lyme Regis, I found a parking spot for the car with some difficulty and walked through misting rain and spreading puddles to get to my appointment with Tom Hardie. Once inside the Angry Badger, I shook the rain from my jacket and cleared the drops from my glasses, then looked around the room and spotted Mr. Hardie sitting at a table within a few feet of the fireplace, his pint glass reflecting the lazy, intermittent licks of flame. He raised it to me in a silent toast as I approached, pointing towards the bar to signal that I should stop there first for my own drink, which I did. As I made my way to his table, trying not to spill my beer, I noticed the water stains and scuffmarks on the wooden floor and wondered whether its planks had been there back in Thomas Hardy's day. Surely the pub had had the same dank, yeasty smell, even a hundred years earlier. To me, that was a comforting thought: lives may fall apart, nations fall and rise again, people move in and out of lunatic asylums, but the village pub remains.

"Sorry to keep you waiting," I said as I sat down, cradling the pint glass in my hand. "I had to park way up the hill."

"No matter," said Tom Hardie, and took an

impressive gulp from his mug. He swallowed, wiped his lips on his shirt cuff, and said, "I don't mind waiting here. It's pleasant enough, and the ale is good." He took another sip, as if to emphasize his point, and then placed a square sheet of yellowing paper on the table before us. I sipped my own beer as I watched him unfold the paper as carefully as if it were a lost page from the Book of Kells. He spread it out on the table, right on top of the wet spots from our own pint glasses, leaned back, and gazed at it with affection.

"This here's the house where you live, you see?" His finger lay on a rectangular box drawn with a dark pencil in the middle of the page. "Here are the outer grounds, down towards you. Here's the forest at the top of the hill. And here," he said, putting his finger down a few inches away from my glass, "right about here is where I met you this morning. You see all this?"

I nodded. "And all of this land belonged to the asylum? Is that what you mean?"

Tom nodded and took another a sip of his beer. He seemed pleased with himself. "It took me a quite a few months to map it all out, but I can tell you what I think these things I've outlined in black are now. Look-see, this here was probably a wash-house of some sort, and back here we have a carriage house and stable, and this—well, they're still gardens, so there's no reason to think they were ever anything else. And here..." His voice trailed off and I looked up from the crude map to see him staring at me. I waited for him to go on, but he didn't. I felt as if he had been submitting me to some kind of appraisal, and that I had come out of it in arrears.

"What do you think it was?" I said, trying to re-direct his attention.

"Not sure," Tom said, his words suddenly clipped and short. "Could be anything, really. Have to do some more scouring of that area." He tipped his glass to his lips and I knew then that he had changed his mind about telling me something. It made sense—he had just met me, after all; why should he share a significant discovery with a stranger? I was willing to be patient.

"Ready for another?" Tom stood up. He had finished his beer while I was still only half done with my own. I shook my head. "I'm ordering a fish pie for myself," he added. "What'll you have, Carrie?"

"'Kerys,'" I corrected him. "I'll have a ploughman's. And I'm supposed to buy, remember?"

"I'll do this. You take the next round, Kerys." He said my name carefully, as if learning a word in a new language. "I'll be back in a few."

I stared at Tom's map while he was gone, noting his odd, childish handwriting and the various marks on the page. He had taken some time with this, and I could see why he was proud of it. He was probably battling the urge to tell me all about it while trying to keep his discoveries safe. I smiled. What he was doing with his metal detecting work wasn't all that different from what I was doing with my own scholarly work on Thomas Hardy: we all learned to protect the things we loved from the reckless plundering of others.

Tom came back to the table and sat down with his new pint. "So, Kerys," he said, wrapping his lips around the second half of my name, "why are you so interested in

Warrinder House? That's what it was called, you know."

"Oh, I know. I've been reading all about it."

"Ah, yes. I've read Gladys Nuttall's book on it, too."

"Gladys Nuttall?"

Tom nodded "Charming name, right? Fitting, I'd say."

"I haven't seen it. What's it called?"

Tom stared at me. "If you haven't seen it, then how do you know about the site?" He squinted at me, suspicion clouding his simple face.

"Apparently, Gladys Nuttall isn't the only one who wrote about Warrinder House, Tom," I said, and, glancing around to make sure there were no undercover librarians on the premises, I pulled *My Time in a Lunatic House* from my backpack. I placed it on his map and carefully turned it toward him so he could read the title easily. Tom stared, touched the cover of the book, and emitted a shrill but soft whistle through his lips.

"Where'd you find this?" He began to turn the pages. "I've never seen this book before." He looked up at me, his fingers resting on the open book. "Did you bring this over from America?"

I shook my head. I had made a calculated decision to confess to Tom Hardie. If I wanted him to share what he knew with me, it only made sense that I had to offer him something first, so I told him all about the book and how I found it—and took it—and how I'd been somewhat obsessed by it for the last couple of weeks. Just as I finished, the bartender called out that our food was ready, and Tom got our plates and another couple of pints (my second, Tom's third, by my count) and sat down again. Tom dug into his fish pie, a dish I'd never order of my own accord, and I picked at the food on my platter. Neither of us said anything for a good five minutes.

At last, I took a good long pull from my beer and made my decision: I was done bargaining. If Tom Hardie didn't want to work with me, that was fine. Setting my mug down, I held out my hand for the book. However, Tom misunderstood my gesture, reached out his own hand, and shook mine forcefully, as if we had just made a bargain. And, apparently, we had.

"Your secret is safe with me, Kerys. I won't tell anyone you stole the book."

"Tom," I said, "I didn't steal it. I merely borrowed it."

He leaned back in his chair, crossed his arms across his chest, and grinned. "Right. I understand."

"What do you mean?"

"Well, you 'borrowed' the book, a rare book, I might add, without bothering to check it out from the circulation desk or tell anyone you were taking it. Have I got that right now?"

I stared at him and pulled the book away from him. "When you put it that way, Tom—"

"It's all right, Kerys. I understand. I'm sure I understand better than anyone else could. Like I said, your secret is safe with me." He soaked up the remaining sauce in his bowl with a piece of bread from my platter and shoved it in his mouth. "We can work together on the site. Isn't that what you want?"

I took the rest of my bread and began to butter it.

"I'm not sure if that's really what I had in mind, Tom. But I do know one thing: I want to find out more about Betony Lodge and its history."

"Well," he said, dabbing at his mouth with his napkin, "I'm your man, then. What say we meet tomorrow morning to do a bit more detecting? I'm off of work—it's Sunday."

"What is your line of work, anyway? Your day job, I mean."

Tom looked at me over his mug, his blue eyes narrowed. "Tree surgeon," he said, and took a sip.

"Tree surgeon? What on earth is that?" An image of Tom, decked out in scrubs and a mask—his scant hair covered with one of those paper caps they give you in the hospital—approaching a tree with a chainsaw and an enormous I.V. tube flitted through my mind, and I suppressed the urge to laugh. It was lucky that I did not even smile, because Tom Hardie was very serious about his work. Tree surgeons, I soon found out, didn't just chop trees down; they saved them, using clamps, screws, and wires, as well as an assortment of other things, to keep their vegetable clients healthy. It was a big business in Dorset, where ecology and the environment were highly valued.

We agreed to meet again the next day in my backyard, when I would accompany Tom on one of his full detecting scans of the rear grounds. As I stood up to leave, my book hidden in my backpack once more, Tom stood up, too, and held out his hand again. Again I noticed how short he was—little more than a couple of inches taller than me. I shook his hand and made my way through a few clusters of people, each of them with a pint mug or a glass of wine in their hand. As I reached the door of the pub, I turned back to look at Tom, wondering whether he was staying on; after all, he'd arrived before I had. Amid the other pub patrons, who were laughing and joking in groups of threes and fours, Tom sat there alone, staring down at his map. A song broke out across the room, some kind of soccer chant, and I felt I was leaving just as the evening fun was erupting.

It wasn't until I was in my car on the road back to Betony Lodge, fifteen minutes after leaving the Angry Badger, that I realized that I had just made a kind of date with a man whom I knew next to nothing about. That, I told myself, was pure carelessness, probably brought on by my unbalanced state of mind, and, to be brutally honest with myself, by my loneliness.

Because it was becoming quite clear to me by then that the only reason a woman would spend two and a half hours in a pub with a complete stranger whom she had met only a few hours earlier prowling around in her backyard was because she was either profoundly lonely—or because she was going insane.

Chapter Twelve

We were often given airings, led out of the building by attendants, and taken across the grounds to walk on sunny days. Some of the women were considered trustworthy enough to walk on their own; sadly, I was never allowed this privilege. And yet I am convinced that fresh air and sunshine would have done more to cure me than any of the assorted treatments that were tried.

After it was seen that their water treatments had no effect on me, and that they actually made my condition worse, it was decided, as I said above, that I would undergo a procedure to have my temporal artery severed and bled. Once again, I was led out of my room, with little idea of where I was going or for what purpose, only this time I was taken to one of the treatment rooms. I was placed in a chair with straps for the arms, legs, and even the throat, and I was secured therein, with an attendant on each side of me to assure the stillness of my head. Dr. B--- approached me with a tool. At this point, I struggled as much as I could. Despite my screams, Dr. B--- punctured the large vein on the side of my forehead; I was made to bleed into a clear glass, and in the middle of the procedure, I fainted. When I awoke, I was in my bed, a bandage on my temple, my limbs weak, my pulse faint, and my mind tottering on the very brink of sanity. It would have taken very little more to separate my body from its soul, I think, but praise God I was saved.

--*Cecilia Davis*, My Time in a Lunatic Asylum

It was dark when I returned to Betony Lodge, and I

felt guilty about having left Diggory all on his own for a good four hours. I had resisted the urge to call Brian on the way home, but was still toying with the idea of sending him a text, just to wish him good luck on his reading the next afternoon, as I made my way into the kitchen to put the kettle on for a much-needed cup of tea. However, when I sat down with my mug, Diggory, newly fed and cossetted with a saucer of milk, climbed onto my lap, and instead of texting Brian, I switched on the television, proceeding to spend the next hour watching a very boring documentary on the evolution of cricket. I have no idea why—then, as now, I have no love for or understanding of cricket—so all I can say is that I was drawn into an inertia of a kind, unwilling to reach out beyond my own thoughts and insecurities, incapable of contacting Brian.

What was he doing, after all, some 200 miles away from me? How had we come to such a pass? It was true that I had encouraged him to go, first to London, and then on to Wales with these new friends of his. After all, I supported his writing, just as he supported my research. That's what being partners was, wasn't it?

But the physical separation between us was beginning to strain our relationship, and unless we could make up the deficit by communicating frequently, it was going to have a serious effect on us as a couple. After all, I was keeping secrets from Brian—not intentionally, certainly, but nevertheless he knew nothing about my inner life, my obsession with Warrinder House, my wayward departure from my own research, my meetings with Tom Hardie. Did he, too, have secrets from me? Who were these new friends of his, after all? Watching the television screen, listening to someone explain the difference between a dead pitch and a dusty pitch, between a maiden over and a wicket maiden, these thoughts flitted through my mind. Still, I didn't pick up my cell phone to call Brian, and to this day, I'm not sure why. Was it resentment? Or jealousy of Brian's new friends? Simple laziness? Perhaps I will never know the answer.

The fact is, the most obvious reason I didn't call or text Brian that night was because I simply fell asleep, sitting there on the couch. The cricket documentary ended, and another program even more boring began, but I dozed off, and after a few minutes, I was curled up on the couch with Diggory on my chest, both of us deeply asleep.

It was my luck to have another nightmare that night.

This time I dreamt that I was on the roof of Betony Lodge, looking out across the fields. It was nighttime: so dark I couldn't see more than three feet in front of me, and yet I knew with certainty that I was on the roof of the building, and that it was a very long drop to the ground. It was a steeply pitched roof, with pipes sticking up in random spots, and I was afraid of slipping down between them, along the slope of the curved tiles, and falling to the ground. Worse still, although I knew I was alone up there, I could hear indistinct voices. Gradually they became understandable.

"Did you tell her yet?" One voice in particular carried up to me, a deep-toned male voice with clipped British intonation—perfect, pure, and logical. "Does she know?"

I thought I recognized the voice, and I scrambled

from one pipe to another, putting my ear up to each opening, trying to get closer to the voices, hoping that they would be amplified by the pipes. All the while, I wracked my brain, trying to remember where I'd heard the man's voice before.

"No," came another voice, this one a woman's. "She doesn't know, and she doesn't care. She's not to know, and she's not to care." It was said in a singsong tone, as if it was a line from a fairy-tale or one of those songs little children sing when they're skipping rope. She began to repeat it over and over again.

"Well," the first voice said, interrupting her, "where is she?" I waited for the response, as if my life hung in the balance. I began to back away from the pipe I'd been holding on to.

"On the roof, right where she should be." Her response terrified me. It was as if I had been hiding, not wanting them to know where or why I was hiding from them. And now I was afraid, because I knew that they'd discovered me; they had uncovered my secret and knew of my fear.

"Then get her and bring her to me." The most terrifying thing about these words were not what they said, or even what they implied, but rather how they were said: in a quiet whisper, as if the person saying them was right beside me. I wanted to scream, but I couldn't. I turned to run, willing even to jump from the roof's edge to escape, only to find that my way was blocked.

A large man dressed in a white apron stood before me. He approached me quickly, put his hands on my arms and pinioned them as I tried to shrug him off. I looked up at his face, but he was wearing a cricket helmet with a face guard that obscured his eyes and his expression. The man's grip tightened on me, and I found I couldn't feel my arms, much less move them.

Then he was wrapping me in a straightjacket, pulling the straps behind me tight and tying them, spinning me around as if I were playing a desperate game of Blind-Man's-Buff. I lurched away, only to be caught and spun again, the stars circling above me as I was wrung around and around in the darkness. I could hear laughter echoing from one of the pipes—female laughter, I thought, and I grew angry and tried to fight back, but it was useless. I couldn't use my arms.

Then, in one of those strange, dream-like transitions, I was in my own flat, still in the straightjacket, my arms pinioned to my sides, and I was being pushed by the man in white across the room to the dining area, where I was made to sit down at the table, shoved into a chair with rough pressure on my shoulders. I sat waiting, until I saw a man coming towards me with a scalpel and another tool that I didn't recognize. Though no one said anything, I knew that I was guilty of a heinous crime, and that my punishment was for these men to open a vein in my forehead and let me slowly bleed to death.

I screamed, long and loud in my dream, yet I have the impression that in reality it was a mere whimper, because when I woke, Diggory was still on my chest, mewing his concern for me. I tried to sit up, but found my arms had gone to sleep. It took me a few seconds to catch my breath, and when I did, I lurched into a sitting position, shaking the feeling back into my arms. Diggory, bless him, settled onto the cushion beside me, and began to purr.

All was well. It was just a dream, I told myself. I went back to sleep, in my own bed this time, and I had no more dreams that night.

But to this day I have an aversion to cricket.

I was up early the next morning, little the worse for wear, the memory of the nightmare I'd had swept aside in the excitement of meeting up with Tom and doing some real metal detecting. As I drank my second cup of tea, I pulled the locket out from its hiding place and unwrapped it. It glinted bright and golden in the morning light, and I turned it over several times, inspecting it. I wondered what Tom might make of it.

He was waiting for me when I reached the forest; he'd obviously come down through the woods, not by way of the road out in front of Betony Lodge. I wondered whether he came that way because he lived in that direction, or because he wanted to do some detecting on his own before he met up with me. He had his metal detecting unit, of course, and was wearing his jacket. In addition, he had a heavy web belt with all kinds of tools: fold-out shovels, little pick-axes, knives, rulers, and even a set of brushes of different sizes. Apparently, he took his hobby seriously.

But I was to be disappointed in metal detecting. That afternoon with Tom, I did little more than watch him wave his detector over the ground. He was intent on finding artifacts, and I, feeling guilty about having already found one without any help, mechanical or human, watched him as he listened to the machine emit its clicks and beeps, then pausing to examine the dirt at times, his shoulders hunched over, bent almost double in his zeal to discover something buried beneath his feet. Occasionally he would set the detector on the ground, or hand it to me if I was close by, and kneel on the dirt, as if he were about to perform a religious ritual, taking out one of his tools to extract the object that had set off the detector. It was a grueling job, scraping and sweeping in the dirt in an attempt to uncover something of value, but Tom Hardie enjoyed it.

Yet I soon tired of the work. I kept looking over towards the garden area, where I'd found the locket ten days earlier amid ankle-high weeds that hid stone foundations, and I wanted to tell Tom that we should move over to that area. But I just couldn't find the will. I knew he would ask me why, and I would have to tell him that I'd found something there, and then I'd have to show it to him, and then he'd end up feeling envious, or worse still, completely deflated by my random beginner's luck. Having thought all this out, I ended up sitting on the ground, my back against the same tree I'd been leaning against when I had met Tom Hardie the day before, dozing in the cool afternoon sunlight.

My pleine-air nap was interrupted when I heard Tom exclaim, "Lord bless me!" I opened my eyes to see him on all fours, with his chin almost on the ground, gazing with awe at a dirt-encrusted object before him. I stifled my laughter, because with his rear end high in the air and his face so close to the dirt, he looked quite comical. There was something about Tom Hardie that always made me want to laugh, even though I knew he would be hurt by my amusement. Somehow it was always a struggle to keep a straight face when I was with him.

"What is it, Tom? Did you find something?"

"Aye, did I ever!" Without taking his eyes off the object, Tom signaled to me with a wave of his right hand to come over and see what he'd uncovered.

I stood up and walked over to him, and he held his hand out behind him, upside down, fingers splayed out in a cautionary gesture to make me stop before I reached the sacred spot.

"Just look at this, Kerys," he said, his voice soft and reverent. "I can't believe it!"

I peered over his shoulder at the object. He had just taken out a piece of yellow terrycloth and was laying it upon the object with the kind of care that a jeweler might take with the Koh-I-Noor diamond.

I could tell he was excited by the quaver in his voice. I asked, "What is it, Tom?"

"I think it's a buckle of some kind—a belt buckle perhaps." He folded the cloth over the object, wrapped it up, and dropped it into one of the many pockets on his vest. Then he seemed to remember that he was on his knees in front of me, and he stood up quickly, dusting the dirt from his hands. "It's one of the better finds I've made this year," he said, in a business-like tone.

I started to say something, but stopped myself short. Poor Tom, I thought. I can never tell him about *my* discovery, my wonderful find. That locket would kill him. He would never get over the shock of me, an absolute novice, finding it, or the knowledge that as many times as he'd been over this site, it had eluded his sharp eyes and his vigilant scanning.

"It's getting late, isn't it, Kerys?" Tom said, cutting short my thoughts. "Could be time we pack up for another day."

I knew he was excited and wanted to get his buckle—or whatever it was—back to his home or workshop or wherever he did his work, in order to clean it and polish it up. Besides, I was tired myself. Doing nothing for hours on end can be even more exhausting than being productive, after all. I nodded and said, "I have a lot of reading to do."

Tom was already packing up his gear, his back towards me. "I'll let you know what this turns out to be, Kerys, right?

"Yes, thanks, Tom," I said, to be polite. "Thank you for letting me go detecting with you today."

"Ah, well, you brought me good luck now, didn't you?" He lifted his machine over his shoulder and paused for a brief farewell smile. "I'll be in touch when I find out what this is."

"Yes, do," I said. "See you soon, Tom."

He said goodbye, and then went back into the woods, the way he had come three hours earlier. Just before he disappeared among the stiff, dark trunks that were waiting to envelope him, he turned around and waved at me, and I waved back. Only then did I breathe a sigh of relief, happy that my detecting ordeal was over.

I walked back to Betony Lodge, my lower back a little achy, ready for a nice hot bath. As I passed by the area where I had found the locket, I swallowed a feeling of guilt and hurried past it, just in case Tom was looking back from his path through the woods.

When I reached the gate to the inner garden, I turned to shut it and paused, looking out across the grounds. I tried to imagine what it had once looked like with a series of buildings, washing houses and greenhouses perhaps, with a tended garden instead of the little wilderness that met my eyes. I stared out at the landscape and took it all in: the sprawling betony, the rocky outskirts of the larger garden, the sloping green hill on which slender trees grew, sliding up into a more mature forest higher up on the hillside, and on up to the peak of the hill, from whose summit I had yet to climb to look out over the sea, spreading its blue haunches across the horizon. My eyes closed for a moment as I stood there in the waning sunlight, my thoughts adrift and aimless.

Then, in the midst of my peaceful reverie, a woman screamed. She was close by, her scream a thin wail that clawed the afternoon in half. I opened my eyes and scanned the grounds, searching for a woman in pain, thinking that perhaps Leanne had tripped and twisted an ankle, but there was no one. The scream came again, now a raucous sound of defiance, and I wondered whether what I was hearing was just a different register of the sobs and moans that I'd already been hearing in my flat at night. I was backing away from the gate, preparatory to running up to my flat, when I bumped into someone and emitted my own version of the scream I'd just heard.

"What's wrong, Kerys?" It was Leanne, perfectly uninjured, who'd come out to pick up her children's toys. "You look like you've seen a ghost, woman. What's happened to you?"

I opened my mouth to answer, but the scream came again. "That," I said, my chest heaving. "Did you hear that?"

In the half second between my question and Leanne's response, I thought, panic-stricken, that she might say that she had heard nothing, proving that this sound, too, was all in my own head, the product of a fevered imagination. But instead, Leanne just laughed.

"That's what's put you in such a fright, Kerys? Really?" I did not give her the satisfaction of an answer; the truth was, I was still trying to catch my breath. "It's a fox, love. They have those in America, now, don't they?"

"Foxes? Yes, but I've never seen one in the wild, and I've certainly never heard one make a sound like that."

"Oh, they do that around here, from time to time, especially towards the end of the day. They're just getting ready to go out hunting, perhaps. It's nothing unusual for Betony Lodge, Kerys. You'll get used to it, I'm sure."

Leanne held open the door to the house, and I went in ahead of her, my eyes struggling to get used to the darkness of the back hallway. "Anyway," Leanne continued, "who was that out there with you in the back? What were you two doing out there all afternoon?"

"He's a metal detector. He invited me to go detecting with him today."

I had reached the staircase and started up. Leanne was just staring at me, obviously questioning my judgment, if not my sanity.

"Good night, Leanne," I said.

"Good night, Kerys," she said, still staring after me as I climbed the stairs to the door of my own flat.

Chapter Thirteen

O were it but the weather, Dear,
O were it but the miles
That summed up all our severance,
There might be room for smiles.
--Thomas Hardy, "The Division"

I was tired from my day in the field and the
needless excitement I'd just experienced, so the first thing I
did when I reached my flat was start my bath. While it was
running, I heated some water for tea and fed Diggory, who
was attacking my feet, searching for attention and food. I
was ready for a long, hot soak with a cup of tea and my
own thoughts. Much as I would have liked to have read
Mrs. Davis's book while bathing, however, I wasn't about
to take a rare, perhaps a precious, book, so close to the
water. At least I had that much self-respect left, I told
myself, as I stepped into the hot tub.

I sat there for a few minutes, easing lower into the
water, my only challenge for the moment being to keep
from spilling my tea into the bathwater. I sipped at it,
watching Diggory, who had sauntered into the bathroom,
licking his chops, looking curious but satisfied. He settled
into a turtle position, his legs tucked under him on the
bathmat, his eyes still on me. I closed mine for a minute,
relishing the heat on my aching lower back and hips.

The next thing I knew, my mug was slipping, and I
had to grab it to keep it from falling into the tub with me.
My movement alerted Diggory, who popped up, surprised,
and then made his way to the tub, standing on his hind feet,

his front paws on the rim of the tub, peering into the water. I laughed at him, took a sip of tea, and at that moment, I heard the sound I'd been dreading all day long.

This time, like the others, it was a low moan, but it was somehow more intense. It was the kind of sound that you think of old women making when they've lost everything they've ever loved, when they sit wailing their misery, oblivious to everything around them. It's the sound you think of refugees from war-torn countries making; amidst bombed-out rubble, they lift their voices in a frail but enduring song of pain, unwilling to suffer their misery in silence. I had seen images of such women on television, but I had never really heard their voices—until that moment.

There's something about the articulation of pain that is both universal and accusatory. When that sound reached my ears, I felt responsible for it, even though I wasn't, even though the sound itself was, in all probability, not even real. Nevertheless, when I heard the unearthly moan, infinitely more human in its misery than the vixen scream I'd heard minutes earlier, I cringed, shut my eyes, and slithered below the surface of the water to avoid the pain it carried with it.

But eventually I had to breathe, and when I surfaced, I realized two things: I had spilled my tea into the bathwater, and my cellphone was buzzing on the washbasin where I had left it. The phone stopped just as I surfaced, so I didn't bother to answer it. I was left with only Diggory's puzzled stare while I washed myself in my tea-infused bath. Perhaps, I said out loud—I had long since begun talking to myself out loud by this time—tea-water was good for bathing. Maybe it would settle my nerves.

As for the phone, I did check it when I got out of the tub, after I had toweled off and dressed myself in comfortably baggy sweat pants and a flannel shirt, but I did not push "redial" to return Brian's call. Because of course it was Brian, checking in after his poetry reading at the bookstore, which I had completely forgotten about. While I was out digging around in the dirt with my strange new friend, I'd completely forgotten about Brian's poetry reading.

And so, in the end, I resorted to the coward's solution: I texted Brian instead of calling him, and said I hoped it went well, followed by a few ridiculous emojis, the kind I'd have been ashamed to use the week before. But these things do have their uses, and within five minutes Brian texted me back, saying he was celebrating at the pub, and that it had gone well, followed by equally inane emojis. When I read his message, I knew I wouldn't hear from Brian again that night.

After a dinner of leftover take-out curry, I curled up in my bed, Diggory snuggled next to my right hip, and opened Mrs. Davis's book. But losing myself in her story was not possible, because in the chapter I was reading, Cecilia Davis recounted an experience that was almost identical to the dream I'd had the night before.

I tried to keep reading after that passage, but I could not concentrate on the words. Despite the heavy comforter, I shivered. My fingers trembled on the pages of the book as I fought to control my growing unease.

Finally, I shut the book, put it on my nightstand, and with a decisive movement, turned out my light. It was half past ten, according to the clock. I closed my eyes, wondering if the "Dr. B." in Mrs. Davis's book was the Dr. Bellemeade, the physician who had left Warrinder House and gone on to treat Thomas Hardy's adolescent case of measles, as evidenced by his journal in the Museum archive room.

Just as I began to drop off to sleep, I thought I heard a stifled moan, but I was prepared this time and did my best to ignore it. I pulled Brian's pillow over my head and snuggled down under the covers. I was learning to take precautions for these odd episodes: all I needed to do, I told myself, was to ignore the noises, and they would simply fade away.

What I wasn't prepared for, however, was the distinct sensation of someone sitting down on the side of the bed. I knew it wasn't Diggory, because I could feel him purring and kneading dough on the other side of me, curled up next to me. The pressure I felt was on my left side, on the edge of the bed. It was just a slight weight, as if that of a young child, but I felt it.

I am sure I felt it settle right next to me.

I was desperate to turn on the light again, but I was too frightened to stick my arm out from the beneath the covers, exposing it in the darkness, in order to turn the switch. I knew it would take a mere fraction of a second— but I did not have the will to brave that tiny segment of time. Instead, I clenched my jaw, my eyes shut tight against my fear, and I waited.

It was a moment later that I felt the soft, almost rhythmical movements beside me. It was someone weeping: I could feel the sobs gently shaking the bed, just as I could feel the silent gasps for breath. I knew then that Cecilia Davis was with me, in my room, and that she was sobbing as she sat on the edge of the bed, divided from my touch only by the thin material of my bed-cover.

What happened next remains a mystery. I don't remember falling asleep, but the next thing I knew, it was broad daylight, and Diggory was lying beside me, grooming himself, each lick of his fur making a tiny, rasping noise. I turned over and watched him as, completely unconcerned, he licked his paw and washed his face, his pupils mere slits in the morning sunlight.

Had I really been visited by a ghost, the unquiet soul of Cecilia Davis wandering through the rooms of the lunatic asylum where she had once been so miserable? Or had I dreamed it up? I didn't know, and I was afraid to think about it too much.

My instinct was to go downstairs and talk to Ethan and see whether he'd had a similar experience that night. Perhaps he'd heard the sad lady again, too, and even if he hadn't, he was the only person I could talk to who would understand. Never mind the fact, I told myself, that I now felt that the only person who could understand me was a six-year-old boy with a willful attitude and a domineering mother. That piece of embarrassing information was something I could deal with later. Right now, I had a more pressing matter to think about.

I needed to decide whether I was being haunted, or whether I was simply going insane. The evidence for both was good, and I could not decide between the two possibilities. I rather hoped that it was a haunting, an emanation of the deep pain and misery that this house, Betony Lodge cum Warrinder House, had witnessed, because I had already discovered one important fact the previous night as I slept, or didn't sleep, however it was that I had passed the time until daylight. What I had discovered was this: ghosts and hauntings are much better than madness. With a ghost, you can share your stories and your experiences—and you don't need a summer night and a campfire to do so. You can sit down with a friend—even if he was just a little boy—and describe what had happened to you and compare notes. A ghost was, after all, a form of company, and ghost stories are fun to share with others. When you are visited by a ghost, you may be frightened and terrified, but you can always find someone— someone—to believe you and talk to you about it.

But when you're insane, you're all alone.

As it turned out, I didn't get to speak to Ethan that morning; he and Gemma and Leanne were just leaving their flat as I left mine, and they were obviously in a rush to get to their school on time. Besides, how was I to bring up the subject with Leanne standing right there? I said good morning to them in the drive as we were getting into our cars, and if my eyes lingered longer on Ethan's round, boyish face, searching for the answer to my question ("has the sad lady ever come and sat beside you on your bed while you were trying to sleep?"), who can blame me? But of course I received no answer, and we each drove our separate ways.

I had decided, however, that it was high time to go back to the Thomas Hardy Museum. I would wrench my attention away from Betony Lodge and its sordid history by force if necessary, in an attempt to return to the reason I was in Dorset in the first place: my research. After all, the Museum's midseason break had ended the previous week, and I was due back for my cataloguing work. In the throes of this desire to return to normalcy, when I arrived at the museum, I parked my car and dialed Brian's number. Maybe if I called early enough, I'd catch him before he set out on his walking tour with Melissa and Jack—it occurred to me that I didn't even know their last name—and tell him I'd been thinking of him all the previous afternoon, during his reading. It was a lie, but it was also the least I could do to keep our relationship alive, after all. Brian picked up on the third ring. His voice had the sound of someone who had been roused from a deep sleep yet was trying to sound awake and alert.

"Good morning, Brian," I said, doing my best to sound cheerful. "How did it go yesterday? I thought about you all afternoon." I cringed as the words escaped my lips, but I couldn't help it; it felt like a well-told lie was all I had left to preserve both my marriage and my self-respect.

"Hi, Kerys," he said. "It was fantastic. You should have been there."

I could hear him stifling a yawn. I knew he wasn't saying it to make me feel guilty, but his words had that effect on me. I started to say, "I wish I had been there," but before I could get the words out, I heard a woman's voice, sleep-tinged and very near, say, "Brian, too early for phone calls!" Then came Brian's sharp intake of breath.

And suddenly, just like that, I was fighting off a tidal wave of nausea.

Brian's voice changed timbre at once, and I heard a rustling sound as if he was moving about. "It was a great reading, Kerys. There had to be about forty or fifty people there, all crowded into this tiny bookstore. I sold about a dozen copies of my chapbook, and three other booksellers asked me to come to their stores, too." The words rushed out, and I knew they were designed to camouflage the reality of his situation.

"That's great," I said, still reeling from what I thought I'd heard. "And you're setting off on your little walking tour today?"

"Yes, only we've decided to stretch it out a bit. I didn't think you'd mind."

A pause followed. I stared out my windshield, watching normal people shoulder their backpacks and walk past my car into the museum. It was a gorgeous day, with a bright blue sky and sunshine that looked like it would last forever, and I sat there in my car, trying to talk to Brian, but feeling numb and sick. "Kerys? You don't mind, do you? I feel I should stay out here a bit longer, you know, to follow up on these bookstore visits. This could be a kind of turning point for my career."

It could be a turning point for our relationship, too, I thought, but didn't have the guts to say it. "Yes, Brian, I know." I paused for a moment, listening closely to the phone, hoping that I had only imagined that other voice. But I could hear someone in the background, a muffled sigh, and someone saying, "come back and give us a kootch." I sucked in a big breath and said, "It's fine. I know you've worked hard for this. Just let me know when you get back from your trip, ok?"

"Sure thing, Kerys." Brian sounded chipper, if not actually happy. I could hear his footsteps as he paced the floor, perhaps moving away from the bed and the incriminating voice of the woman who was calling out to him. Part of me wanted to say something to him, to confront him, but another part of me, a much bigger and more cowardly part, I'm ashamed to say, wanted to hang up as quickly as possible and get into the safety of the museum and the boxes upon boxes of Thomas Hardy memorabilia. It was the coward in me that won.

"Bye, Brian," I said, leaving off my habitual "love you."

Brian said, "Bye, Kerys. Love you." I didn't answer, and a moment later, a very long moment full of pain, suspicion, and the dull aftershock of anger, I pressed "end."

I sat there, staring out my windshield, still in shock. A second later, my phone rang, and, like an automated operator, I answered it. "Yes?"

"I was thinking, Kerys," said Brian. "Why don't you come over to Wales and go with me on the walking tour? That would be fun, don't you think? Couldn't you come along with me—with us?"

I took another deep breath. "No," I said. "No, I can't possibly get away right now. Too much cataloguing, and I have all this research to do. And there's Diggory, too. Sorry."

"Okay." Brian sounded as if he was saddened by my refusal. "I'm sorry you'll miss it. There should be some great scenery."

"Me, too." I was getting used to lying by then.

"Look, I've got to run," I added. "Take care. Call me when you get back to civilization." I pressed "end" before he could answer and turned my phone off. Then I dropped it into my purse and, before I could let any of my feelings catch up to me, I hurried into the building to begin a day of cataloguing.

"Hello, Kerys!" George Marten-Douglass smiled at me as I came through the front door. "It's been a few days. I hope you're well?"

"Yes, thank you, George. How are you?"

"I'm well, thanks. Care for some tea?"

I shook my head. "I'd better get right to the archiving. Don't want to lose my momentum." I started to walk to the door to the archive room.

"Suit yourself," said George. He stood up and hobbled over to the cupboard. "We're just about out of tea, anyway. I used the last bit up from the kootch this morning. I'll have to go out and get some today."

"What did you say?" I turned around to look at him. George stopped with a spoonful of tea hovering over the pot and stared at me. His eyebrows were raised.

"I didn't mean anything by it, Kerys—it's just an expression. You know, like 'go ahead and please yourself.' Don't you say that back in the States?"

"I meant that other word," I said. "Where did you say the tea was? In the 'kootch'?"

"Oh, that." George laughed. " '*Cwtch.*' It means 'cupboard,' or 'safe place.' But it's Welsh, so it can also mean other things. You want to be careful about that. Welsh is odd that way. If someone asks you for a *cwtch*, it means they want you to give them a hug."

"I get it," I said. "How do you know so much about Welsh, though? I thought you were English?" Asking lots of questions, I'd found, was a good way to cover up all the emotions I was feeling.

"My gran is Welsh. I used to spend the summers in Wales. Llangollen."

"I see. Interesting. Well, I'd better get started," I said, backing away. Then I turned and went through the doors to the archive room.

Chapter Fourteen

I was not a good patient, Reader, I will warrant that. After I had gotten my bearings, after I had learned about the true nature of Warrinder House and all those who purported to work for the benefit of those benighted souls who were kept there, I rebelled. I acted out, I challenged my keepers—indeed, I sought solace in the smallest of insurrections, if only to remind myself that I was, after all, a free woman, born of English parents on English soil. If I were to be held against my will in a madhouse, so be it; yet I would not yield without a fight. And a fight for one's independence can be fought in the smallest ways.

This is not the place to recount those miniscule battles. I am not particularly proud of them, and I myself would prefer not to recall such episodes from the past. Indeed, some of them seem quite shameful to me now. It is more important, dear Reader, for you to know that though I suffered greatly at their hands, I did indeed escape from the clutches of Mr. Warrinder, Mr. E---, and Mr. B---. In the end, I learned a great deal about myself and, even more, about human nature.

I will share one lesson I learned from my experience. Every human being is held captive by something: be it a love of gain, an overriding ambition, or a passionate nature that cannot be restrained, all of us must struggle against our "mind-forg'd manacles," as the poet Blake puts it. And, while these chains certainly exist, it is of paramount

*importance that we struggle to escape them, and that
we believe that we can in fact effect our escape. Most
important, until escape is possible, we must keep
ourselves ready for the real struggle ahead, by
keeping healthy, strong, and alert in mind and body. I
enjoin you, my readers, to remember my words when
you face troubles in your life, so that you will be ready
for the fight when you find yourself on the field
awaiting whatever battles you must face in this
uncertain life.*

--*Cecilia Davis,* My Time in a Lunatic Asylum

It was while I was driving home that afternoon that
the tears came. I didn't try to stop them. There was only me
in the car, after all, and no one was watching. So I cried
until my nose started running, and then I sobbed a bit,
which is challenging when one is driving a stick shift on
the wrong side of the road, and once or twice I slammed
the steering wheel with my fist, overcome by righteous
anger. In other words, by the time I got back to my flat, I
was one hot mess.

I won't describe the hours that followed. I was
consumed by grief, anger, and not a little self-
recrimination. After all, hadn't I simply ignored Brian for
the past two weeks, ever since I'd started exploring the
history of Betony Lodge? Why hadn't I gone to London, or
for that matter, Wales, with him? Wasn't he just acting the
way any other man would? In the triumph of his literary
success, he succumbed to the urge for a carnal celebration.
It was the same old story. Yet this time I was not just an
observer, but a pathetic participant in the story, and I was

disgusted and enraged and saddened by the whole tawdry episode.

When I finally turned my cell phone back on that night, I saw that Brian had tried to call twice.

Apparently, that was all I was worth—two attempts at calling and no texts or emails. I turned my phone back off and set it on the table, determined not to turn it on again until I was certain Brian had left on his wilderness hike and I could expect no other communication from him. As much as I wanted him to call, I didn't want to talk to him. I wasn't sure I wanted to talk to him ever again.

How easy it is to give up and fling your happiness, even your soul itself, away into the darkness of despair! The thought flew into my head, and I wondered whether it was mine, or whether I had borrowed it from *My Time in a Lunatic Asylum*.

Later that night, I crawled into bed and pulled the covers over my head. That night, it was I, not she, who shook the bed with my sobs. My tears were real ones, burning with misplaced shame, outraged fury, and the kind of pain that seizes up your insides and churns your feelings into jagged, sharp pieces. It was a long time before I fell asleep, but when I did, no dreams came to me: a small and tender mercy in the midst of the emerging shipwreck of my life.

When I woke up the next morning, I felt as if I'd been run over by a bus, and one of those large, red, double-decker London buses at that. Emotional trauma can create a kind of hangover every bit as real as an alcoholic one. The swollen eyes, the sore throat, the sense of disconnect, as well as the bemused wonder at the horrific state of affairs that come in those first moments of wakefulness and memory: these things are shared by both kinds of hangovers.

All that morning, I wandered around in a kind of daze, turning my cell phone off and on at random intervals to see if Brian had left any messages for me, calling George to let him know that I would be in later that day, if at all, blaming a migraine headache. Neither a sick head nor a wounded heart, however, was enough to keep me from delving again into the pages of *My Time in a Lunatic Asylum*.

During the next few days, I received great solace from Mrs. Davis. It was she who taught me that all things pass. With her stoic example before me, I was able to endure the pain, the fury, the whole gamut of twisted emotions I was feeling. I went to the Museum as scheduled, forcing myself to continue my normal activities as much as possible. I tried not to picture Brian tramping through the green Welsh hills, tried not to think about what kind of woman was with him, holding his hand, sharing his sleeping bag. I was mostly successful, but it took a great deal of energy, and at nights, after petting Diggory and eating dinner, I would tumble into bed, drained, and fall into a deep, dreamless sleep. There were no noises, either, during these few days, no more sobs emanating from the walls of Betony Lodge: all of the sobs and moans that echoed through those walls during the next week were produced entirely by me.

As I said, it's an old, old story, and there's nothing terribly interesting about it. Breakups occur at a prodigious rate in our society, and they all occur in more or less the same way. I suppose my story was no different: a couple grows apart, little by little, and if there's not enough between them to tether them to each other, well, that's how it goes. Maybe in Mrs. Davis's time, when life itself was much more precarious, it was easier to stay together. If you live only so long, perhaps it's easier to be happy with what you have and with who you are. When death peeps around the corner at every turn, whether from illness, or accident, or from complications of childbirth, it might be more important to treasure whatever relationships you have, however tenuous they may be.

The point is, I'm not blaming this all on Brian. I know now, and I think I knew even then, that I'd been neglecting him. Perhaps I had never put enough into our relationship—perhaps neither of us had—but recently, my own internal life had become richer and more rewarding than the life I'd been making with him. That was my own fault, probably due to selfishness and a personality quirk I don't really want to explore. The point was, as I saw it, I had made my own bed, and now I was doing my best to lie in it.

And so there I was, lying in my own bed, pillows propped up behind my back, just as if I had a cold or flu, seeking comfort in—what else?—brave Mrs. Davis's saga about her time in Warrinder House. What did she have to say about love, about broken hearts? Not much, to be honest. But I found strength in her words nonetheless. In a strange way, I felt as if she was personally exhorting me to be strong, to hold on to my own sanity, to maintain the fight. But even more, I felt that Mrs. Davis was on my side: I felt that she had anticipated my feelings and was helping me surmount the problems I was facing in my own life. Silly, I know, but by then I was fully engaged in her book, and I had begun to think of her as an ally in my own pathetic struggles.

Four days after that phone call to Brian, and presumably three and a half days after he had left for his walking tour of Wales, I was eating a bowl of soup and watching Diggory eat his own dinner and reflecting that he was enjoying his far more than I was mine, when there was a knock on my door. My heart skipped a beat, and I put my spoon down on the table with careful deliberation, forcing myself to take a breath before I went to open the door. I won't lie: a part of me, and a big one at that, really wanted it to be a bedraggled and penitent Brian on the other side of the door, come home to throw himself in my arms, at my feet, and tell me how much he'd missed me, how he could never be happy apart from me. Between the time I put my spoon down on the table and walked to the door, I had actually convinced myself that it was Brian, and I was all set to accept his hugs and his apologies without asking too many questions. I took a deep breath when my hand was on the doorknob, and then pulled it open with a little too much force.

Of course, it wasn't Brian.

At first, I thought it was yet another strange emanation from "the other side," as I'd begun to term it, because there was, initially, no one at the door when I opened it. But I had been expecting Brian, so I was looking up, towards where his face would have been. When I saw only darkness, I looked down, expecting to see a package, perhaps, left by my door, and that's when I realized I was facing Tom Hardie.

"Oh," I said, my voice flat. "Hello, Tom."

He pursed his lips, and I wondered if my lack of enthusiasm in seeing him hurt his feelings. I felt badly, so I invited him in.

"I really can't stay, Kerys, and I didn't mean to crash in on you like this, but I did try to ring you on your mobile. I couldn't reach you."

"Oh. Right. I'm having a bit of trouble with the phone right now. I guess that's why." We were standing in the doorway, and I had to force myself to look into his blue eyes as I told such an obvious lie.

"Well," Tom said, his voice sounding uncertain but his eyes bright with excitement, "you were right! I thought you'd want to know."

"Right? What was I right about?"

"It was a belt buckle after all, Kerys! I had Ned Dewy take a look at it, and he says he's sure it's a buckle, and that it probably dates from the 1920s."

"Oh," I said for the third time in less than three minutes. "That's great, isn't it, Tom?"

"Yes, it surely is, Kerys," said Tom in his thick Dorset dialect. "I'm going to present it at our next meeting. And I brought you something as a thank-you gift."

"Thanking me for what?"

"For helping me locate the buckle and dig it out. You were in on the discovery, you know, Kerys. I couldn't have done it without you."

"Oh, Tom," I said, "it was nothing. There's no need to thank me."

"Never you mind that, Kerys. Here," he said,

holding out a small paper bag.

"What is it?" I was reluctant to open the bag, because by this point in our conversation, it seemed to me that things were getting very awkward between us.

"Now, then, I'm not telling. You'll have to open it up yourself, Kerys." Tom just stood there grinning at me, so I took the bag from him and reached inside, pulling out a thin book with an old-fashioned cover. "Warrinder House: The History of an Asylum" by Gladys Nuttall.

"Oh," I said, for the fourth time. "How nice. You shouldn't have, Tom."

"Well, I know you're interested in the history of this place," Tom said. "I hope you enjoy reading about it." He turned to go, pulling open the door. "Listen," he said, "why don't we go detecting again this Sunday? I think we should follow up on this first discovery fast and hard. There's probably a great deal more stuff for us, just waiting to be uncovered."

I felt sorry for Tom, which is why I reluctantly agreed to go with him. It wasn't like I had anything else to do, anyway.

"Brilliant," he said, smiling. "I'll meet you out back at two, will that suit?"

"Yes," I said. "And thanks for the book, Tom."

"Least I could do," he said. "You're a tremendous help, you know."

I didn't know what to say, so I just said, "Thanks, Tom. Good night."

I watched as he went down the stairs. I could see from the play of light on his shoulders that the downstairs door—the door to Leanne's flat—was open, and I walked to the bannister and leaned over to see if Ethan was playing on the steps. He wasn't, but I heard Leanne say something softly to Tom and his soft chuckle in return as he went out the front door of Betony Lodge.

So much, I said to myself, for a simple, scholar's life. I was living in a house that had once been an insane asylum, and it was pretty clearly haunted. My brand-new husband was off gallivanting around Welsh mountains with a couple I had never met, and, in all probability, with a new girlfriend as well. And now, apparently, I had accepted a date to go metal detecting on Sunday with a man who became inordinately excited when he unearthed rusty belt buckles. I shook my head. This was not what I had been expecting when I had made my plans to come to England.

I shut the door behind me, tossed Gladys Nuttall's book on the couch, and went straight to the liquor cabinet. A life such as mine surely called for a stiff drink. I poured out the Scotch and added just a bit of cool water, as I'd seen Leanne do a few weeks earlier. Then, shaking my head in disappointment, I put the glass to my lips and tilted it back, taking a huge gulp, seeking solace in its smoky, burning taste.

After a few sips, I freshened up my drink. I stood for a moment and listened, but all I could hear was Diggory purring. "You keep doing that," I said, stooping to pet him. "Somehow it makes this place a lot less lonely." I took my glass, sat down on the couch, and picked up the book I'd just mistreated, thinking that I would at least thumb through it in order to show Tom my gratitude. Still, I wished he hadn't brought it over. It was definitely creepy to have two books about my current residence in my possession, each of them focused on its history as an insane asylum. I had just opened Gladys Nuttall's book, fully intending to read at least through the first chapter, when I heard it again: that low, plaintive moan that sounded so close and so familiar it almost seemed to have come from my own lips. I felt my heart speed up, and I glanced over at Diggory, who, curled up on the kitchen rug in a tight, compact ball of fur, seemed to have heard nothing, as usual.

It stopped, then began again, and I closed my eyes, listening. I allowed myself to hear it, to welcome it into my home, to identify it as a distinctly human sound, not as an animal's cry or a mechanical noise. It came again, this time as a long moan, with a clear beginning and end. Listening to it, my eyes closed tight, I found nothing to fear in it but the very real human pain and heartache it expressed.

That evening, for the first time since I'd begun to hear Cecilia Davis, I allowed myself to feel a kind of kinship with her, a sense of shared experience, of suffering and longing for companionship. I wondered whether Ethan was hearing her, too, and resolved to ask him the next morning, even if it meant knocking on the door of Leanne's flat and asking to speak to him. As the moan trailed off, I listened again for a third wave of its unearthly sound, but it didn't come. I walked to the kitchen and set my glass in the sink, then headed for bed. As I changed into my nightgown, I wondered whether my newfound acceptance of these eerie sounds might be a sign of my own descent into madness. Could it I actually be losing my sanity? Do insane people wonder whether they are in fact insane, or does the fact that they can wonder about their own sanity demonstrate that they are sane?

These questions made my head spin—or perhaps it was the Scotch that was responsible. At any rate, I told myself, Gladys Nuttall could wait. I lay down in my bed. A few minutes later, Diggory joined me, and I fell into a deep sleep almost instantly.

Chapter Fifteen

A tranquillising spirit presses now
On my corporeal frame, so wide appears
The vacancy between me and those days
Which yet have such self-presence in my mind,
That, musing on them, often do I seem
Two consciousnesses, conscious of myself
And of some other Being....
    --William Wordsworth, Book II, The Prelude

When I woke up the next morning, the first thing I thought about was Ethan. I needed to talk to him, if only for a minute or two, to see if he was hearing what I had been. I dressed quickly, making sure to time my departure from the flat when I thought he and his mother and sister would be heading out the door to drive to school. As a matter of fact, I parked myself on the top stair, where I could hear their door open, and sat there for a full five minutes, car keys in my hand and my backpack by my side, ready to move at the first sound of them leaving.

I was in luck: when the door opened at last, it was Ethan who came out, alone. Leanne and Gemma were usually a bit slower to emerge from their flat, and Ethan often played on the steps with his favorite toy car while he waited for them. He was running the little blue sedan along the third stair when I approached him.

"Hi, Ethan. How's it going?"

He looked up at me but didn't answer. I searched for something to say, something to break the ice, but time was short, and I couldn't think of anything, so I simply blurted out my question. "Have you heard the sad lady lately?"

Ethan's round green eyes grew even rounder, and he nodded without saying anything. "I have, too, Ethan."

"Really?" He seemed relieved. "She seems sadder to me the last few days. She's very unhappy."

"I know," I said. "I wish I could make her happy. I think she's a nice lady."

"Oh, she is!" Ethan seemed very sure of it. "I know what you could do to make her happy, though."

"What?" I had come down the stairs and was sitting on the step with him as he ran his car along its edge. I was staring so intently at him that I didn't hear the door to the flat open and Leanne come out. "What is it I should do, Ethan?"

It was Leanne who answered. "You should leave my boy alone, Kerys Markham, that's what you should do!" She was staring at me, looking down at me with her blue eyes blazing in anger. She grabbed Ethan's wrist and pulled him off the stair to her side. "I don't want you talking to him anymore, do you hear me? You're upsetting the child, and I won't have it."

"Leanne," I began, but she cut me off.

"We're late, and I can't discuss this now, Kerys. Please, just leave Ethan alone. I don't want him talking to you. Do you understand?"

"But Leanne," I began again. And again she stopped me.

"Do you understand me, Kerys? I don't know why you think it's amusing to play these games with the child, but you're not to do it again. No more ghost stories, or whatever you choose to call them. Just leave him alone."

She didn't give me a chance to answer. I watched as she went out the door with Gemma's hand in one of her hands and Ethan's wrist in the other. She fairly dragged him along behind her, and he looked back at me, his little forehead furrowed. I felt sorry for him then, because I knew that more than anything else, he wanted to talk to me about the sad lady, since I was the only person who would listen to him. I stood in the doorway, watching them get into their car. As Leanne drove through the gate and onto the road, Ethan stared out the back window at me, and, when I waved goodbye, he held up the two fingers of his right hand and bobbed them twice in an abbreviated, furtive wave. Then the car turned onto the road, and I went back into Betony Lodge to pick up my backpack and purse.

I drove to the Hardy Museum, prepared to brave George's kindnesses. But I had questions about the value of my work, just as I had questions about everything else in my life at that time. I had found nothing of interest in the archive room since the journal of Mr. Bellemeade, the alienist at Warrinder House, and I had not thought to explore it further at the time of my discovery. In fact, I had forgotten about it, as it had been eclipsed by all my other discoveries over the past two weeks.

And, in a strange way, it all made sense. I was used to keeping a slight but real divide between my professional life and my personal life. I tried not to impose my own interests, passionate as they were, on those who were unfortunate enough to be in my general vicinity. But in this case, these two aspects of my life had collided and dovetailed; they had folded into one another, and at first, unused to such an occurrence, I didn't take note of it. Armed with Mrs. Davis's juicy tell-all book about Warrinder House, I didn't think to follow up on Mr. Bellemeade himself—ostensibly the link between Thomas Hardy and Warrinder House/Betony Lodge. But on that day, I decided I would.

George was busy with museum patrons when I arrived, and so I was spared the pain of being polite and cordial at a time when I had little patience for social amenities. I simply waved, like Ethan, as I passed through on my way to the archive room. Once there, I located Bellemeade's journal and flipped through it, hoping to find something significant. But there was nothing about Warrinder House, aside from that sketch of the house on the first page of the book. I turned the pages carefully, studying each one, hoping for something—a sketch, a doodle, initials—anything that could tell me more about Mr. Bellemeade and his earlier vocation. I couldn't find anything—until the penultimate page.

There, at the back of the book, he had drawn a heavy line beneath his typical journal entry in the catalogue of adolescent ailments he diligently kept, and had scrawled in his thin, cramped handwriting what looked like a personal note to himself below it. I leaned forward, my eyes inches away from the page, my breath surely dampening the paper. I could just make out Bellemeade's words: "*Mrs. Davis from W.H. requests information, June, 1851.*"

I leaned back in my chair and took a deep breath. There could be no other Mrs. Davis who would contact Dr.

Bellemcade, could there? Here, then, on the table before me, was evidence of a connection between Bellemeade and Mrs. Davis. The "Mr. B" that she referred to in her account had to be Bellemeade—I was sure of it.

I felt a flush on my face and put my hand up to my cheek as if to ward off the feverish excitement that coursed through me. The thrill I felt at this paltry discovery was, I can see now, pitiful. I was the only person in the entire world who would care about it at all. Well, Tom Hardie might care, but then again, I told myself, perhaps he cares only for his bits of metal and his rusty belt buckles.

And then a somber thought hit me: at this moment, when I had made the most interesting discovery of my professional life, pitiful as it was, I had literally no one to share it with.

I shoved that thought from my mind. Instead, I did some research on Bellemeade, looking him up in the copied archives of the Dorchester church registry, also conveniently housed in the archive room, in the hope of finding him listed there. For a few minutes, maybe a half hour, I forgot about Brian, about whomever he was with and whatever he was doing with her, about poor Ethan and his forceful mother, and even—and this was the most merciful forgetting of all—about myself. For a few minutes, that is, I was completely absorbed in the tiny mystery I was working to solve, and I was happy.

I retained some of that feeling later that afternoon, when I left the Museum and drove home, part of the way in the dark, and greeted Diggory with a caress. It was threatening rain, and there was a bit of a chill in the air, so I made myself some tea and sat down at the table. Before I pulled Mrs. Davis's book to me, though, I thought to turn on my cellphone to check for voice messages.

There was one from Brian: *Having a great time, Ker, wish you were here, no regular cell phone coverage but I'll check in whenever I can.* There was one from our bank: *No problem, just checking to be sure you're satisfied with the service so far.* And there was one from a number I didn't recognize.

"Hello, this is Dana Murchison." It was a woman's voice, and it sounded confident and professional. *"I've just become the Lyme Regis Library Archivist, and I was calling all the users to introduce myself."* I felt a nasty jolt of dread fingering my insides as I listened to the rest of the message. *"We're beginning a new project to catalogue all the holdings of the Archive Room, and we wanted to enlist the support and the aid of all of our patrons. Thank you for your time, and please stop in to say 'hi' the next time you're in the Library!"*

I listened to the message a second time, trying to determine if it really was just a "hi, this is me call" or whether Dana Murchison had called because she had realized that Mrs. Davis's book had gone missing.

Could Tom Hardie have told her anything about my discovery? As far as I knew, the only way she could have known about my theft of the book (I saw no reason to mince words) was from Tom. Perhaps they were related in some way—cousins, or romantic partners, or old school chums. Who knew? I pulled the book to me and stroked its cover, my fingers tracing its smooth, marbled surface. I picked it up, along with my mug of tea, and moved to the couch. Diggory jumped on my lap and began to purr.

Petting him, I said, "We're in trouble now, Digg. I think I've done something really stupid this time."

But somehow, I didn't feel guilty, nor did I feel particularly worried or frightened. Instead, I felt liberated, almost empowered, and I put my feet up on the coffee table as I opened the book and entered Mrs. Davis's world once again.

The patients treated in Warrinder House were all women, and they were a piteous lot. One had some kind of religious mania: she thought she was guilty of the most heinous sins, although she could not, when pressed, explain what those sins were. Another thought she was made of glass—literally made of glass—and had to take great care where she walked so that she would not fall or bump into something and break herself into tiny, sharp pieces. One woman, according to Mrs. Davis, died in suspicious circumstances shortly after she herself left Warrinder House; in fact, Mrs. Davis all but accused Mr. Warrinder, Mr. E, and Mr. B of murdering this woman in her bed, referring to a court case that took place over the matter in the late 1840s. Delicacy forbad Mrs. Davis from mentioning any names, she wrote, but there were several "ladies" incarcerated in the house, and their plight was similar to hers, although she refrained from going into any details. She continuously railed against the treatment of the insane; it was something of a mantra in this small book. "*We must find another way to deal with mental illness*," she says at the midpoint of the book, in a strident tone, "*for the ways in which we treat it now surely do not work, and those who undergo such treatment, particularly ladies of refinement and grace, suffer greatly at the hands of those who treat them.*"

I closed the book and stood up, listening for her sighs as I readied myself for bed, but there was nothing. At the time, I didn't even think it was strange that I was disappointed at her silence. I went to bed that night wishing I could hear more from her.

Chapter Sixteen

My gift to God seems futile, quite;
The world moves as erstwhile;
And powerful Wrong on feeble Right
Tramples in olden style.
My faith burns down.
I see no crown;
But Cares, and Griefs, and Guile.
--Thomas Hardy, "The Church-Builder"

The rest of the week passed. I received several more messages from Brian, all in more or less the same vein: *Enjoying myself, beautiful scenery, no regular cell service, will call when I get back to Aberystwyth.* Though I listened for it, I could hear no background dialogue, no one calling him "*cariad,*" a Welsh term of endearment which I learned from George, who, with the best intentions, took it upon himself to expand my Welsh vocabulary with a few words each day when we drank tea together at the front desk.

Brian must have seen the need to be extra cautious, I decided. Did he realize that I had guessed about his new activities? I wasn't sure, and, a coward by nature, I didn't want to broach the topic. I was content to let things ride, to see what move he would make next. The longer his walking tour lasted, I said to myself, the better.

I see how wrong, how unhealthy, that attitude is now, but back then, I didn't. And yet, chances are, even if I knew that I was burying my head in the sand, it wouldn't have changed the way I was dealing with Brian. I didn't want to face the fact that we had drifted apart in the few short months we'd been married; I was working hard to keep from thinking too much about my domestic situation by immersing myself in my research, and, of course, in my other little obsessions.

I went detecting with Tom Hardie that Sunday, as I had promised, and we spent the better part of two hours out by the woods in the back, rooting around the leaves and trees, turning up stones and digging under soft, inviting clumps of moss. I found metal detecting to be deadly dull, but I loved being outside in the fine weather, crawling beneath the heavy, silent elms and the slender oaks, dirtying my fingers with the rich soil of the Dorset coastal hills. I breathed in the very slight smell of salty sea air, mixed with the delicate odor of new plant growth wafting down the hillside, and, closing my eyes, I could forget, for a moment, that I was engaged in a truly thankless task.

Yet how different, I asked myself again, was metal detecting from literary research? That thought struck me as I watched Tom grow red-faced with excitement, his breath coming in short, powerful little bursts, as he negotiated a new find in the dirt. When it turned out to be nothing but an old pull-tab from a can of beer, I felt sorry enough for him to suggest that we move closer to the house, to the grounds where I had found the locket.

"Why there?" He looked up at me. I was standing by the tree where I had been sitting when I'd first met Tom, looking down at Betony Lodge. I turned to look at him.

"Because I've already found something there." I am not sure why I blurted this out. After all, I half suspected that Tom had had something to do with the worrisome call

I'd received from Dana Murchison. But the words were out of my mouth before I could stop myself.

Tom just looked at me. Now I no longer felt just sorry for him; I felt guilty as well.

"It was before I met you out here," I said, my words rushing out. "It was just a locket. Probably nothing of note, anyway."

Tom still didn't say anything, so I walked towards him and took his arm. "Look, I'll show you, Tom. Come up to my flat and I'll show you what it was. And I'll show you where I found it, too."

He switched off his machine and hiked it over his shoulder, as if he were a doughboy shouldering his rifle. He still hadn't said a word, and I was worried that I'd done something wrong, had offended him even before he had seen the locket, but I said nothing and simply led him towards the house. We set off like that, a couple of misbegotten infantry soldiers fighting in the war against time, struggling to save a few random fragments of history from oblivion.

"Here," I said, as we passed the spot where I had found the locket.

Tom looked at me. I explained, "This was where I found it. Here, you can see the outline of stones right there. There must have been a building here once, don't you think? Look how regular the stones are."

Tom's glance followed my finger, and I could see that he was taking it all in. He was studying the dirt, staring at the stones, following the pattern they made in the ground, now barely visible through the long strands of grass and moss that had worked so hard to obscure them.

He squatted down to examine the spot even more closely, and with a short, stubby finger reddened by outdoor work, he traced the edge of a square stone. I saw him nod twice, and then he stood up and said, "Let's go take a look at your find, then, Kerys." His voice was low and gruff.

I turned and led him through the back door and up to my flat. I knew better than to suggest he leave the metal detector outside, leaning against the house in Ethan and Gemma's play-yard; it was Tom's prize possession, and so he carried it up the stairs on his shoulder, while I worried that he would bump its dish into the wall or the ceiling. But he must have been used to carrying it that way, because it arrived in my living room intact.

"You can put that over here, against the wall," I said to Tom as we came through the door to my flat. But either he didn't hear me, or he didn't want to follow my direction; I watched him as he set the device on the sofa as carefully as any mother would put her infant down for a nap. Then he turned towards me. I went into my bedroom to retrieve the locket from the sock drawer where I kept it. When I returned, I placed the terrycloth bundle on the dining room table. I looked up at him and nodded, and he walked to the table and looked down at the lump in the middle of the cloth.

"Well?" Tom looked up at me.

"Let me show you," I said, unwrapping my treasure. A moment later, it sat exposed, its fine gold curves incongruous against the faded blue dishtowel. I heard Tom gasp, and I watched him as he bent low over the locket. He stayed in that position, staring at the piece for what seemed like a minute or two, without touching it. Then he used a corner of the towel to flip it over. He bent down even closer, hovering over the locket, and pulled a magnifying glass out from one of the many pockets on his vest, staring at the back of the locket for at least a minute. I could hear him breathing; I could hear my own heartbeats as the seconds passed.

Just when I was beginning to run out of patience and was wondering how to interrupt this examination, Tom looked up at me, his eyes shining. For a moment, I thought he was tearing up: he had a strange, lop-sided smile that looked excited but somehow sad at the same time.

"And you found this outside, Kerys? At the spot you showed me?" His voice was sharper than I expected, contrasting with the almost sublime look on his face.

I nodded. To be honest, I was a little afraid to speak just then. I'd never seen a person more intent on getting an answer. The brightness in his eyes pierced me like uncut diamonds.

"Do you know what this is?"

I didn't, not really, so I shook my head. He bent down over it.

"Look here, Kerys. See these initials? And the dates? It's a mourning locket. Usually there'd be a lock of hair from the deceased inside it. Very fashionable in Victorian times, although we think of it as pretty weird these days."

"Well, there were a few strands of hair in it when I first opened it, Tom. Not a complete lock of hair, but a few of them…"

He stared at me and I realized then that I'd said something wrong. "What do you mean? You checked? Did you try to open this locket, Kerys?"

"I didn't try. I did open it. And there wasn't anything inside it."

Tom sputtered like a Fiat with a missing sparkplug. I watched him, surprised by his evident outrage. He stared at me for a second, then turned his back on me, walked over to the couch, picked up his metal detector, and made for the door.

"Wait a minute! Where are you going? What on earth is the matter?"

"You know very well what's wrong." Tom's lips formed a big, ugly circle as he said the words, and only then did I realize that this was more than mere jealousy. He was clearly furious with me. He set his metal detector down and stared at me, green eyes blazing in anger.

"No, I don't know what's wrong. Tell me, Tom. You owe me that at least. After all, I showed you what I found!"

"You don't even know what you found, Kerys. You have no idea what you're doing out there, mucking about, and you'll ruin it for all the rest of us." He shouldered his metal detector again, took a breath, and added, "I'll call you later." As he slammed out of my apartment, I heard him add, *sotto voce*, "Maybe."

I stood there in the middle of my living room, staring at the door, listening to him as he clattered down the staircase. I heard the angry bark of the front door closing behind him. Stunned by the force of his anger, I moved to the window in time to see him walk through the front gate of the grounds and into the road, where I lost sight of him.

What had I done? Was it just that I had opened the locket? Or was it something more? I suspected that it was the fact that I had found the locket at all, without his aid, that really set Tom off. Unable to control his jealousy, Tom couldn't stand being in the same room with me, not even with the lure of a recent find lying on the table in front of him.

I tried to control my disappointment, tried to ignore that nagging voice in my head that was declaring how unfair life—in particular, my life—was, but it was just too much for me. I sat down on the couch and cried, my sobs coming in out in irregular, ugly bursts, backed by salty tears. Diggory jumped on my lap, more curious than sympathetic, but for the most part, I ignored him, sparing him only a couple of strokes down his head and back. I didn't like crying, didn't like the way the moans erupted from my lungs like some kind of unwelcome autonomic response, but I couldn't help it. Between Brian, Leanne, and Tom, I felt like I'd been wronged in every one of the human relationships I'd had, and, powerless to control myself, I gave way to my sorrows, even though I told myself I was beginning to make this crying thing a habit.

I don't know how long I sat there, melting in my tears. I know that Diggory tired of my antics after a few short minutes and jumped down from my lap, and that the sunlight soon faded from the window, shrouding my view outside in darkness. When at last I stopped crying, night had come, and I could hear a commotion from downstairs. I sat up straight, blew my nose, and listened for the knock on the door that I knew must be coming.

Nothing. I began to wonder if I had heard

something that was not really there. For that matter, I told myself, it had been several days since I had heard any ghostly moans or cries, so perhaps I was due for another visitation of sorts.

But I was wrong. A moment later, a series of sharp and hurried knocks erupted on my door, making me jump. I walked over to the door and pulled it open, half expecting to see a contrite Tom Hardie on my doorstep, ready to explain his recent behavior.

But it was Leanne, looking pale and worried. I assumed she had heard me crying—I had not really tried to hold back, after all, and in Betony Lodge, the floorboards let sounds through easily enough. I started to tell her I was ok, that it was nothing, but she cut me off.

"Kerys," she said, breathless from her ascent up the stairs, "have you seen Ethan?"

"No," I said, surprised into silence. I waited for her to go on, then said, "You told me –"

She broke in to say, "He's missing. I thought he was in his room playing, but I can't find him now. I wondered whether he was up here with you."

"With me? Why would he be here? Especially after you told me to stay—"

Leanne waved away my objection as if it were a noxious insect of some kind. "Kerys, I don't have time to explain. I just thought he might be here. I've torn up my flat downstairs looking for him, and I've just been through the back garden. I can't find him anywhere, and I'm starting to panic." Her eyes watered, filling with tears, and her lower lip was beginning to tremble.

"It's okay, Leanne," I said, coming through my

door and out onto the landing. "Have you looked in the other flat? The one across from you?"

Leanne sniffed and shook her head. I offered her one of the tissues I had in my hand, hoping I hadn't yet used it myself. She blew her nose and said, "How could he get inside that flat? It's kept locked up, isn't it?"

"Well, yes, of course it is, but little boys have ways of getting around locks and barriers, Leanne."

"I need to find him before Gary gets home, Kerys. He'll be here in thirty minutes, and I don't want to worry him with this. Please, can you help me?"

I didn't bother to answer, just trotted past her and began to go down the staircase. "Where's Gemma, Leanne? We don't want her to get lost while we're looking for Ethan," I called out over my shoulder.

"She's fine—I made her promise not to leave the living room. She's watching the telly." Leanne and I had reached the downstairs landing. "I'll just make certain she's where I left her, Kerys." Leanne opened the door a crack, peered in, and then closed it softly. "She's sitting in front of the telly, just like I left her. I don't want to distract her—she's better off staying right there."

I nodded and turned to the other flat, the one I had never been in. "Does your key work in this door?"

Leanne pulled her keys out of her sweater pocket and looked at them. "I don't know. I've never tried."

I took them from her and put them into the lock, but they didn't fit. I tried my own key with the same results. Then I put my ear against the door and motioned Leanne to be silent.

"I think he's in there, Leanne," I said, my voice a

whisper.

"But how? And why?" I put my finger to my lips, convinced that we needed to be as silent as possible.

"I don't know why or how he got in there, but I just have a feeling that that's where he is," I said. "Can you take me into his bedroom?"

Leanne was looking at me as if I was crazy, but she was worried sick about her son and had no choice. Desperate, she nodded and we went into her flat. Gemma looked up as we passed by, but quickly decided that *Blue Peter* was more interesting than whatever antics her mum was getting up to. She turned back to the television, which was blaring loudly as some live-action forest animals sang a duet about stranger danger.

We rushed through the hall in silence and into Ethan's room. It was very messy, with pillows and blankets tossed about. I went to his bed, which was stripped to the mattress cover, and pushed it away from the wall. There was a sheet of wood against the wall, painted the same color, and I pulled it. It came away easily.

"What are you doing, Kerys?" Leanne was staring at me. "He's not behind the bed. I've already looked there."

"I know," I said. "Just a minute." I had pulled the wood away from the wall and found what I somehow knew would be there: a small access door, which was hanging ajar. I heard Leanne gasp, but didn't stop to look at her. The doorway was just big enough for me to crawl through it, and in another few seconds, I found myself next door, in the empty apartment.

It was very dark and very dusty. The window shades were all down, making it difficult to find my way. I stood up and started to call Ethan's name, but something made me stop, some internal warning that was telling me to be silent. Instead, I tiptoed out of the room and into the hallway. I made my way to the front part of the flat, towards what would be the living room if the apartment had been inhabited. Despite my care, my footsteps sounded to me like the clicking of a telegraph sounding out an SOS.

I entered the front room and stopped. My eyes were growing used to the darkness, and I could see a small form huddled in front of the door to the flat. I walked over to it and looked down.

It was Ethan, of course.

Before I picked him up, I unlocked the door. Then, with some effort, I scooped him into my arms, opening the door with difficulty, and carried him across the hallway into Leanne's flat. It was a relief to lay his dead weight on the couch, and I did it so quietly that Gemma, still transfixed by the singing badgers, didn't even turn around. I wiped at the dirt on Ethan's face with my sleeve, but it only made the dusty gray streaks worse. Not knowing what else to do, I covered him up with an afghan and went to get Leanne.

She was still waiting in Ethan's bedroom, still staring at the small doorway I'd crawled through a few minutes earlier. "Leanne," I said, coming up behind her and touching her shoulder. She jumped and swung around, her eyes wide and her mouth open. "I found him. I brought him back. He's asleep on the couch."

She shoved her way past me, trotting through the doorway and running down the hall. I followed. When I got to the living room, she was already wiping at Ethan's face with a damp cloth and calling his name, tears trailing down her cheeks.

"He's fine, Leanne," I said. "He was just sleeping. He probably fell asleep trying to get out through the front door of the flat. You know how children are."

She turned, and I saw two deep parallel lines on her forehead, just above her eyes, which were glaring up at me. "What do you know about how children are, Kerys?"

I took a step backwards, so harsh was the tone in which she hurled those words at me. "Leanne," I began, but she interrupted me.

"How did you know where he was, Kerys? How did you know about that door in his room?" She stood up and took a couple of steps towards me. "What have you been doing with my son?"

"Mum," said Ethan, who was now sitting up on the couch and rubbing the sleep from his eyes. "Don't be mean to Kerys. She didn't do anything wrong. She was the one who found me and brought me back."

Leanne paused and turned back to look at her son. I took advantage of her momentary distraction and slipped through the door and into the hallway of Betony Lodge. As I made my way upstairs, I heard the sound of tires crunching over gravel. Gary was home from work. I sighed with relief.

Back in my own flat, I made myself a strong Scotch and water and sat down on the couch. Once again, Diggory jumped into my lap, and this time, I scratched him under his chin, eliciting a contented purr from him. I drank my Scotch and sat there petting him, thinking hard about what had just happened.

Leanne was right. How *had* I known about the door? I couldn't say, but I had to admit that I had known it would be there when I moved the bed away from the wall, just as I knew precisely where I would find Ethan in the neighboring flat. It was as if I had been operating from some prescient instinct, a kind of foreknowledge that led me right to the boy. Whatever the reason for this ability, I was glad that I had been able to find him, but I also was beginning to worry, especially after Leanne's outburst, that I would be blamed for his disappearance.

I wondered again about my mental state. Could I be losing touch with reality? Losing my mind, in fact? Then again, I thought, why is insanity always perceived as a loss of some kind? People always talk about losing your mind, about losing your sanity. But does anyone ever talk about madness in terms of gaining something?

I didn't like the direction my thoughts were taking. But it was difficult to find something pleasant to concentrate on. Between finding Ethan and showing Tom Hardie the locket I'd found, I just couldn't catch a break. Blame seemed to find me no matter what I was doing or whom I was with. I shook my head at the irony, raised my glass in a silent, sarcastic toast, and drank deep, shuddering as the Scotch burned my tongue and throat.

It was a good night to get drunk, I thought, and I was well on my way to that estimable goal when my phone buzzed. A little tipsy by then, I hit "Receive" before I looked at the number, which is how I ended up speaking to my husband for the first time in a week.

"Kerys?" His voice was deeper than I'd remembered. I paused for a moment before answering.

"Yes?"

"It's Brian."

"I know." I took another sip of my drink, a long one. I was preparing for an awkward conversation.

"How are you?"

"I'm fine, Brian. How are you? How's your walking tour?"

"It's good." Another long, uncomfortable pause. I waited. After all, he was the one who had called, not me. "How's your research going?"

"It's fine," I said, unwilling to engage. "I'm making progress."

I could feel Brian's tension on the other end, but at this point I had no pity, and certainly not a shred of sympathy, for him. So I waited. Tonight, for some reason, after a busy and emotional day, I had endless stores of patience. Besides, I was enjoying Brian's discomfiture.

"Well," he said, finally—and I could hear the note of desperation in his voice, a small catch at the end of the word that almost made me feel sorry for him—"I just called to say hi. We're staying in a guesthouse tonight and tomorrow, and heading towards Abergavenny the next day."

"Oh," I said, making sure my voice stayed flat. "Nice."

"We should get back by Thursday," Brian offered.

"And then what?" I hadn't meant to say it, hadn't meant to give Brian the slightest opening, but it slipped out before I could stop myself.

"Then…well, I thought I'd come back home."

I didn't say anything, and there was a long silence.

"Kerys?"

"Yes, Brian. I'm still here."

"Kerys, I've got to go. I need to get back to the others—we're planning our route. I just wanted to say hi and tell you I'd see you soon."

"Yes," I said, watching the ice melt in my drink, the auburn patches of scotch swirling amid tiny currents of water. "See you soon, Brian."

"I love you," he said, almost as an afterthought.

But it was too late; I'd already taken the phone away from my ear, and though I heard the words, they were muffled and distant, as if coming from a thousand miles away.

I put the phone on the side table and put my drink to my lips, tipped it back, and swallowed the rest of it, ice chunks and all, in one gulp. Then I picked up Diggory and cradled him on my lap, petting him. After a moment, I chuckled. Funny, I told myself, that someone like me, a serious student of Thomas Hardy's novels, would be so naïve as to be surprised to discover that life is not fair.

Chapter Seventeen

" 'Tis hard; but,' I thought, 'never mind it;
There's gain in the end:
And when I get used to the place I shall find it
A home, and may find there a friend."
--Thomas Hardy, "The Curate's Kindness"

I woke up the next morning a little worse for the wear, my head aching and my eyes feeling like I'd spent the night reading—though of course reading had nothing to do with my headache. I had already dressed and had my first cup of tea when I heard footsteps coming up the stairwell. I waited, expecting a knock on my door.

Sure enough, it came, and a moment later I was standing in my threshold, looking at Leanne.

"Good morning," I said, staring at her. She was cradling an oblong object in her hands, something like an old-fashioned bowling pin. "How's Ethan?"

"He's fine," she said, staring at me with a flat gaze. "Thank you for helping me find him yesterday." But the words sounded forced, as if she'd memorized them from a script.

"You're welcome, Leanne. Would you like to come in? Maybe have a cup of tea?"

She shook her head, then looked down at her hands. "Ethan asked me to give this to you. Actually," she said, proffering the object, "he insisted. He wouldn't eat his breakfast or get dressed this morning until I promised him that I'd bring it to you. He said you'd know what to do with it."

I looked at the object she was offering me: it was a doll, but like no doll I'd ever seen. This one was wooden, with an awkwardly shaped head and torso made from a single piece of wood, and arms and legs that were jointed, held together by a set of pins. The doll's face was painted, and though faded, I could make out a rather grim set of eyes, a narrow nose, and a tiny, pursed mouth. One cheek was pink, but the other had been rubbed to reveal an ivory color. The hair, too, was painted on, as were the socks, or perhaps they were meant to be shoes. I took it from Leanne and held it up to look at it more closely.

"What is this?" I turned back to Leanne. "Where did Ethan get it?" I was struggling with a wave of nausea that had hit me at the moment I had taken the doll from her hands.

Leanne shrugged. "I don't know. He said you'd understand. I have no idea where he found it."

I stared at her for a moment, looked down at the doll, then looked back into Leanne's narrowed eyes.

"I'll take it to the museum in Dorchester," I said at last. "They'll know what to do with it."

Leanne nodded. "Whatever you do is fine. Ethan just told me to give it to you."

"But why would he do that? I don't understand."

"I don't know, Kerys, but I think you'll understand if I ask you once more to keep your distance from him. I don't think you're a good influence just now."

"Leanne, I don't know what's come over him, but I hope you know I've had nothing to do with it. After all, I found him yesterday, didn't I?"

She stared at me and said nothing. I pulled back

164

from the doorway, and then she turned around to start down the staircase. I shut the door without either of us saying goodbye.

It was raining that morning, and I left in a bit of a hurry, eager to get back to the Museum, where I knew I could keep my emotions and my thoughts in order. I took the doll with me, but when I got to the car park of the Museum, I changed my mind and decided to leave it under my seat. I couldn't face the barrage of questions I assumed would follow if I simply presented it to the museum collection. Besides, I told myself, I wasn't even certain they'd be interested in such an artifact.

And, while I was there that day, duly cataloguing ancient invoices for false teeth, shirtwaists, and Westminster collars, I realized that the Hardy Museum wasn't the place to take the doll, anyway. I would take it to the Lyme Regis library on my way home.

Of course, the natural thing to do would have been to call Tom Hardie, who, with all his experience in antiquity hunting, would have known just where to take it, but I wasn't sure we were friends any more, not after his outburst the previous night. So, after a brief stop at the front desk on my way out of the Hardy Museum, where George and I spoke about the awful weather we were having, I left, running through the pouring rain to my car, and drove away, rather damply, towards Lyme Regis.

There, as usual, I had to hunt for a parking space, even though it wasn't high tourist season, or any season other than wet season. But at last I found one, and, stuffing the doll deep into my backpack, I walked four blocks downhill to the library in a misting, thick rain that worked to muffle my senses. I knew the sea lay before me, an iron-gray space of limitless proportions, the one flat feature in the landscape, but the mist and fog hid it from my view.

I arrived at the Lyme Regis Library only thirty minutes before closing time. Rushing into the building, pausing only to shake off the drips from my raincoat, I hurried to the circulation desk. I shrugged my backpack off my shoulders and hugged it to my chest.

"Yes?" The woman working the desk looked up at me, and I could sense her irritation at being engaged in any kind of conversation that could delay her departure for home.

"I was wondering if I could talk to the person who is in charge of the Special Collections," I said, wishing I'd come earlier in the day.

"She's not here," said the woman, adjusting her glasses and looking back at her computer screen.

"Oh," I said. "When will she be back? Should I come back tomorrow to see her?"

She shook her head, still gazing at her computer. "She's out for a bit. And we've closed off the Special Collections, anyway."

"Closed it off? What does that mean?"

"It's inaccessible."

"For how long?" I was beginning to get impatient with the woman.

"For the foreseeable future."

"Why?" My hold tightened upon my backpack, and I could feel the hard outline of Ethan's doll through the canvas.

The woman stood up and rearranged a few papers

on the desk. I could tell it was a dismissive gesture, that she wanted me to leave her in peace so she could lock up the library and go home, but I wasn't willing to go gently.

I repeated my question. "Why is the Special Collections closing?"

"It's been decided that it needs more attention—cataloguing materials and such. No one knew what we had down there. That's a bad state for a library to be in, so it's been closed until further notice."

"Does everything happen in passive voice around here?" I was frustrated and upset, and my temper got the best of me. The woman just looked at me for a moment, then turned and put a pile of books on the rolling bookshelf behind her.

I was dismissed, that much was clear. I hitched my backpack onto my shoulders and left the library. As I walked out, I could feel what must have been the doll's elbow, or knee, digging into my right shoulder blade, and I walked back to my car, the rain coming down harder now, with that little reminder of my failure to find it a home.

I sat in the car for some minutes, partly because of inertia, partly because I still had time on the meter and felt it was my prerogative, my right, to use that time up completely. And all the while I sat there, it occurred to me that the closure of the special collections might be due to a traitorous phone call from Tom Hardie.

As soon as the idea flitted back into my brain, I was convinced it was the truth. Tom was angry with me, jealous because I had found something by accident that he couldn't find despite months, perhaps years, of dedication. He had probably called the Lyme Regis Library up that very morning and told them about *My Years in an Asylum,* about how I'd spirited it away from its unknown resting place and was keeping it illegally. Their response, apparently, was to shut down the Special Collections for the foreseeable future.

Correction: their *first* response. There were other measures to come, certainly. I could expect a phone call or a visit from the library officials, a reprimand, perhaps something even worse, maybe a black mark on my career as a scholar. I could feel my panic begin to get the better of me as I sat there contemplating the situation. My head began to throb with every one of my heartbeats. I drew in a ragged breath, forcing it into my lungs, which seemed to have lost their ability to expand.

How could I ever have trusted a stranger like Tom? But then again, trust was such a silly thing to place in anyone. Look at the trust I'd had in Brian: in a few short weeks, it had been blown to smithereens, with hardly any shards left to pick up. Anger surged through me as well as panic, and I hit the steering wheel hard with a tight fist. My hand would hurt later, I knew, but I couldn't restrain my temper, and I couldn't keep from allowing it some kind of outward expression.

Just then, from the left side of the car, came a tap on the passenger window. I looked up, and saw Tom Hardie staring in at me through the rivulets of rain making their way down the window. Instead of rolling it down, I got out of the car and spoke to him over the top of the car.

"What do you want?" The words came out in a sharp and angry burst, just as I'd intended them to.

He looked surprised. "I was passing by, and I saw

you sitting here. Is everything ok, Kerys?"

"I don't know," I said. "Why don't you tell me?"

"What do you mean?"

"I mean you ratted on me, Tom. Just because you were jealous of my find."

"Look, I'm sorry about that, Kerys. I flew off the handle last night, and it weren't—wasn't—right or seemly of me. I'm sorry, truly I am."

"You have an odd way of showing it, Tom."

"What do you mean?"

"I'm talking about the Special Collections at the Library. You told them that I took the Davis book, didn't you?"

Tom stared at me. Then he shook his head, and walked around the front of the car to face me. "Kerys," he said, "I didn't do any such thing. I wouldn't ever do that." He paused, watching for my reaction, then added, "Look, there's no use us standing out here in the rain, getting drenched and bibbering like this. Come round with me to the Badger, and we'll sort this all out."

I looked at his broad face and felt my resentment melt away. I saw no dishonesty or subterfuge in his green eyes. Besides, I wanted to believe that he could be my friend. Nodding, I reached into my car for my backpack and walked back down the hill with him to the pub. It was worth a pint to listen to him explain his behavior, anyway, I told myself.

The Angry Badger was packed; it seemed that a rainy day in Lyme Regis was a call to all inhabitants to make their way to the nearest pub and take in a few pints in an effort to find consolation for the wet weather. But we managed to find an empty table, or rather a corner of a table, and sat down.

"Look-see," said Tom, "First, I want to apologize for storming out last night, Kerys. I was overcome, sort of, by how lucky you'd been, and how you found things that I've not. It's unfair, you see, with all that I've put into it."

I took a pull of my beer, in no hurry to answer Tom. Besides, I knew all of this already; he was offering me nothing new. After a moment, I said, "So you didn't call anyone at the Library about me?"

"Of course I didn't. Kerys, I might have a bad temper, but I'm not a noggerhead. I wouldn't get you in trouble. You know that, don't you?" He was staring at me, his pint forgotten for the moment.

"I guess so," I said after a moment, staring at the table, refusing to meet his gaze after he'd finished speaking. The group next to us erupted into laughter, and we both looked over at them, a group of young adults smiling and chuckling, in a playful mood that contrasted with the somberness of our discussion.

"Kerys," Tom continued, "I acted like a footy idiot, and I'm that sorry for it."

I didn't know what "footy" meant, but I assumed it was bad, and that Tom had abased himself enough for his behavior the previous night, so I said, "That's all right, Tom. Let's just forget about it."

"Really, Kerys? You forgive me?"

"Sure, Tom. I'm sorry for accusing you of being a ratfink."

"Ratfink?"

"Never mind." I took another long sip of my beer,

and Tom, his duty now complete, drank from his as well.

"Another round?" he asked. The eager, chastened look in his eyes reminded me of a puppy that had just been disciplined.

"Look," I said, "I'm sorry we had a misunderstanding. Let me pay for this round, anyway, Tom. We'll put it all behind us, ok?" I reached for my backpack and unzipped it, thinking to pull out my wallet to pay the bill, but the doll that Ethan had given me fairly jumped out of the zipped enclosure. I put my hand over it, ready to stuff it back in, but I was too late. Tom had already seen it.

"What's that?"

I saw no reason for subterfuge. I was tired of keeping secrets, anyway. "It's a doll of some sort, I think. The boy in the flat below me found it. He gave to me."

Tom leaned back in his seat and stared at me. I knew what he was thinking, so I said, "Go ahead and give it a look, Tom. I'll go get the next round."

While I hadn't meant to show Tom the doll that day, not wanting another display of angered jealousy so soon upon the heels of the last one, I didn't care enough to keep it from him. I took my time at the bar, deliberating between a house ale or a local cider, and then made my way back through the throngs of damp people to our table, trying not to slosh too much of our drinks onto the floor.

"What do you think of it?" I said, as I sat down and slid his mug over to him. "Kind of a nasty thing to give a small child to play with, in my opinion."

Tom pulled his eyes away from the doll and handed it back to me. "Put it back into your satchel," he said. "No point in waving it about here, in this crowd."

I did as he said, but asked why it was so important to keep the doll a secret.

"It's not so much to keep it a secret, Kerys. But you don't know who's in a place like this when it gets crowded. There are people about who might want to get their hands on your stuff, you see."

"You mean like competitors? Like other metal detector types? What is it about you, Tom—do you people have a contest of some sort to determine who gets the most discoveries? That's kind of juvenile, if you ask me."

Tom shrugged. "Maybe. I'm not worried about other people with metal detectors, to be honest. It's the treasure-hunters that are the threat. Lyme is crawling with people who are looking for the next big find, and they're none too careful about how they get it, if you know what I mean."

I didn't, but I didn't want to take the time to listen to a full-blown, drawn-out explanation of what he meant, so I tried to change the subject. "What do you think about it, Tom? I don't know where it was found or what it is—it was just given to me by a small boy who must have happened upon it."

"Lucky little lad," said Tom, almost under his breath. "Well, it's clearly a doll, a plaything from the late nineteenth century. No clothes, they must have rotted away. Painted face and head, rubbed away on the right side, but, all in all, in fairly good condition. I'd say it's worth a small fortune—if you could provide any information about where it came from and who it belonged to."

"No such luck," I said, almost relieved to know that without the all-important "provenance" I really didn't have anything valuable on my hands. "I told you, I don't know where it came from. It was given to me. But listen, Tom—what about my book?"

"What book?"

"You know, the one I – the one I borrowed from the Lyme library. What do you think I should do with it? Now that they've closed the collections, I mean."

"Silly question, Kerys," said Tom, after a sip of beer. "Keep quiet about it. No sense dragging your own self into trouble if you don't have to."

I was already down to the last two inches of my cider. "You really didn't say anything, Tom? You didn't try to get me into trouble with the library?"

Tom sighed. "Look, Kerys," he said. "I admit I was jealous to the point of anger last night. I know it was right silly of me, and I'm sorry I had a pelt. But I wouldn't turn you in like that. I'm not that kind of man."

"I'm sorry," I said. "I know that you're not. Listen, why don't you come back over later this week and we'll have a look at the book? And the locket. And the doll, for that matter. What do you say?"

"Thought you'd never ask," he said, smiling. "How about Wednesday evening? Would that suit you?"

"That's fine," I said, standing up and grabbing my backpack. "See you then."

I left the Angry Badger wondering why on earth I was dragging Tom Hardie back into my orbit when I had had the chance to be free of him. As I sat behind the wheel of my car, only a little the worse for the two drinks I'd had,

I realized I had no good answer to such a question. I shrugged, kicked the car into drive, and made my way back to Betony Lodge.

It had become the kind of rainy evening that calls for a cup of tea, a good book, a soft couch and, if luck is with you, a nice, purring cat to sit on your lap as you read and sip your way through it all. Raindrops streamed down the windowpanes, making strange patterns that seemed to be set out for them in advance by an unseen hand. As the daylight failed, slipping away like a thief, I plopped myself onto my couch, cup in hand, Diggory by my side, and Mrs. Davis's book on my lap. I had reached a chapter in which she discussed an outing to the Cobb, one of the sights to see in this area of England.

Strange, I thought, that I had been here in Dorset, living so close to Lyme Regis for several months now without ever having visited one of its most famous landmarks. I would go the next day, I told myself as I got up to get more tea. It was then that I heard the voices, soft but clear enough to discern some of the words, though they made no sense to me back then. "It's fair mizzy out," said one, while another said, as if answering the first, "Aye, and it looks as if it'll be raining nicely afore long." I looked towards the television, thinking I might have turned it on by rolling onto the remote control when I got up from the couch, but the screen was dark. I went to my front door and pulled it open quickly, expecting to see the speakers in the hallway, but there was no one.

And, because I was under the influence of Mrs. Davis and her story, doubtless also because I had been living with a degree of stress and worry that I'd never known before, with no one to talk to or to counsel me, I decided that the voices I was hearing were part and parcel of the strange emanations of Betony Lodge. I no longer distrusted my assumptions; in fact, from that time on, I believed them without question. Betony Lodge, once Warrinder House, had a life of its own, a history that was so rich in human misery and suffering that it could not simply recede, well-behaved and silent like most other houses, into its dark past, but instead clamored for attention from those who would or could acknowledge its presence. In other words, my house was alive with its history, and I was therefore not merely a witness to the strange and multiple lives it harbored, but a participant in those lives as well.

I don't know if I reasoned all this out at just that moment; it could be that I figured it out later, when I had ample time to think and muse upon my experiences. But I know this: that night I went to bed in a calm and accepting mood, without even a trace of worry or fear. I was part of the house now, I told myself as I dropped off to sleep, Diggory curled up beside me, and I knew I had nothing to fear from it any longer. I knew then, just as I know now, that whatever else happened in my chaotic life, I belonged here, in Betony Lodge.

Chapter Eighteen

We were rarely allowed outside to wander about the gardens on our own, but when we pleased the doctors by our behavior—in other words, when we submitted to their orders and took their medicines and treatments, horrible as they were, without demurral or question—we were allowed to visit Lyme Regis, the closest town to Warrinder House. Two or three of us would be loaded into a carriage and driven, our attendants sitting beside us, the three miles down to the town. Once there, we were ushered from one shop to another, allowed only a glimpse of merchandise we could not buy, as people pointed at us and whispered when they thought we could not hear them.

The misery of those outings I will spare you, my dear Reader. To be thought a lunatic, to be talked of in my own presence, incurred a pain so sharp I sometimes thought it was physiological in origin; my heart heaved within my breast, and tears of shame, of frustration, yea, even of anger, made my eyes burn. One day, we were taken onto the Cobb, the long pier that juts out from Lyme, to take some sea air. Ever since I first came to Warrinder House, once I realized that it was situated on the southern coast of England, I had longed to see the ocean, to feel a salt breeze on my face, to breathe the seaside air, and on that day, at least, I was not disappointed. The Cobb is an imposing structure, its ancient stones worn with the imprint of so very many feet through the centuries. Walking upon it that day made me realize that there is a permanence in life, that some things are indeed real and

*unchanging. I date my recovery, such as it was, from that
moment of realization, and were I a poet, with the power
of Miss Rossetti or Mrs. Browning, I would sing the
praises of that wonderful structure, so fondly do I
remember its firm presence beneath my feet, as from its
secure and safe heights I watched wave after wave break
against an ever-changing shoreline.*

      --*Cecilia Davis,* My Time in a Lunatic Asylum

     The next morning, I lingered in my flat. My urge
to immerse myself in the lifeless stacks of books, boxes,
and papers in its antiseptic artifact room had waned; I had,
much sooner than I would have thought, grown tired of
the impartiality, the remote nature, of the things I was
cataloguing. How could I pull myself away from Mrs.
Davis's narrative, whose pages I felt compelled to read
again and again, from the locket, and now the doll—these
things, these treasures that were living reminders of a
history that surrounded me at every turn in this house—
trading them in for meaningless scraps of papers that no
one could really care about? I dragged my feet getting
ready for work, and in the end, I forced myself out the
door, feeling very proud of myself for putting duty before
pleasure.

     I nearly tripped and fell, however, because Ethan
was crouched right on my doorstep. I looked down at him
in surprise, and began to say something, but he held his
finger up to his lips, and, taking the hint, I sat down on the
floor next to him.

     "You shouldn't be here, Ethan," I whispered. "You
know your mother doesn't want you talking to me

anymore. You'll get me in trouble."

"I'm sorry, Kerys," he said, his large eyes on mine. He looked solemn and very serious, and in that moment, I felt sorry for this little boy, for like me, he, too, was caught up in something he didn't understand, and yet he was so young, so innocent. He leaned towards me. "I had to talk to you. Are you taking care of the doll?"

"I am," I said, matching his serious demeanor. "But why did you give it to me? And where did you find it?"

"It was in the wall, through the doorway between my room and the other flat," he said. "It was just sitting there, and I thought I was meant to take it, so I did."

I nodded. "But why did you have your mom give it to me?"

"Because I knew she wouldn't like me having it. I knew she wouldn't let me keep it. She would have taken it away from me. I thought you would be able to keep it safe, because, well, you know…"

"Because I hear the voices, the sounds, just as you do?" I stared at him, and for a second he didn't answer. Then he nodded, as if reluctant to put his feelings into words.

"Listen to me, Ethan," I said, moving closer to him and taking his hand in mine. "I need you to promise me something."

"What?" The boy may have been innocent, but he was smarter than to make a promise before he knew what he was getting himself into.

"I need you to promise me that you won't do what the voices say any more."

He started to object, but I raised a hand and hushed him.

"Ethan, I know that you were told to go into that flat. I know it was the voices that told you to, because you wouldn't have thought of doing it on your own, would you? You wouldn't have known about the hidden door if the sad lady hadn't told you about it. Would you have?"

He shook his head, biting his lip.

"Well, then, listen to me. You mustn't do things just because the voices tell you to. The voices aren't mean or bad, but you need to remember that your mum is the person you have to listen to. If they tell you to do something that you know would upset her, then you must not do it. Do you understand me?" Ethan nodded and I continued. "Your mum doesn't want you to talk to me, so you'll have to stop coming up here. But you know I'm your friend, right?"

"Yes, Kerys." I was sorry for him. He looked sad, much sadder and wiser than a six-year-old boy ever should. "I just wanted to be sure you had the doll and were taking good care of her."

"I am, Ethan. And you be sure and remember what I've told you. You can listen to the voices. But don't try to find them, and don't listen to them if they tell you to do something you know isn't right. If that happens, you go out and play, or turn on the telly, or ask your mum to take you out to the stores, ok? Can you promise me that, Ethan?"

He nodded. "I promise, Kerys," he said.

"Now, then, off with you back to your own flat before your mum realizes you're gone. We can wave to each other when we see each other, as long as your mum doesn't see, but don't come up and visit me again unless your mum knows about it and approves."

He stood up before I did, and for a moment I was looking up at him. "Bye, Kerys," he said, and ran down the stairs, treading softly. For some strange reason, I had to fight back tears as I watched him descend the staircase without a backward glance. A profound sense of loneliness washed over me, and I sat under its weight for several minutes before I picked up my backpack and headed out to my car.

George Marten-Douglass was at the desk when I arrived at the Museum. He looked up and smiled at me. "You're here early today, Kerys." He offered me a mug of tea, which I took and thanked him for. "What gives? Some kind of deadline?"

I shook my head. "Nope, just felt like coming early to get some work done." It was a lie, but, I hoped, a therapeutic one. I took a sip of my tea and sighed. "Of course, you've derailed me already, George. But thanks for the tea, anyway."

"You're welcome. You work too much, Kerys. Whatever's in there waiting for you, it's not that important."

"Maybe not," I said. "But it's part of my fellowship. I'm supposed to be doing something for my stipend, after all."

"Yes, that's true, but you need to save time for yourself. You should get out more."

I laughed and pointed to the window. "In this

weather?"

"Kerys," George said, his dark eyes on mine, "you've lived in England long enough now to know that a bit of rain never stops us. In fact, it's a blessing when it does rain, since it keeps the tourists away."

"I was just thinking I ought to go out onto the Cobb," I said, warming my hands on my mug. "I haven't been there yet."

"You haven't seen the Cobb?" George raised his eyebrows, then shook his head, as if in pity. "Kerys, you're worse than I thought. You really must get out more often. You don't want to get ill now, do you? Fresh air is absolutely necessary for those engaged in scholarship. You must know that!" The singsong quality of his slight Welsh accent came through in the last sentence, and I thought about how different the British were from Americans. In the States, going outside in bad weather was what led to illness; here, however, it was the opposite. It was staying indoors too much that could lead one to getting sick. I was beginning to wonder whether the British had the right idea about this.

"Listen, Kerys," said George, uncapping a pen and pulling a piece of paper towards him. "I'm going to make a list of places you need to visit." He was writing very quickly, and I hoped I'd be able to read his handwriting. "Think of it as homework, or a prescription, if you want. But the point is," he said, pushing the paper back to me, "you need to do all these things. The sooner, the better."

I looked at his list. There were five things on it: the Cobb (in capital letters and underlined, as if to make certain I'd understand the importance of it); Brownsea

Island; Sherborne Abbey; Corfe Castle; and Durdle Door. The only one I'd heard of was the Cobb. I was duly chastened and admitted it.

I asked about the places, and when George told me about them, I resolved to visit them all. But where to start? "Well," said George, "the Cobb is the easiest, obviously. It's right in Lyme, and you can do it in less than an hour— maybe even less than thirty minutes. Corfe Castle is where all the school trips go, so you'll want to be careful when you choose your time to go there—maybe wait until the long summer holidays. But my personal favorite has to be Durdle Door."

"And what on earth is Durdle Door? It sounds like something you'd find in a Tolkien novel."

George laughed. "Not unless it's one about Norse gods and ice giants. I guess that's would be C.S. Lewis and not Tolkien, wouldn't it? Durdle Door is a gigantic rock structure, an arch, that rises right up out of the water, as if someone placed it there on purpose. It's surrounded by this lovely cove, too—Lulworth Cove. That's where Sergeant Troy goes missing in *Far From the Madding Crowd*: remember how he goes for a swim and a fishing boat picks him up, and then he stays away from Bathsheba Everdene for years? Lulworth Cove is where he goes swimming, which is just a stone's throw—literally—from Durdle Door. Hardy calls it something else in the novel, as usual, but there's no doubt it's Lulworth. You know, Kerys, as a Hardy scholar, you simply have to go see the area. It's required viewing. If I weren't still nursing this silly ankle, I'd take you myself."

"You're right, George. I'll go as soon as I leave

here today," I said. I finished my tea and set the mug down. "But first I'll go do my stint of cataloguing, so I can say I earned my stipend this week." Before I left the room, I called out, "Thanks for the tea! And for the tourist information!"

"My pleasure," said George, turning back to his computer.

It was some three hours later that I emerged from the storeroom, my eyes sore and bleary from trying to decipher old-fashioned handwriting in faded ink. I thought briefly about stopping at Lyme on my way home in order to walk the Cobb, but I was tired. I wanted to relax in a hot bath, not walk in a cool mist, and it was a very "mizzy" (or drizzly) afternoon. I took the turn off the Charmouth Road to avoid Lyme and go direct to Betony Lodge, but then, perversely, I changed my mind. At the very next turnout, I used it to reverse direction and head back into town. I would see the Cobb today, I told myself, this very afternoon, and cross one of the items off George's list right away.

Parking was easy that day, no doubt due to the rain. Indeed, as I walked towards the Lyme waterfront, I heard a few comments about the weather from shoppers and other errand-runners as they walked in pairs past the shops. "'Tis raining nicely now," said one old man to a woman, presumably his wife, as the rain started coming down harder. "Aye," said the gray-haired woman, her scarf pulled up over her head. "'Tis fair tipping it down." Yet no umbrellas came out; these were Dorset people, and a bit of wet was nothing to them. I, on the other hand, was getting soaked to the skin despite my anorak jacket, and I had trouble controlling my shivering. Yet I was determined to make it to the Cobb, to walk on the same stones Mrs. Davis had all those years ago, and to try to derive the same comfort from its permanence that she had.

But first there was a long walk along the beach front, which would have been lovely, I'm sure, if it had been summer or even just a sunny fall day, but it was wet and blustery, and I felt like I was performing some kind of Navy SEAL exercise just to reach the point at which I could get up onto the Cobb. My shoes dug into wet sand, which sucked at the soles as if they were made of glue. It was an ordeal just to get to the base of the long stone pier that jutted like a spear into the Channel.

Some ten minutes after I had passed the last of several lonely fish and chip stands, their faded fronts boarded up and looking derelict, I reached the beginning of the Cobb. I climbed up the gray granite steps, onto the break wall, to start my walk.

I wish I could say that I was profoundly affected by the experience of walking the length of the Cobb, that I felt as if I really were treading in the footsteps of Mrs. Davis, and that it was a meaningful experience for me. But I can't. I shivered in the cold gusts, and I was pelted with hard raindrops. The rocks were slippery, and I was afraid of losing my balance and skinning my knees, or worse still, winding up with a twisted ankle, like poor George. And while the sea was an impressive shade of gunship gray, so was the sky; the only thing that distinguished them from each other were the angry whitecaps that appeared and then disappeared at intervals upon the water's surface.

Yet I forced myself to walk the whole length of the Cobb, all the way to the bloody end of it, where it stopped abruptly, its stones lagging off into the bay. And I made myself stand there, taking in the sight, the smell, and the sounds of the place. Intending to stay for a while in order to immerse myself in the scene, so that it would etch itself into my memory, I gave up and bailed after a grand total of two minutes. "To hell with this," I muttered, and turned back, pulling my jacket around me to ward off the slicing wind.

In fact, I muttered obscenities pretty much all the way back to the shoreline, and once there, my muttering grew somewhat louder as I picked my way down the steps, now pooling with the rainwater that was collecting in treacherous puddles on the uneven surface of the stones. When I got to the shoreline, no longer a sandy beach but rather a blistered mess of wet sand, I felt grateful to be unscathed, and profoundly irritated by my pointless excursion. I trudged back across the stand, the empty food booths and brightly colored cabanas mocking my ill-fated mission. Only a fool, I told myself, would come out here on a day this miserable.

And that's why I was surprised when I heard someone call my name as I reached the town.

Looking up, I saw Brian.

"Kerys," he said, "I thought I recognized your jacket. Didn't you see me?"

I stared at him. He pointed across the street. "I've been waving at you and calling your name from way back there," he said. His dark hair was plastered against his forehead, making him look like a kid, and raindrops were lingering on his eyelashes. He blinked them away. "I came home early. Cam Jarvis was driving this way back home, and I hitched a ride. I just got here about half an hour ago. I was looking for a ride back to Betony Lodge."

"Oh," I said. "You're home early, then." I was trying to process all that information at once. Was Cam Jarvis a man or a woman? I didn't know, and I didn't really care. All I knew was that I was not ready to talk to Brian.

Brian opened his mouth to say something, but stopped. He stood there, just nodding his head for a few seconds. Finally, he said, "Look, we need to talk, Kerys."

"I know," I said, fighting a wave of nausea.

"Do you have the car here? We can go back home, you know, and—"

But I didn't want to go back to Betony Lodge with Brian that evening. I stalled.

"Let's go to the pub, Brian. I don't have anything at home to make for dinner, and it's too late to go to the shops now." This at least was true; in the weeks during Brian's absence, I had perfected the art of eating from bare cupboards: tinned soups, noodles, apples and other storable fruits, along with copious amounts of tea, had made up most of my diet. To say nothing of my new favorite beverage: Scotch and water.

Brian nodded, and we walked to the Angry Badger without saying another word.

Chapter Nineteen

Ache deep; but make no moans:
Smile out; but stilly suffer:
The paths of love are rougher
Than thoroughfares of stones.
    --Thomas Hardy, "The End of the Episode"

It was early still, barely evening, so it was not difficult to find a quiet seat in a corner of the pub. Brian pushed one of the chairs aside and put his backpack in it, at the front of the table, as if to block us off from other customers. Then he went to the bar and returned with a beer for himself and a glass of white wine for me. I hadn't drunk white wine since he left, and I remember wishing he'd gotten me a beer instead. White wine belongs to the summer, with its long days and plentiful sunshine, not to the winter months, when you need something substantial to provide refuge from cold, wet, hopeless days. But I said nothing, not even "thank you," and simply took the glass from his outstretched hand.

He took a long sip from his pint, and I wondered if he was looking for some liquid courage to begin our discussion. I almost felt sorry for him, but I was determined not to help him in this conversation—a conversation that he had asked for, and indeed had created a need for ten days earlier.

At last, he cleared his throat and spoke. "Kerys," he said, "I need to tell you something."

"Actually, Brian," I said, "you don't."

Brian looked at me, his blue eyes squinting. I

noticed that his hair was beginning to curl around his ears from the damp air. "What do you mean?"

"You don't have to tell me anything," I said. "I don't really care what you've been up to."

He leaned back in his chair, his eyes on my face, and sat there for a moment, staring at me. Then he took another sip of his beer. When he put down his mug, he sighed and wiped his mouth on the back of his hand and ran his other hand through his hair, shaking a few wayward drops of rain from it. All the while I stared at him, fingering the stem of my wine glass. I had not yet taken a sip of it.

Finally he sat up and leaned forward, across the table. "I get it," he said at last. "You're not going to make this easy for me, are you, Kerys?"

"Why should I?" I was trying to control myself, desperate not to give into the fury that was churning up my stomach and making me clench my teeth, but I couldn't help my voice breaking under the stress of the hostile words I threw at him. I bit back still other words that were struggling to come out, words of recrimination, anger, pain. If I begin to speak now, I remember thinking, I might never stop.

Brian leaned back into his seat again, holding his mug in his hand, and looked down into it as he rocked it lightly, watching the beer swirl round. "You're right," he said, after a few minutes of uncomfortable silence. "I deserve this. I totally deserve this kind of treatment." He looked at me from across the table, his eyes watering— were those tears, or lingering raindrops? "All I can say is that I'm sorry, Kerys."

"Really?" The word escaped my lips before I could stop myself. And, because leaving that word out there, hanging between us, seemed like something a teenaged girl would do, I allowed myself to go on. "That's it? You're sorry?" My hand came down on the table unnecessarily hard as I thumped it to accent my words.

Brian was surprised at my reaction: his head snapped back as if I'd slapped him, and his hand jerked, spilling his beer. He set his mug on the table carefully and looked down at his feet. We sat in silence for another long moment. He was probably thinking of what to say next; I was seething with anger and resentment, trying hard to keep my mouth shut and wondering how much longer I could make myself sit there with him.

After a few minutes, Brian looked up and smiled at me. He said, "Come on and drink your wine, Kerys. I got the kind you like, the moscato. Remember?"

Honestly, I'm not proud of what I did next. Yet I have to admit I enjoyed seeing Brian sitting there, the sweet, sticky wine rolling down his nose, dripping from those long, lovely eyelashes, his blue eyes wide with surprise and, behind that surprise, ill-concealed anger and frustration. After I emptied the moscato over Brian's head, I slammed the empty wineglass down on the table hard enough to break the stem, which is when I became conscious of all the other patrons turning towards our table to see what was coming next.

But I didn't care, because by then I was already on my way out of the Angry Badger. I started to walk to my car, but by the time I had it in sight I was trotting. Even before I had pulled out from my parking space and into the street, my cell phone began to buzz, but I didn't bother to look at it—I just reached into my pocket and shut it off. It was getting dark now, and with the rain and the wind, and my own tumultuous frame of mind, the last thing I needed was to become distracted by a conversation I didn't want to be having.

At first, I forced myself to drive slowly. After all, I told myself, there was no way Brian could follow me; he had no car, no way to get out to Betony Lodge. For tonight at least, I told myself, I was safe from his awkward and infuriating attempts to apologize to me for screwing another woman, for getting lucky with some young groupie who worshiped him and his wretched poetry. I refused to let myself think about her, about them together. I pushed wayward images from my mind and concentrated only on the road before me, whose black surface, now slick with rain, was merging into the dark in an uncomfortable and seamless way. I squinted harder and clicked on my bright lights.

That's when I saw her.

In the road in front of me, just at the bend in the road as it swung west to climb up to Betony Lodge, I saw the figure of a woman—at least, I thought it was a woman. It was hard to tell, because she, or he, was wearing a very long raincoat of some kind, and lurking along the edge of the lane. The roads in Dorset are narrow, with either hedges or walls on the sides of them, so I braked to avoid the person, wondering who would be out on such an evening. My tires squealed, and I pressed harder on the brake pedal, cursing the rain that had made the Vauxhall's wheels slip on wet pavement. They caught at last, and the car juddered to a stop. I took a deep breath and unclenched my hands from the steering wheel, wiping them on my pants leg. The light from my headlights glared on the empty road in front of me.

I exhaled and put my hands back on the wheel and lifted my foot from the clutch, putting the car into first gear and preparing to continue on to Betony Lodge. I didn't know what had happened to the woman in the road, and to be honest, I didn't care. Maybe she was a ghost, a phantom. But I wasn't up for more scary stories; it was enough, I thought, to have to live with sobs and moans emanating from a two-hundred-year-old house that was once a lunatic asylum. No, I was done with this melodrama. I needed some cold, hard reality in my life. I put the car in gear and started to ease forward.

Just then the passenger door opened, and a very wet woman got into the seat next to me.

I will admit now, after all these months, that I was close to losing it at that moment. The only thing missing, after all, was a miasmic fog that parted occasionally to reveal a full moon, with the sound of baying wolves in the distance. When I turned my head to look at my uninvited passenger, I was shocked to find, not a Victorian phantom shimmering in an unearthly light, but rather a woman as real as I was, with very short, dark hair beneath a floppy hat, a diamond stud in her nose, and oversized glasses with green frames. I stared at her, not knowing what to say or do.

"Well," she said, taking off her drenched hat and running her fingers through her cropped hair, "that was kind of close, wasn't it?"

I didn't say anything.

"I mean," she continued, taking her glasses off and rubbing them on her coat, "you could have stopped a bit earlier, couldn't you?"

At last I found my voice. "Who the hell are you? And what are you doing in my car?"

The woman laughed, a soft chuckle that put me on alert. "My name's Bronwyn," she said. "I'm just a woman looking for a ride, that's all. I took a bit of a wrong turn a couple of hours ago—got off the bus a couple of stops too early. I've been trying to find my way ever since."

I watched her put her seatbelt on and finally said, "I can take you back to Lyme, if you want. It isn't safe to be walking on the road on a night like this."

"Don't I know it," she said, in a high voice, much higher than mine. "But the truth is I'm not exactly sure where I'm going. Then again, if you could take me on to Lyme Regis, I'd appreciate it. I'm not going to a place so much as I am looking for someone."

I had put the car into gear and accelerated, searching for a turn-off so I could head back to Lyme. But at the sound of her words, something inside me seized up, like an engine does when it runs out of oil. My stomach went into lockdown mode for the second time in less than an hour.

"Looking for someone? Who would that be? Lyme Regis is a pretty small town, and there's a chance I might know whoever it is you're looking for." That was a lie, of course; I knew no one in Lyme Regis, but I had a profoundly uncomfortable feeling that I'd know just who it was my passenger was looking for.

"His name," she said slowly, playing with her earrings like the coquette she was, "is Brian. Brian Markham."

I whipped the car around in the lane, not waiting to find a convenient turnoff for a U-turn. I spun that Vauxhall around as if I had been driving British cars on tiny country roads all my life. My passenger exclaimed when I pressed my foot hard on the gas pedal as we straightened out.

"Brilliant job! You did that like someone on *Top Gear*! I'm impressed."

"Thank you," I said, keeping my voice flat.

"Listen, thanks for stopping back there," she said. "Not everyone would pick up a passenger, even on a night like this. It's very nice of you to do it."

"I wish I hadn't," I mumbled.

"What?" Bronwyn leaned toward me, and I could smell her fragrance—a blend of chamomile tea, Persil detergent and pure tobacco that was not unpleasant. "I didn't catch what you said."

"I'll let you out at the local pub," I replied, ignoring her question. "I'm sure you'll find whatever you need there."

"Hey," she said, "you're American, aren't you?"

I nodded. "I love the way your accent sounds," she said. "British people tend to think a Welsh accent the most attractive, but being Welsh myself, I never really hear it. For me, an American accent is just about the loveliest thing in the world."

After that, we didn't speak for a few minutes. But Bronwyn just couldn't keep herself from talking. "I'm chasing down a guy—I might as well tell you. Funny, he's American, too."

"Really?" I made sure my tone was non-committal. "That's interesting. Apparently England is crawling with us right now."

"Oh," she said, laughing, "come on now. You've done the same thing. Don't you say you haven't. We've all done it, one time or another. Sometimes a man just needs a little push to fall into your arms. As my gran used to say, there's no harm in administering that push yourself, if there's no one else to do it."

We were coming into the town, and I made it look like I was busy with driving so that I wouldn't have to respond to her. "This is a tough intersection," I said. "Lots of cars come tooling by here, going much too fast."

I made my turn and pulled up to the Angry Badger, stopping short right in front of it. The pub's sign, with its stern-looking badger, was rocking in the wind overhead. "Well, here we are, Bronwyn." I said her name carefully, exaggerating each syllable, turning towards her. "Good luck finding what you want here."

"Thank you so much!" she said, gathering up her things as she stepped out of the car, leaving a damp spot where she'd been sitting. "You never did say what your name was, *cariad*."

I waited until she got out of the car. "Kerys," I said, through the open window. "My name is Kerys." She started to move away. "Wait a second," I called out, and Bronwyn turned and stuck her head almost inside the car. "Do me a favor, Bronwyn, will you? When you see Brian, can you give him a message from me?"

"Sure," she said, although she looked puzzled, and perhaps a bit alarmed.

"Just tell him that I'm only sorry the glass wasn't bigger."

Then I peeled away from the curb and made another uncivilized U-turn. For the second time that night, I heard my tires squeal, but it was worth it. In my rear-view mirror, I saw Bronwyn standing in the middle of the street, staring after me with her mouth hanging open.

I drove back to Betony Lodge, this time with no stops. It was almost ten o'clock when I opened the door to my flat, and I found Diggory in the kitchen, looking for some food. I hadn't meant to be out this late, and I felt badly about leaving the kitten so long, so I filled up both his food bowl and a little saucer of milk as well. Then I sat on the floor with him, petting him as he lapped it up, listening to his deep-throated purring.

When I'd first left Lyme an hour earlier, I was worried that Brian might somehow find a way to follow me home. But I was pretty sure that now, with Bronwyn on his hands, he wouldn't. I was safe in my solitude, and to tell the truth, I was grateful for Bronwyn's appearance.

But that didn't mean I was fine with the situation. I wasn't. I paced the floor for about thirty minutes after Diggory finished eating, and then I sat down with a cup of tea. I didn't want alcohol—that was certain, since I felt that in the days ahead of me I would need all my wits. I wasn't sure what was going to happen between Brian and me, but I was determined not to just go along with the flow, not to make things easy for him. I'd done too much of that, and I was beginning to realize that that was precisely how I had ended up in my present situation.

I can't say I was calm and rational that night. In fact, I was angry, and hurt, and full of resentment— against Brian, against Bronwyn, and against life itself. Why, of all people, was I the one to pick up Brian's newly cast-off lover and deliver her to him? I had to laugh in spite of my own pain: that incident was certainly worthy of a Thomas Hardy novel, where plot is less an element of story than an emanation of blunt-fisted fate.

I sat and stewed, and I paced, and I drank tea for the next two hours. I had turned off my phone, so I wasn't worried about Brian contacting me; I felt safe from his intrusive attempts to apologize, to set things right between us—which was, I now knew, an impossible task. But despite this protection from him, I knew sleep would elude me after my eventful and emotional evening, and I was in no hurry to go to bed. By midnight, I was sitting on the couch with a blanket around me, Diggory on my lap, my mind churning, running over the events of the last two weeks.

Because I needed a break from my own thoughts, an escape from my own little domestic tragedy, I picked up Mrs. Davis's book, eager to find a respite in someone else's troubles. And yet, I found no solace; in fact, I ended up having to read its blurry words through my tears. All through the evening I had resisted what I had thought a senseless emotion, but now, softened by advice from a woman who had been dead over a hundred years, I allowed myself to feel grief as well as anger, and I cried. I wept for myself, for my delusions about Brian and our life together, for the future we no longer had. I wept for Mrs.

Davis and the injuries done her in the name of medicine. I wept for little Ethan, caught up in something he didn't understand, without any friends to talk to and only the telly for companionship. I even cried for Brian and Bronwyn, who were going to have to figure out where they would go from here. And as I cried, sitting on my couch, my cheeks slick with salt tears, I heard a soft moan. I stopped crying. I sat there, expecting—no, hoping—to hear Ethan's Sad Lady join in.

In the silence that followed, I heard nothing, no sobs, cries, or moans, just my own sniffing. But I felt something, and though I hesitate to describe it now, months later, it's only because that moment has become one of my treasured memories, something I think about every single day. I felt a sense of ease, of calmness, settle over me, and all at once I was at peace. Don't get me wrong: I wasn't exactly happy about the circumstances in which I found myself. But I realized at that moment that I could accept the situation and move on. I had lost my life with Brian, true. But hadn't I gained something, too? Hadn't I gained freedom, and autonomy, and an independence I hadn't sought but now welcomed? The truth is, before that moment, I was a hopeless mess, a broken woman who'd been cheated on and treated badly; after that moment, that watershed instant when I felt peace glide inside my soul as if it were a physical entity, I was a whole person, somewhat bruised but fully able to go on with my life.

I went into my bedroom, lay down on my bed, and I went to sleep. I slept long and deeply, without any dreams to disturb my cleansing rest, and when I woke up the next morning, the rain had cleared. It was a bright and sunny morning, a kind of reward for the dismal weather of the past few days. I dressed quickly and set some food out for Diggory, eager to get to the Museum. I had immersed myself in a world of emotions for too long.

Chapter Twenty

O vision appalling
When the one believed-in thing
Is seen falling, falling,
With all to which hope can cling.
Off: it is not true;
For it cannot be
That the prize I drew
Is a blank to me!
--Thomas Hardy, "At Waking"

I drove to Dorchester and arrived at the Museum early enough for George to be surprised, again, at my appearance. "I thought you would be in later this morning," he said. "You usually don't arrive this early. Certainly not two days in a row."

"I woke up early," I said.

"I assumed that," said George, stirring his mug of tea. "Care for a cup?" When I shook my head, not trusting my voice to answer, he leaned across the counter to look at me more closely. Instinctively, I looked down into my backpack, sorting through my books and papers, pretending I was looking for something. I found my mobile phone and pulled it out, holding it in my hand lightly, as if it were a stiletto or a hand grenade. I still had not turned it on, because I did not want to field a phone call or a text from Brian, and I had feeling there would be several of both if I did power it up.

"Are you all right, Kerys?" George seemed genuinely concerned about me.

"Oh, yes, I'm fine," I said, looking up at George at last. "Maybe I'm feeling a bit under the weather. I went out to the Cobb yesterday, per your instructions, and it was quite windy and cold." I got ready to go through the doors into the archive room, shouldering my backpack again and setting my phone on the counter.

"Did you?" said George, breaking into a wide smile. He seemed happy that I had taken his advice. "And did you like it? Quite a view, isn't it?"

"It was lovely," I lied, then added, somewhat more truthfully, "Very dramatic." I looked at him and then said, "Well, I've got to get to work. Talk to you later, George." I started to walk towards the double doors to the archive room, but George called my name and I turned around.

"You forgot your phone. It's here, on the counter. You set it down just now and left it."

"Oh, right," I said. I was disappointed: I had meant to leave my phone there, hoping that it would be placed in the Lost & Found and that I would not have to worry about ever turning it on again. Defeated, I walked back and took it from George's outstretched hand.

"Thanks," I said, trying hard to sound like I meant it. I took my phone and shoved it deep into my backpack, then left the reception area, with George, his empty hand still held out before him, staring after me.

At lunchtime, I emerged from the archives, rubbing my eyes and thinking that a cup of tea sounded pretty good. George was typing at his keyboard while talking into his own cell phone, so I made the tea, risking criticism, and poured myself a cup, signaling to him that there was plenty of tea for him, too. He nodded and mouthed the words "thank you," and I handed him his cup.

Although I busied myself with looking at the displays, I couldn't help hearing George's side of the conversation. "Certainly it is.... No doubt about it.... Oh, come off it, mate. Don't be such a fool as that." George was arguing with someone; I wondered who it could be.

After a few minutes, he came, mug in hand, and sat down next to me. We were sitting on a bench against the wall, near the birthplace exhibit. Only two patrons were in the museum, and they had gone to look at the exhibit of Hardy's manuscripts.

"Thanks for the tea, Kerys," George said, flexing his sore ankle. "I need it right now. That was my brother. He was going off on me for forgetting my dad's birthday. And I didn't even really forget it. I just sent the bloody card late. Anyway, this tea was just in the nick of time." He took a sip and sighed, then turned and stared at me. "You sure you're doing ok, then, *cariad*? I was a little worried about you earlier today."

I couldn't help it. At the sound of the word, which I would forever associate with Bronwyn and Brian, I flinched, drawing back as if he'd insulted me.

George noticed my reaction. "You can tell me what's wrong, Kerys. You know, I'm here if you need someone to talk to."

"No, I'm fine. Really. Just a little under the weather, that's all." I looked at him and saw his eyes cloud a little. He leaned back for a moment, staring at me, then shook his head very slightly and stood up.

"Well, if you do need to talk to someone, Kerys...." He let the sentence drift in the air between us, and then, when I didn't respond, he turned around and walked back to his desk, leaving me alone to contemplate the blank wall in front of me.

A minute later, I finished my tea, set my mug in the sink behind George's desk, and disappeared back into the Archive Room without another word.

I spent the rest of the afternoon making a list of the items in the box I'd been working on and checking it off against the master list of holdings in the Archive Room. It was a boring, mindless task, which explains why the entire time I was busy with it, my mind was wandering on a continuous loop. What were Brian and Bronwyn doing right now? Where were they staying? Was Brian pleased to see his girlfriend, or dismayed? What would the next scene in this tawdry little melodrama be?

I tried to shove these thoughts out of my mind, but from time to time, they got the better of me, and I stopped my scribbling and box-checking, and looked up at blank walls, with tears welling up in my tired, scratchy eyes. At those moments, as a tide of anger and pain washed through me, I also felt a nagging concern about my phone. All I had to do, I told myself, was to turn it on, and I would probably have numerous voice and text messages from Brian outlining just what he was doing and thinking.

I didn't want to. I didn't want to know his thoughts, didn't want to see his messages or hear his voice. But what was I to do with the phone? As I'd found out that morning, I couldn't just leave it somewhere—too many people were too helpful and too ready to return lost property. I thought about tossing it under the wheel of a passing car, but with my luck, the physics of tire meeting pavement wouldn't work in my favor, and the phone would survive such carnage. I wished I could bury it somewhere, out in the woods, but with people like Tom Hardie out in the countryside waving their metal detectors, it probably wouldn't stay lost for good.

There was only one solution, I told myself as I was packing up for the day. I would have to throw it into the sea. The best place to do this from, however, was the Cobb, and I wasn't eager to go back there. Brian might very well still be in Lyme Regis, mooning about, waiting for another opportunity to talk to me.

I could just wait, I told myself, and try to forget the fact that I was carrying this time bomb in my backpack. Yet, at any moment I knew that I might yield to the impulse to turn the damn thing on, and I wanted that temptation gone.

As I left the Museum that afternoon, I made a special effort to be nice to George, thanking him for the concern he'd expressed earlier that day, and offering to help with washing up the tea things. Smiling, he dismissed my offer and told me to get out and get on with doing the things on the list he'd given me the day before. "You've only seen the Cobb, Kerys. That's a start, but you've got more to do. Go out there and see the rest—there's still plenty of the day left!" I felt like I'd been forgiven, but I wasn't quite sure what my offense had been.

Thinking about his advice, I was considering a drive to Corfe Castle, but I lost my ambition and my energy as soon as I got behind the wheel of the car. I would drive back to Betony Lodge, I told myself, even though it was a sunny, brisk day, with no hint of the wind and rain the day before, and I would watch television, do the laundry, keep busy somehow. Diggory would appreciate my company. The truth was, I really didn't want to see anyone else that day, not even strangers touring the same landmark I was.

And so I drove back to my flat. About half way there, I began to worry: did Brian have his key to the flat with him? Would he have effrontery to use it, to go in there while I was gone? I didn't think so, but then again, it was his flat, too, and he had left all of his things there before his trip to Wales.

It was my flat now, anyway; Brian knew nothing about Warrinder House and Mrs. Davis. It was I, and I alone, who belonged in Betony Lodge. As for Brian, I no longer knew where he belonged, and it was during that drive home that I realized I didn't care to find out.

I pulled into my parking spot, right next to Leanne's car, and got out of my Vauxhall, looking up at the second-floor window to see if I could tell whether Brian was there, trying to prepare myself for a chance encounter, if one were to occur.

And then it hit me. I had looked up like that, standing in that very place and in exactly that time of day, when Brian and I had first looked at the flat, a lifetime ago, when all was well between us. I drew in a ragged breath, closing my eyes against the pain of memory. It's funny how a flimsy little thing like memory can inflict such misery.

"Kerys? Are you ok?" I opened my eyes to find Leanne staring at me, a look of real concern on her face.

"Do you need help getting up to your flat?" Ethan and Gemma were standing beside her, staring at me with the kind of detached curiosity a small child often has when things go wrong in the grown-up world.

"No, thank you, Leanne. I'm all right."

"It's just that you looked like you were in pain for a moment."

"No, not at all. Just a bit of a headache, that's all."

We all started walking to the front door of Betony Lodge. Ethan and I exchanged a surreptitious glance and a quick smile, and a few moments later, I was climbing the stairs to my own flat, wondering what I would find when I opened the door.

What I found was, thankfully, nothing other than the usual: Diggory waiting for his dinner, a mess of papers on the dining table, and the blanket, empty mug, and book I had turned to for comfort the previous night, amid a sea of wadded tissues littering both couch and floor. No sign of Brian.

I let out a long sigh of relief. Maybe, just maybe, he'd gone back to Wales with Bronwyn. That would be perfect, in my view. We could end our relationship with a safe distance between us, and it would be all neat and tidy and impersonal—civilized and hygienic, just like the mature adults we were.

I sat down and thumbed through Gladys Nuttall's book, one of those ambitious but drab little books sold in local history museums, and drank a mug of tea, and then I think I dozed for a few minutes, just long enough to drop the mug onto my kneecap, causing me to wake up in pain, grabbing at my scalded knee, which in turn sent Diggory, who'd been asleep by my side, scrambling to get under cover.

I was wiping up the puddle of tea on the floor when I heard footsteps coming up the stairs. I walked over to the front window and looked down into the car park, but there was only my car and Leanne's, so whoever was at the door must have walked up to Betony Lodge. The knock on the door made me freeze, and I hesitated before I answered it, wondering indeed if I needed to answer it at all. If it was Brian, I thought, he might go away if I didn't open the door.

Or he might just open the door with his key and come through. After all, I had to admit that he had every right to come in and claim his possessions. That would be awkward, especially since it would be obvious that I had stood there, listening to him knocking, hoping he would just decamp.

So, I took a big breath, walked over to the door, and pulled it open.

It was not Brian standing there, however, but Tom Hardie. "Hello, Kerys," he said, a smile on his broad, round face. "I tried to call before I came, but you didn't answer." He squinted a bit, drawing his eyebrows together over his somewhat flattened nose, adding, "Actually, I've been a bit worried. You didn't answer my texts, either, and I thought you might have been tampin' mad with me."

"Tamping mad?" I stepped back, and Tom came into the flat, shrugging off his ridiculous jacket with its millions of pockets. I hung it up on the wall and went into the kitchen. "What's that mean?"

"Oh, it's just Dorset for 'annoyed.'"

"I see. No, I'm not mad. Do you want some tea? Or something stronger?"

"Yes," Tom said, sitting down at the dining room table. "I'd love some tea. Actually, you ought to get your phone looked at, Kerys. I think it might be broken."

"Yes," I said, "I'm looking into it. Milk? Sugar?"

"Both," said Tom. "Say, how about going detecting again on Saturday? Are you up for it? That's really what I came for—to ask if you wanted to go out again."

I didn't. I'd had enough of sitting against a tree, watching Tom wave his detector over a patch of dirt, scraping away at a piece of metal that would turn out to be another pop top from a beer bottle or a button from some field worker's sleeve. But I stopped myself from declining his invitation. If Brian had not left the area, he might come round over the weekend, and the less time I stayed in the flat, the less chance there was that I would encounter him. So I said yes as I handed him his mug of tea, hoping I wouldn't regret it.

"Excellent! It'll be great fun, Kerys. We'll go over the area where you found that locket. I'll bet we turn up something else just as interesting. By the way, might I have another look at that locket of yours? You don't mind, do you?"

I went to fetch it. When I came back into the living room, Tom was sipping his tea, his eyes closed. I wondered whether he was overcome with emotion at the prospect of seeing a real discovery, or whether he was just fair made up, as he might put it, with the cup of tea I'd given him. While I had gone to get the locket, he'd gotten his jacket down from the peg and had taken out a couple of his detecting tools: a jeweler's magnifying glass and a probe that looked more like a screwdriver than anything else. His jacket lay in a heap behind his chair. He'd probably meant to drape it across the back of his chair and it had slipped off; I couldn't imagine him just dropping it on the floor. I cleared my throat as I approached the dining table and put the locket down for him to examine.

"It's lovely," he said in a low voice, bending low over the golden necklace. "I cannot believe you found it with your eyes alone."

I could detect a note of wistfulness in his voice, so I said, rather quickly, "It was just dumb luck, Tom. You know that."

He didn't answer. He was looking at the locket through a strange little magnifying glass that he held close to his eye. "Amazing," he said, almost under his breath. He bent down and studied the object even more closely. It was clear that he had forgotten everything in the world at that moment but the locket, so enthralled was he as he poked at it with his index finger, flipping it over and probing it with that strange screwdriver-type tool. I could hear him mumbling under his breath.

I stepped back and picked his jacket up off the floor, but Tom didn't notice. It was heavier than I'd imagined; God knew what he had shoved into his pockets, I thought: he may never empty them fully.

That was when I got the idea to slip my phone into one of those cavernous pockets. He probably wouldn't discover it lurking there, and consequently I wouldn't have to worry about what to do with it any more. So, while Tom sat drooling over the locket I'd found, exploring it from seventeen different angles, I walked over to the couch, opened my backpack, grabbed my phone, and dropped it into a deep pocket on the inside flap of his coat. I didn't dare zip it shut, thinking the noise might alert Tom; instead, I trusted to fate that he wouldn't find it for days, if not weeks—maybe even months—and I hung it back up on the wall peg near the front entry.

I offered Tom another cup of tea. He glanced up at me, his eyepiece still in place, looking as if he'd forgotten where he was. I held up the teapot. "Oh, yes, thank you, Kerys," he said, letting the jeweler's glass fall from his eye into the palm of his right hand. "You know, this is an amazing find. It's not every day that you see a mourning locket."

"A locket to commemorate someone's death," I said. "How gruesome."

"No, not really gruesome at all," said Tom. "Not for Victorians. They did this kind of thing all the time. They had rings and bracelets made from their loved ones' hair after they died. They even had little vials called 'tear-catchers'—to preserve the tears they cried for their dead relatives. Wouldn't I like to find one of them some day!"

I thought about how many of those little vials I could have filled up with my own tears in the last few days. Then, because I didn't want to continue that train of thought, I said, "How do you know for certain that it's a mourning locket, Tom?" I had picked up the loupe myself and was trying to look through it.

"See here, Kerys." He used the probe to open the

locket. "There's nothing in it, no lock of hair, no miniature picture or anything, but if you look closely enough, you can see the date: August 23, 1841.' And then, when you look at the back—" Tom gently closed the locket and turned it face down on the table.

"I know there are letters there, but they were too small for me to read. I figured they were Latin. Or just initials."

Tom shook his head. "No, it's not Latin, Kerys. Take another look. Use my loupe this time."

So I picked up the loupe and studied the back of the locket while Tom took another loud sip of his tea, waiting for me. What I saw took my breath away.

Frederick Whiting Davis. I looked up at Tom. This time it was I who had forgotten to take the loupe from my eye.

"Could this be? Is this really?" I began to ask him, then stopped, remembering he hadn't read Mrs. Davis's book. But that didn't matter, because Tom had misunderstood my excitement. He was nodding, a wide grin on his face.

"Yes, of course it is, Kerys! It's an amazing find— a real, authentic, Victorian mourning brooch. Pretty good for your first discovery! And without any tools at all, to boot! You'll have no problem at all becoming a member of the Dorset Dirt-Diving Club." I must have looked shocked, maybe even dismayed, because Tom hurried on, saying, "I know, it's a horrible name. I've been after them to change it for two years now, ever since we started up. But it doesn't matter: they're still the best club around, for my money. And I want to propose you as a member—if you're willing, Kerys."

I stalled for time. I needed a few minutes to digest the fact that the locket before me had once belonged to Cecilia Davis—my own Cecilia Davis.

"Kerys?" Tom was still waiting for my answer.

"Oh, well, yes, I guess that would be ok," I said. I got up and went into the kitchen, opening the refrigerator. "Do you want some toast or eggs or anything, Tom? I was just going to make something to eat for dinner."

Tom stood up, looking stricken. "I'm sorry, Kerys," he said. "I didn't mean to stay here so long. I just wanted another look at the locket, and to ask you about the club, you know." He paused, thought a moment, then asked, "Say, do you want to go out for dinner? I don't have a car—I walked here through the forest—but if you don't mind driving, we could go down to the Angry Badger. Just a pint and a bite to eat, you know."

I shook my head. The last thing I needed was to show up at the pub where I'd last seen both Brian and Bronwyn. "No thanks, Tom. I've got a lot of work tonight." There, I told myself, with pride. I had finally been able to say no.

Tom took it well. He grabbed his jacket from the wall and started to put it on as I held my breath, wondering if he'd feel the extra weight of my phone. For a moment I thought he did, because his face wore a puzzled look when he turned around. But then he said, "Just as well, Kerys. There was a big dust-up at the Badger last night. I only saw the last bit of it, but I heard it was quite a show. Seems there was this flash—"

"'Flash'? What's that?"

211

"Oh, you know—a dazzler, a fellow with fancy clobber. Clothes, I mean. Anyway, apparently he'd said something to make his girlfriend tamping mad—you know what that means—and it seems she dumped an entire glass of wine over his head. So there he sat for a few minutes. This happened before I got there, but believe me, I heard about it. Everyone was still talking about it by the time I arrived half an hour later. So he's sitting there, trying to look normal, you see, and then another girl comes in. I was there for this part, Kerys, and let me tell you, it was priceless. She comes in, soaked to her skin, and looks round the pub, sees him, and makes a beeline right for him. Then she sits herself down, and the two of them start talking, and before you know it, she grabs his pint, or what's left of it, and throws it right into his face! Can you believe it? That poor sod, sitting there bibbering in front of the entire pub, for the second time in one evening! I can't remember the last time we had such a good show at the Badger, Kerys. You should have been there!"

I put the egg I was holding down on the counter and came out of the kitchen. "What happened next, Tom?"

He stopped chuckling, and said, "Well, he got up and left. The girl had already cleared out—upended her chair, she was in such a fair hurry to leave. I've an idea she was going out to catch the white bus, if you know what I mean."

I shook my head. "I don't. What's the white bus?"

"The one that takes you to the loony bin. She must have been off her rocker."

"What about the man? Maybe he's the one who was insane."

Tom didn't say anything. He just stood there, chuckling, obviously enjoying the memory of Brian's double disgrace. "Anyway," he said, getting control of himself, "it's bound to be boring there tonight. Lightning never strikes in the same place twice, now, does it?" He put his hand on the doorknob and said over his shoulder, "I'll see you Friday night then, Kerys."

"Friday night? What's that?" I had no idea what he was talking about. "I thought we were getting together on Saturday afternoon."

"It's the Dirt-Divers' meeting. You're coming, right? You said you were. Be sure to bring the locket with you."

Before I could answer, he pulled open the door, to reveal Brian standing there in the darkened hallway, his hand poised as if to knock.

Chapter Twenty-One

Through vaults of pain
Enribbed and wrought with groins of ghastliness,
I passed, and garish spectres moved my brain
To dire distress.
                    --Thomas Hardy, "A Wasted Illness"

Why hadn't we heard him coming up the steps? The only reason I can think of is that Tom and I were both too involved in his story, he in telling it, and I in hearing it, to pay attention to the sound of footsteps on the stairway. And now it was too late to go back. I could hardly shut the door in Brian's face, much as I wanted to. The three of us just stood there for a second, staring at each other.

"I'd like to come into my own flat, if you don't mind," said Brian at last. He had been looking Tom up and down, and now he turned his eyes towards me.

I stepped aside to let him in, but unfortunately, Tom chose this moment to be both protective and inquisitive. "Kerys? You know this man? He's the wanker who—"

"I know him, Tom. Come in, Brian," I said, stepping aside and letting Brian enter. Then, turning to Tom, I said, "He's my husband."

Now it was Tom's turn to stare at me. I nodded, and he adjusted his jacket, unaware that he was doing so, as his eyes widened and his eyebrows went up. "You've got a husband, Kerys? But you never...."

"Well," I answered, while watching Brian, who

was pacing through the flat, picking up books and cups and looking at them as if he was trying hard to remember them, "you never asked."

Brian stopped his prowling at the table. He looked at both of us.

"What's all this? He pointed to the locket. "Kerys, what's been going on here while I've been gone?"

Tom started to speak at the same time I did, but my voice was louder than his. "Nothing, Brian. Absolutely nothing. Don't you wish you could say the same? Where's Bronwyn, by the way? Did you send her packing?"

"This isn't about Bronwyn, Kerys." Brian's eyes shot an angry look at me, then at Tom. "This is about us."

"It seems to me that Bronwyn has become a part of 'us,' as you put it, Brian. At the very least, she has a claim on you."

I heard Tom gasp and turned to look at him. "That girl," he said, staring first at me, then at Brian, then back at me. "The one who dumped the wine—"

I sighed. "Yes, Tom," I said.

"Look, I don't want to stay here a minute longer. This is all beyond me. I never meant to get caught up in anything like this." He took a step towards Brian. "Look, mate. I didn't—"

"You're not my mate, you clown," said Brian, taking a few steps towards Tom. "And if you know what's good for you, you son of a—"

"That's enough! Brian, shut up. You have no right to talk that way. Tom is just a friend."

"That's right," said Tom. "I didn't touch her. I never knew she was married."

"That's not even relevant," I said, coming between them. "This is ridiculous, Brian. Only someone like you would feel it's okay to cheat on your wife and then turn around and accuse her of the very thing you've been doing all along. You make me sick."

"*I* make *you* sick?" I had never seen Brian so angry. "I come home to find another man in our flat—*my* flat—and you expect me to simply accept it? You're just as bad as I am, Kerys. Admit it!"

"Now just a minute," said Tom, entering the fray. "You can't hurl accusations like that. There's another person involved, and—"

"You shut up," snarled Brian, glancing at him. "I'm not interested in anything you have to say. This is between Kerys and me. And I intend to have it out between us, Kerys, right now." He moved towards me.

I took a deep breath to calm myself, then said, "You think everything runs on your timeline, don't you, Brian? Well, it doesn't. Get your things and get out of here. I don't feel like talking to you tonight."

"It doesn't matter whether you feel like it or not, Kerys. You owe it to me. You owe it to our marriage."

"How dare you say that?" Despite my best intentions, my voice rose up to an operatic octave. I was just about to add a few choice words about Bronwyn and go up yet another octave when there was a knock on the door, which was half open. It was Gary from downstairs.

"Hullo, what's going on here? Any problems, Kerys?"

Tom, Brian, and I stared at Gary, who loosened his tie and said, "You're making a hell of a ruckus up here, and we're trying to get the children to bed. I just popped up to see if there was anything I could do."

Gary was a big man, and in the five seconds of silence that followed, while we were all taking stock of the situation, I knew that both Tom and Brian were busy sizing him up. I walked over to Gary, put my hand on his forearm and steered him back to the staircase, saying, "I'm awfully sorry, Gary. We were having a little discussion, and I guess it got out of control. We'll take it down a notch or two, I promise."

Gary looked at me, then at Tom and Brian, uncertain of what to do next. But he was saved from making a decision by the arrival of Leanne, who was running up the stairs, breathless and pale, her hair out of place and a look of panic on her face.

"Gary," she said, grabbing his free arm, the one that I didn't have my hand on, "Ethan's gone. He just disappeared!"

Gary turned to his wife. "What do you mean, 'disappeared'? The boy was in the tub when you sent me up here. I saw him with my own eyes! How could he disappear in three seconds?"

Leanne was near tears. "I don't know! I just got Gemma to bed, had just tucked her in, when I went back to check on Ethan. He was supposed to be getting into his pajamas, but when I went into the bathroom to tell him to brush his teeth, he wasn't there! He wasn't in his bedroom, either. He's gone! And it's getting dark out, too. Gary, should we call 999?"

"Don't be silly, Leanne," said Gary. "Where's Gemma? We don't want her getting lost too, do we?"

Together they charged off down the stairs, leaving Brian, Tom and me looking after them in a supremely awkward silence.

Finally, after a couple of seconds, Tom said, "Well, I should be getting on back home. Nice meeting you—Brian, was it?" I stared at Tom. I was having a hard time believing he could pretend what was almost a three-way fistfight had been some kind of polite social occasion.

"Just a second, you," said Brian. Apparently he was having the same difficulty I was. "I have a few questions for you."

"Such as?" Tom was backing his way out the door.

"Such as how long have you been screwing my wife?"

"Brian! How dare you!" I grabbed Tom by the arm, keeping him from leaving the flat. "You'd better apologize this minute. Tom doesn't deserve this kind of treatment from you."

I could feel Tom shrinking away towards the door, trying to make his exit, but I was long past the point of caring about his comfort. I couldn't let Brian get away with such brutish behavior.

"Really?" Brian's voice was harsh, filled with anger. "He was at the pub last night, laughing at me with the rest of the jokers around here. Apparently, he has nothing better to do than dig around in other people's lives."

That was truer than Brian realized, but I knew it was not the time to comment on it. "Listen, Brian. For the last time, there is nothing between Tom and me. We're just friends. In other words, this is nothing like what went on between you and Bronwyn."

"Bronwyn?" Tom's timing, I was beginning to understand, was unbelievably slow. "Was she the other—"

"Never mind!" Brian and I both said it at the same time, and Tom looked hurt, as if we'd ganged up on him in a playground and taken a ball out of his hands. There was a silence while we all took a deep breath, which was broken a few seconds later by the clatter of Leanne's footsteps barreling their way up the stairs again and calling my name.

I rushed past Brian and Tom and into the darkened hallway. "What is it, Leanne?"

"I can't find him! He's gone. I checked the door behind his bed, and it's still nailed up. He's vanished without a trace. You've got to help me, Kerys. Just this one more time! Can you find my boy? Please?"

I squinted at Leanne in the darkened corridor. Her hair flew about her head as she spoke, and even in the shadowed hallway I could see her lips trembling. I grabbed her hand and pulled her towards the stairs. "Come on, Leanne. Let's go find Ethan," I said, leaving Tom and Brian facing each other in the living room.

Leanne kept talking as we charged down the stairs to her flat, telling me about Ethan's disappearance in a shaky voice. When we got to her living room, Gary was pacing back and forth in front of the sofa in his stocking feet. He stopped, looked up at us as we came in, and held his finger to his lips. "I just got Gemma to sleep," he said in a low voice. "No thanks to you, Leanne." He sighed, then added, "Look, there's no sense getting hysterical about this. We'll find Ethan. He'll probably turn up himself in a few minutes, none the worse for his little adventure."

Gary, while trying to be cool and level-headed, didn't look very calm himself. His blonde hair was spiked up on the sides, a result of him running his hands through it repeatedly, and his eyes darted from Leanne to me and then back again. I could tell he was wondering why Leanne had involved me, and I suspected that she had never told her husband about Ethan's earlier disappearance.

"Have you looked for him outside, Leanne?" I turned towards her; it was clear that I was reporting to her, not Gary.

"Outside? At night? Why would he be outside, Kerys? Don't you think he's just somewhere in the building?"

I shook my head. "I think we need to go out to be sure. You know, search the back garden and maybe the car park. I'm sure if he is outdoors, he hasn't gone far."

I watched the look of panic come into Leanne's large blue eyes and immediately regretted my words. Taking her by the arm, I pulled her out of the flat and to the front door of Betony Lodge. Above us, we could hear Brian and Tom shouting; apparently, they were continuing their altercation without the benefit of my presence. Leanne and I went out the front door and trotted through the car park in the front of the building, calling Ethan's name. It was now fully dark, and the moon was lurking behind a thick layer of clouds. A chill breeze rustled the dried stalks of betony that surrounded the house, and I shivered, dressed only in my light flannel shirt and an old, thin pair of sleep pants. I had not even put on my shoes before I'd run out the stairs of my flat with Leanne.

"Ethan?" I called out his name, tentatively at first, then a bit louder. "Come out—this is no time to hide. Remember what I told you? You were supposed to listen to your mum, not to anyone else! You promised, Ethan!"

There was no response: just the wind skirting through the bushes and rattling the front gate, which was rocking in the breeze. I waited, listening for Ethan's high-pitched voice, then left Leanne out front and ran around to the back of the house, pushing my way through the stalks of betony and the other tall bushes to make my way, biting back my exclamations whenever I stepped on a rock or a hard clod of dirt. As I passed by the empty downstairs flat, I looked through the window, thinking that I might spy Ethan inside, but I could see nothing but my own reflection, which, to be honest, frightened me. I looked like a madwoman, my tousled hair blown this way and that by the wind, my eyes wide and piercing, their whites showing plainly in the dark pane of glass. I looked away, then hurried along the edge of the house towards the back garden, where my progress was stopped by the low wall that separated the house from the open grounds behind it. While I'd been making my way to the back of the house, tracing its perimeter, I had lost track of Leanne in the car park out in front.

The wind was picking up, rustling through the leaves of the trees around me. It ruffled my hair, a sharp breeze against my face, cooling my fevered cheeks. I started to climb over the wall; it was only waist high, after all, meant to be a visual rather than a physical break from the outlying gardens. But my climbing skills must have been rusty, because somehow I slipped and fell, and the next instant I was lying on my back, staring up at the sky, struggling to get my breath.

I could see the clouds racing over the moon, their tattered edges like fingers stroking a crystal ball. For a couple of seconds—it could not have been more—I lay there and stared at it, fascinated by its round fullness, by the filmy curtain of thick clouds drawn across its bright face. Then I heard it: a low wail, barely audible, hiding in the sound of the wind, moving in and out, up and down along the breeze.

"Mrs. Davis." My voice came out as a whisper through dry lips. "Cecilia, please help me. Help me find the little boy."

I got to my feet, still craning my neck to watch the clouds racing across the sky. I had gotten the breath knocked out of me, and I struggled to breathe now, my throat making strange, rasping sounds as I forced the air into my lungs in a struggle that took all my strength. But when I heard something—a faint whimper, rather like a kitten mewling—I forgot my discomfort and looked up to the second story window, thinking that Diggory, tired of watching Tom and Brian squabbling, had come to an open window of my flat. But it was not Diggory who had made the noise: it was Ethan.

He was perched on the edge of the roof, looking down. To be honest, at that moment, I couldn't have sworn it was Ethan, because I couldn't see his face. In the flitting moonlight, all I could see was the dark outline of a small head peering down at me.

"Ethan! Stay where you are. I'm coming up for you!"

"She's here! The sad lady is with me, Kerys!" I could make out his voice now, its high-pitched child's timbre cutting through the rising wind.

"Don't move, Ethan. Stay right there!"

To this day, I don't know how I accomplished what I did next. I have an impression, too vivid for a dream but too hazy for a real memory, of scrambling up the side of Betony Lodge, using exposed bricks and trellis rungs to gain purchase for my ascent, grabbing at metal pipes with my fingers and scrabbling at the bricks and mortar on the side of the house with my toes. I remember slinging myself over the eave, pushing fear away as if like a tangible object that I had no interest in, and flopping down next to Ethan as I finally pulled myself onto the roof. The little boy was crouched next to a pipe, hugging it as if it were his favorite stuffed animal.

"Kerys," he whispered. "You came for me."

I reached for the pipe with one hand and took hold of one of his arms with the other. "I did, Ethan. But why are you here? You told me you wouldn't listen to the voices any longer. You promised."

"I know," he said. "I tried not to, but I couldn't help it. Please don't be mad at me. And please don't tell my mum."

"We'll worry about all that later, Ethan." I looked around. There were pipes sticking up all over the roof, randomly dispersed in a way that reminded me of a soccer field full of inept players waiting for a pass. "We've got to figure out how we're going to get down from here." I took a deep breath, then added, "How did you get up?"

"I crawled up through the chimney in the empty flat. When Mum and Dad were giving Gemma her bath, I heard you upstairs having a fight, you see. I wanted to make sure you were ok. So I snuck out of the flat and started up the stairway. But once I got to the stairs, I felt the lady telling me—"

"You *felt* the lady telling you? Ethan, that doesn't make sense!"

"You know what I mean, Kerys," he said. I nodded and told him to go on.

"I went over into the empty flat—you and Mummy forgot to lock the door, you know—and I found the chimney that she told me about, and then it just seemed like I had to go and stand in it. Don't tell my mum, please, Kerys. Anyway, on the inside of the chimney, there were metal bars, almost like a ladder, and I climbed up them. I was following the noise, see, and then I came up out of the top of the chimney and onto the roof. But then I slipped, and…. I've been too scared to get back up there."

I looked past Ethan and saw the chimney sticking out of the steep roof. My heart skipped a beat. That was how Ethan had made it out onto the roof, and that was how we were going to get back down. At least that was how Ethan would get back down—but would I fit through the chimney as well? On the lawn below, I heard Leanne's panicked voice still crying out for her son, pleading with him to come out of his hiding place. Ethan heard her, too, and began to sniffle.

"Don't cry," I told him. "I'll get you back to the chimney. You crawl first, in front of me, and that way, if you slip, I'll be able to stop your fall."

I count it as a miracle that Ethan actually believed and trusted me, because I knew then, just as I know now, that if he had slipped, there was no way I could have stopped him from tumbling off that roof: we would both have ended up in a pile on the ground below, our bodies maimed and broken. But he let go of the pipe and moved away from the edge of the roof, inching up the slope towards the chimney, and I followed, my hands and knees clutching at the hard slate tiles.

We reached a large pipe coming out of the chimney, which was when we heard the voices. "Did you tell her? Does she know?" I trembled when I heard them. Ethan gave me a knowing look, tapped my hand, and whispered to me:

"They're talking about you, Kerys."

I said nothing. The voices went on. "No. She's not to know, and she's not to care." My breath came faster, and my heartbeat rose in my ears over the sound of the brisk wind.

I tried not to give in to panic; instead, I used my fear, my sense of urgency, to propel Ethan forward, up the slope of the roof. I pointed towards the chimney and urged Ethan on. The boy scooted along the slope of the roof, his plump fingers reaching out in front of him, and I followed, grateful to put the voices behind me. Together we crawled inch by bloody inch to the base of the chimney. Then I pulled myself into a standing position, clutching at the chimney, and looked over its edge into the darkness.

I remember the rush of fear that made it hard to catch my breath; it produced a metallic taste on my tongue. The chimney was dark and narrow, and although Ethan had made it up, he was a five year old, and I was an adult. True, I wasn't large or muscular, and I thought I would fit without a problem, but I have never been a fan of enclosed places. Without actually being claustrophobic, I still didn't like the idea of going down that dark hole into the empty flat below.

But Ethan had already climbed over its rim and was dangling his feet into the abyss. I started to yell at him, but I didn't want to startle him and make him fall. If Cecilia Davis had gotten him up here, for God knows what reason, I told myself, maybe she'd take care to get him back down safely.

"It's easy, Kerys," said Ethan, smiling at me. I was accustomed to the flitting moonlight now, and could see his face clearly. I smiled back. "Just follow me and do what I do."

I had no choice, so, when Ethan's head disappeared below the rim, I swung my leg over the edge of the chimney and followed him into the darkness.

I still have nightmares about that climb down the chimney of Betony Lodge. As my feet found purchase on the metal rod, stuck two hundred years earlier into the brick to serve as a ladder for the poor little sweeps who must have once cleaned the chimney, it took all my courage to let go of the inside edge of the chimney pot to descend. I had to find a handhold, so I felt around the bricks until I located another rod, and then, with Ethan below me, coaching me, I dropped myself, ten or so inches at a time, down the length of the chimney. I told myself repeatedly that I should not be afraid: that this makeshift ladder had been created for just this purpose: to allow those who cleaned the chimney, boys probably not much bigger than Ethan, to move up and down the chimney with their brooms and brushes.

But would the bars hold my weight? Would they be secure after a century and a half of disuse? And even if they did hold me, would I fit down this shaft, or would the space narrow as it descended to the ground floor? I fought off panic more than once in the three minutes it took me to get to the bottom of the chimney. Each time, I told myself that it was my duty to get Ethan back to his flat in one piece—and I sent out a silent, whispered plea to Cecilia Davis, across the centuries, begging for her help.

At last I neared the bottom. I could feel the air circulation change, hear the sound of my own hands grabbing the rails grow muffled as they clutched at them, and, always, in the background, the whispered encouragement of Ethan, who must have already reached the bottom. My toes scuffed against the dusty brick bottom of the fireplace, and then I ducked below the lintel and emerged, filthy and shaken, from the chimney. I brushed my hands off and turned to find Ethan, who was sitting on the floor, waiting for me. Apparently, he thought my performance was amusing, because even in the darkness of the empty flat, I could see him smiling.

"Made it!" I said, smiling back. But then I realized that encouragement of any kind was not what Ethan needed just then. I grabbed him by the shoulders. "Promise me you will never do anything like this again, young man."

Ethan put his hand over his heart. "I promise, Kerys. I'm sorry I didn't listen to you. I didn't do what you said. I listened to what the voices were telling me to do instead." He sounded like he was about to cry.

"That doesn't matter now, Ethan. Let's go across the hall to your flat and let your parents know you're ok."

We started to walk away, towards the door of the unused flat, but I turned around to look at the fireplace so I could see what it was that had attracted Ethan's attention to it in the first place. I blinked in the darkness: even in the shadows, with no proper light but that which crept in through the tall, narrow windows, I could tell that the chimney itself had been papered over. The paper was now dangling from the top of the mantel in one long strip. I touched the end of it and pulled it off, dropping it in a heap upon the dusty floor. Then I turned to Ethan.

"How did you know chimney was here, Ethan?"

He looked at me, and then put his finger over his lips, calling to mind his father's gesture some twenty minutes earlier. "It's a secret," he said in a whisper.

"It's ok," I said, also in a whisper. "You can tell me, Ethan."

He hesitated, then said, "She told me I'd find it here if I looked." He paused, then added, "She was right."

Chapter Twenty-Two

At dawn my heart grew heavy,
I could not sip the wine,
I left the jocund bevy
And that young man o' mine.
           --Thomas Hardy, "After the Club
Dance"

Together, Ethan and I left the empty flat and went
across the hall and into the Noudies' living room, where
Gary was pacing in front of the muted television. He
stopped to look out the front window, and I could hear
him sigh as he peered through it into the night. Turning
around to continue his worried pacing, he saw us, blinked,
crossed the living room in two steps and scooped Ethan up
into his arms.

"Thank God," he said. "Where's your mum?"

"She's still out front," I said. "I'll go get her."

As I left the flat to go out the front door, I could
hear Tom and Brian arguing upstairs. I had forgotten
about them. I would never have guessed they'd have so
much to discuss. Apparently, they hadn't even noticed that
I'd left them almost half an hour ago. I suppressed a
strong desire to laugh at their self-absorption.

Leanne had seen me open the front door of the
building; she was coming through the darkness, running
towards me. She stared at me, and I realized that although
I hadn't actually laughed out loud, I was smiling at the
incongruity of Brian and Tom arguing while Ethan and I
had been scrambling over their heads on the rooftop.

She stopped in front of me, scrutinized my face, and said, "You think this is funny, Kerys? A little boy is missing, and you're enjoying it?" The fury of her words made me flinch, and I took a step backwards, into the shadowy doorway of Betony Lodge.

"It's all right, Leanne," I said. "Ethan's been found."

"Oh, my God," she said, followed by something between a sob and a sigh of relief. "Where was he?"

"He was on the roof," I said. "But I got him down. He's safe. He's inside with Gary."

"You got him down?" We were both inside the doorway now, and she turned to stare at me under the dim hall light. I watched her eyes turned dark with rage. "You got him up there, too, no doubt." She moved close to me, and I could see her eyes narrowing with anger and something else: contempt. I felt frightened as she reached a claw-like hand out to grab my shoulder. "I've had enough of this, Kerys. I'm calling the police. If I have to get them to arrest you, I swear I'll make you stay away from my boy."

"But Leanne," I said, trying to shrug off her grasp.

"No. Shut up, Kerys. I'm done with you. And you're done with Ethan. Get out of my way." She pushed me aside with some force. I stumbled towards the stairs and fell to my knees, grabbing at the banister. Leanne slammed the door to her flat shut. Rising from my knees slowly, wincing in pain, I took a few steps towards her door, but then I thought better of it, turned around, and climbed up the stairs. I pulled open the door to my flat and walked in.

Tom and Brian were standing very close to each other, each one speaking in that kind of low, intense voice that can be so much more threatening than shouting or yelling. They fell silent, however, when I entered and turned towards me, looking somewhat surprised. I wondered if they'd forgotten that I had left the flat and was out looking for a lost child.

"Don't mind me," I said. "Keep it up. You two are really making a hit with the downstairs neighbors tonight." I grabbed the keys to the Vauxhall and my backpack, and slipped my shoes on.

"Kerys," Brian said, "we've got to talk. I don't care whether you want to or not. You owe me that much, you know."

"I owe you nothing," I said, shouting, causing both Brian and Tom to blink as I hurled the words out. And then, because I had no desire to say anything else, or to listen to either Brian or Tom, I ran out the door, down the stairs, and out of Betony Lodge.

I stood for a moment in the car park, looking up. The weather was changing once again; a few minutes earlier, on the roof, I had seen the moon floating in a clear sky, just beyond reach. But now the moon had disappeared again behind ragged clouds, and the wind smelled of salt, as if it had been whipped up from the sea and carried inland. Through the windows of the building I could see Ethan squirming in Leanne's tight, maternal grasp, and, on the floor above them, both Brian and Tom peering out the upstairs window down at me. I yanked open the door of the Vauxhall, threw my backpack over the seat into the back, and got in. Pulling the door shut with more force than necessary, I strapped my seat belt on and put the car into gear. In a few seconds, I was driving through the gate of Betony Lodge.

The car did a good job of hugging the road, but it was dark and rain was beginning to fall again, so I slowed down on the curves. I knew that I needed to think, to process all that had happened that night, and it was clear that I needed to get away from Betony Lodge in order to do that, so I headed to the Hardy Museum, knowing that it would be closed, but not caring. If all I did was sit in the car park for the five hours until it opened, at least I'd be away from Brian, Tom, and Leanne, away from mysterious voices in the dark of the night, and away from little boys who got themselves lost and for whose disappearance, apparently, I was to blame.

It's a wonder I didn't get a ticket that night; while I didn't speed, my driving was erratic, and I found myself weaving from the right to the left side of the road, forgetting that I was driving in England. Thankfully there was no traffic; I didn't pass a single car between Lyme Regis and Dorchester. It was late, of course, and that was the reason; I hadn't realized how much traffic dwindled in Dorset after midnight, but I was lucky it did.

I arrived at the Museum at 1:30 a.m. in a blinding rain, the water hitting the windscreen so hard that my wipers were virtually useless. I sat in the parking lot for a while, sorting through all my impressions of what had happened to me since I'd come to England. But it was no use. I could not make them coalesce, couldn't force them into any kind of order that would help me determine my next step. I was too confused and emotionally battered. Finally, after several fruitless minutes of churning through my thoughts, I reached back behind the seat to pull out Mrs. Davis's book, intending just to hold it in my hands and feel its comforting weight. But then I remembered that in my rush to get away from Brian and Tom, I had left it behind, on my dining room table in Betony Lodge.

I think that's what finally broke my spirit and corroded what inner strength I had. That's when my mental strength evaporated, and even though I'd recently decided that I'd been spending way too much time crying in the last few days, the tears came—lots of them. I ended up putting my arms around the steering wheel and resting my head upon it, sobbing. In fact, I cried so hard that I could feel the entire car rock with each wracking moan that erupted from my savaged psyche.

I can't say just how long I sat there crying; it could have been thirty minutes, or it could have been two hours. I was not thinking of time. I was not thinking at all. If I had been, I wouldn't have been so surprised when the patrol car turned into the car park.

When at last I noticed a set of headlights facing me, I lifted my head up. I thought about leaving abruptly, pealing out as fast as possible, to avoid talking to the policeman. But I couldn't very well start the car and whip it out of the car park and into the road, since that would draw suspicion and probably involve me in a police chase. So, out of options, when the policeman pulled up next to me and rolled down his window, I rolled mine down, too.

"Everything good here?" He had to shout through the teeming rain.

"Yes," I said. "I was just leaving."

"Bit late to be out! I thought the museum was closed at night?"

I nodded. "Just had some work to finish up. I'm done here, though." I started to roll up my window, but the policeman held up a warning finger and I stopped.

"Isn't safe out here, a woman by herself. Don't stop. Just go on home, that's the girl."

I bit my lip and rolled up my window, put the car into drive and turned onto the road. Would I have gone straight back to Betony Lodge if the policeman hadn't given me that bit of superfluous and patronizing advice? I'll never know, but I think I might have. As it was, the policeman's words added fuel to the fire of my discontent, stoking it and making me burn with anger and resentment. And so I took off into the night with something like a point to prove. The rain was beginning to let up, and visibility was improving. Instead of turning left onto the road, back towards Lyme Regis and Betony Lodge, I turned right.

At that moment, I had no idea where I was going; I just knew that I couldn't stay in the Museum car park all night, just as I knew that I wasn't willing to return to my flat. I drove east along the coastal road, and it wasn't until I saw the sign for the turn-off for Durdle Door and Lulworth Cove that I knew where I would go. A few days before, George Marten-Douglass had praised Durdle Door as one of the top five sights to experience in Dorset, and perversely, I decided that this night, the very point at which my life had burst apart at the seams, was the night to visit it.

As I drove along the hilly roads towards the coast, random unbidden thoughts raced through my mind. Were Brian and Tom still arguing? Had they come to blows? Did Leanne really mean to call the police to get a restraining order against me? What was happening to poor Ethan? But mostly, I wondered what Cecilia Davis would be doing in my position. Like her, I felt alone and misunderstood; as I saw it, the entire world stood leagued against me, and there was no one to listen to me and my complaints. Mrs. Davis, I told myself, would have understood me. She had been by my side throughout the last three weeks, difficult as they were; perhaps, if I called upon her help, she would help me through this, the loneliest night of my life.

I pulled into the car park that led to Durdle Door and Lulworth Cove. Of course, since it was in the early hours of the morning, there were no other cars around and I had my choice of hundreds of spaces to park in. I chose the one closest to the parking kiosk and got out of my car, taking my backpack with me. I glanced at the large map in the display window on the kiosk, but I couldn't see it in the darkness. Without directions, without having any clear idea where I was going, I began the long ascent to the ridgeline that overlooks Lulworth Cove.

It was a long, slow hike for me in mist and drizzling rain. The path was quite steep, and I grew winded within a few minutes, although my backpack was light. If I had made this trek during the day, I might have enjoyed the scenery, but as it was, I couldn't see my surroundings: only a few flashing lights off to my left, which I assumed were distant ships moving slowly across

235

the Channel. Meanwhile, the wind raced over the hill and across my path, striking me full in the face and leaving me breathless; at times I had to struggle to fill my lungs. Yet while my path was difficult, I rejoiced in moving for a change, in forcing my legs to take long, uphill strides and feeling my muscles strain at the unwonted activity. If I couldn't stop my thoughts from racing, I told myself, at least I could tire myself out physically.

It took the better part of an hour before I reached the crest of the hill. I could just make out the path that would continue down to Durdle Door, and I could tell it was narrower than the ascent was. I knew I would have to be careful if I chose to follow this route; going on into the darkness was dangerous, since tripping here could mean a deadly drop down onto the rocks below.

But I went on. I don't remember feeling any fear, only an odd compulsion to continue towards the rock formation, to see it up close. For some reason, I was drawn to it, as if it were a lodestone and I a tiny fragment of iron pulled towards it by some unknown force. I walked towards it. By looking only a few feet ahead of me, I was able to make sure that my feet found the path, and slowly, ever so slowly, I made my way down the rocky cliff path to the famed limestone arch.

It was lucky for me that the tide was out when I got down to the shoreline, or at least that it wasn't high tide. Just a few feet in front of me, I could see the inky, dark surface where waves splashed at the shore. I stood and steadied myself by putting a hand on the rocks that made up Durdle Door, rising up from the sea like a prehistoric bridge to nowhere, crawling up into the sky and then back down into the sea some yards away. Up close like this, in the darkness, it seemed like nothing special—just a large cliff face blocking my view of the ocean. I could smell the sea, and the dank breeze, musty with the odor of wet rock and moss, whipped my damp hair across my cheeks and into my eyes. The rain had stopped now, and the clouds were breaking up, tearing across the sky in thick, light-colored tufts, revealing a star here and there in the darkness behind them. I sat down on the rocks, letting my feet dangle just above the water that had pooled up into the rock depressions, and shrugged off my backpack. I was content to sit for the next little while, listening to the wind whistle through the rocks behind me and the waves lap at those below me.

I must have sat there for a long, long time; I couldn't tell, because I was not wearing a wristwatch, and of course my cell phone was back home at Betony Lodge, in some deep pocket of Tom Hardie's jacket. But I didn't care about the time. I was outside of time, beyond the reaches of time itself. My thoughts were like the clouds themselves, flitting across a blank backdrop, the gaps between them revealing just a series of impressions, a random idea here, a stray memory there.

I sat there until I felt the water begin to lap at my shoes and only then did I realize the tide was coming in. Standing up on stiff legs, I turned away from the sea and made my way back from the rocks, to the sandy strip on my right. I had to walk through about two inches of water, the wet sand sucking at my shoes, as if unwilling to let them go, but I followed the curve of the beach, nestled as it was between the cliffs rising behind it and the incessant waves pulling at the eroding shoreline. It was starting to rain again, yet I was too tired to make the climb back to my car, too numb to care about getting wet. I settled myself against the cliff face, kicked off my useless shoes, and pulled my backpack on top of me. Once again, the sky had completely clouded over, and although it had become as dark a night as I'd ever seen, I sensed somehow that dawn could not be too far off. Still, looking out towards the Channel, I could see only the whitecaps where waves were churning as they foamed over, cresting and returning to the sea that had created them.

I had come to this place because I wanted the time and space to think, to be alone with my own thoughts and emotions. But now that I was here, the only thought I had was how sorry I was that I couldn't help Cecilia Davis and others like her. I wasn't worried about Brian, or Tom, or even about Ethan: my heart ached not for myself, but for those who were prisoners of history, who had been confined, not only by the cruelty of their fellow humans, but by the obdurate, impartial silence of the inescapable passage of time.

Thoughts like these make no sense when you repeat them aloud, and they hardly make sense to me even now, after more than a year. It does no good to examine them, and I seldom do these days. They resemble feelings or intuitions, and thus do not bear analysis. I have never tried to describe them to anyone, because I knew then, as now, that no one would ever believe that such incoherent and inchoate feelings could be the reason I stayed out on the shore all night long, endangering my own life, and indeed, jeopardizing my very sanity as well.

Chapter Twenty-Three

*I, like the other patients in Warrinder house, often
succumbed to bouts of self-pity. I am ashamed now,
looking back, to think of how I used to sulk, and weep, and
walk about in a torpor of apathy, so hopeless was the
situation in which I found myself. I was not always as
compassionate as I should have been, for the other women
patients needed, as I did, a friend in adversity.
Throughout the time I was a patient, I confess I did little
to help the other women: prisoners all of us, we each
could spare so little for the benefit of our fellow-sufferers.
I did nothing to help them, and for this I feel a load of
guilt that I shall bear to my dying day.*

*I say this not to expiate my sins, Reader, for there
is nothing that I can do or say now, so many years
afterwards, that can pay for a sin of omission, but instead
to remind you that we must all remember others, even
when we are immersed in our own private travails and
hardships. The woman who cleans your fireplace may
have a sick child; the man who bakes your bread may
have just become a widower—they will never let you know
by look or word what pain they themselves bear. Be
mindful of others, and take care that you do not hurt them
unwittingly, for there is hurt enough in the world without
a careless wound inflicted by one who is herself in pain.*

----*Cecilia Davis*, My Time in a Lunatic Asylum

I have no memory of being found; by then, I was
beyond consciousness, having slipped into something that

Mrs. Davis and her ilk might have called "brain fever." I do have some dim memories of stirring from my torpor to discover that I was being carried on a stretcher up the coastal path, and of worrying that, due to the incline, I might slide off the end of it and onto the ground, tumbling, perhaps, down to the sea below. I remember, too, the raindrops pelting my face as I lay prone on the stretcher, and thinking that they were tears. Indeed, perhaps they were tears. But I could do no more than blink them away; I had not even the strength to lift my arm up to my face. I remember nothing of the ambulance ride to the hospital beyond the unfamiliar sound of the siren and lights glaring in my eyes.

When I did wake, it was to find myself in the county hospital in the central part of Dorchester, a building I'd passed many times on my way to the Museum but had never visited. Why would I? I had never intended to end up there.

I woke from my haze only after I'd spent the better part of a day in the hospital, I'm told, and even then, I had trouble recognizing people. I could neither say with certainty what day of the week it was, nor answer basic questions about the current events of the day. It was as if I had been suffering from a serious illness for weeks, instead of simply spending one night out on the beach—or, as the Brits call it, "sleeping rough."

Smell was the first sense that returned to me: gradually I became aware of the scent of the fresh-laundered sheets, then felt their crisp, institutional folds against my legs. Opening my eyes, I saw the bland white ceiling above my bed. For several minutes, I just lay there, staring into space, not knowing where I was or who I was. My sense of disconnect didn't bother me; I was well past the point of caring. At that moment, I viewed my own life much as a detached spectator views a not-very-interesting cricket match. I didn't really care who would win or lose, and I wasn't even sure I understood the rules of the game.

A young man in scrubs with dark hair and gray eyes came into my room. "Oh, smashing!" he said. "You're awake." He typed something into the computer tablet he was holding and then looked up at me. "Feeling better?" I nodded, not knowing what to say. He typed some more, then took my blood pressure and my temperature. I felt pliant and weak, so I meekly offered my arm and opened my mouth for him. I was, I think, an excellent patient.

"Feeling well enough for a visitor?" He was folding up the cuff as he said this, or he might have noticed me clutch at the sheets. I was grateful he'd waited until after he'd finished taking my blood pressure before he'd asked the question. He took my silence as assent. "Smashing," he said again. "I'll send him in a few minutes. He's been waiting for you to wake up." Again, I said nothing, just stared at the nurse as he left the room, noting that he left the door slightly ajar behind him.

I lay there, too exhausted to worry, although I confess there was a moment when I remembered Roger O. Thornhill in *North by Northwest* escaping from a hospital room by climbing through the window of his room. But of course, I had neither the energy nor the will to engage in acrobatics, and so I just lay there, my fingers caressing the stiff white sheets pulled up beneath my chin.

The fact was, I had no desire to see Brian, or anyone else for that matter. I felt exhausted, more tired than I had ever been in my life. That's why, after waiting for a few minutes with my eyes on the door, I gave into fatigue and let them drift shut. I started to doze off, but just when I began to sink below consciousness into a welcome absence of sensation, I heard someone sit down heavily in the chair beside my bed. Opening my eyes, I saw Brian peering at me, his pupils large, his eyebrows raised.

Unable to speak, I simply nodded at him and closed my eyes again, reaching after the gray oblivion of sleep in a determined effort to avoid conversation. I think I dropped off again, because the next thing I knew, Brian's hand was on my arm. I felt the warmth of it, and irrationally, I wondered whether he might have a fever. Could it be him, not me, who was ill? I did not bother to open my eyes.

"Kerys. It's me, Brian."

I nodded, wondering what he wanted from me.

"I'm sorry we fought. I didn't mean for you to storm off like that. You could have died!"

I didn't have the heart to tell him that part of me already had died, and that it was not me, Kerys, but apparently just a shell of myself lying there in the bed before him. I just lay there, pretending to be more tired than I really was, with my eyes closed. In a few minutes, I heard him get up from the chair. Then I heard the door to my room click shut, and I was able to breathe once more.

I fell back asleep almost as soon as he left the room.

The next thing I remember was a visit by a doctor, a woman who looked like she had too much to do and not enough time to do it in. It must have been some hours later, because the light filtering into my room was quite different: a soft golden glow, somewhat pleasing, had settled over the lower half of the room. I had pulled myself up into a sitting position and was contemplating the dust motes swirling in the rays over the linoleum floor.

"Mrs. Markham? Kerys?" I looked up into her deep brown eyes.

"I'm Dr. Kirmani. I'll be attending you here."

"Thank you," I said, not knowing what else to say. These were the first words I'd uttered in over 24 hours. My voice sounded foreign to me, alien, as if I'd never heard it before.

"We're running some tests on you right now, but it looks as if you're suffering from nothing more serious than exhaustion and a bit of exposure. There's nothing for you to be afraid of. I'm quite sure we'll have you out of here and back home tomorrow."

I stared at her. She was looking at me closely. I could almost detect the slight shrug of her shoulders I was looking for, the non-verbal signal that meant, "I don't understand her, but she's not my problem." She did nothing to hide it, after all, and so I was not surprised when she left immediately after typing something into her tablet.

Apparently, I was normal, healthy enough to go home, at least according to the physicians at the hospital. I only wished I believed them.

The next morning, when the nurse arrived, I thought he would give me my clothes and tell me to gather my things to prepare to leave the hospital, but he just flicked at his tablet for a few minutes, reading it and making notes. "When do I have to—when do I get to leave?" I asked, finally. But he didn't answer me; he set his tablet down on the tray by my bed and began taking my blood pressure. I waited, feeling the cuff close ever tighter on my left arm, watching him, waiting for his answer. It was hard to resist the impulse to exclaim at the tightness of the cuff, but I said nothing. The nurse looked down at the round dial in his hand, his eyebrows raised.

"Looks like your blood pressure is up a bit, Ms. Markham."

"I'm not surprised," I said. "It's quite frustrating lying here, waiting for you people to decide my fate."

He turned his head towards me, and our eyes met, as humans, not as caretaker and patient, for the first time. "Well," he said, after a moment, "we won't be bothering you too much longer. You'll be out of here this afternoon, anyway."

"Thank you," I said. He gathered his instruments and left, and I sat there for a moment, then swung my legs over the side of the bed, got up, and went to the bathroom. When I returned, Brian was sitting on my bed. I had not heard him come into my room.

"How are you, Kerys?"

"I'm ok," I said, sitting down on the visitor's chair, since Brian made no move to get up.

"Ready to come home with me?"

I stared at him. Then I shook my head.

"Come on, Kerys," Brian said, taking my limp hand in his. "We can work things out. I know we can. You've had a bad time of it, but the doctor says you're on the mend now. She said it was probably a nasty virus, but you're getting over it quickly."

"A virus?" I pulled my hand away from him.

"Yes, some kind of virus that you'd picked up. You were running a high fever when they found you. But you're getting back to normal now—the doctors and nurses all say so."

I laughed. It started out as a derisive snort, dismissing the doctors' judgment, but suddenly I saw the humor of the situation. I laughed until the tears streamed from my eyes and down my cheeks. In fact, I could not stop laughing for a quite a few minutes. Brian was growing impatient, and perhaps a little frightened as well. He took my unresisting hand again and patted it.

"What's so funny, Kerys? Share the joke with me."

"Crisscross," was all I managed to get out. What I meant is that I had effectively swapped places with Cecilia Davis, with a few crucial variations. I well knew, having studied *My Time in a Lunatic Asylum*, that her illness was physiological, the direct result of her typhoid infection; in other words, her delirium, induced by a high fever, was wrongly labeled psychological in origin by those around her. My illness, on the other hand, was clearly psychological, the result of weeks of stress, not only from a failing marriage, but from a growing persuasion that I was experiencing supernatural visitations. And yet it had been labeled physiological by the medical personnel who attended me.

Cecilia Davis and I had begun at opposite ends of the spectrum, crossed in the middle, and ended up where the other began. It was supremely comical, if one had the proper sense of humor to appreciate the situation, and apparently, I did, because I laughed so much that eventually Brian got annoyed and stood up.

"Kerys," he said, "please stop laughing. You're scaring me."

Earlier in our time together, Brian would have understood that when I'd said "crisscross," I was referring to Hitchcock's *Strangers on a Train*, a film about lives getting mixed up and switched in a macabre way. But he clearly had no idea what I was talking about that morning in the Dorchester Hospital, and he didn't think to ask what I meant. The emptiness I felt when I realized this was close to complete, as if the last link between us had vanished without a shadow. It became easier, in that moment, to stop laughing.

"Ok," I said, taking a deep breath. "Sorry. I'm not quite myself these days." I almost started laughing again at my choice of words, but I knew that if I started, I would not stop, so I swallowed, wiped my tears away, and added, "When am I supposed to check out of here, anyway?"

"Soon," said Brian, picking up a card attached to a pot of flowers that had been delivered to my room. "You've gotten several of these, you know. People—aside from Tom—that I've never heard of." He winced when he said Tom's name, and again I wondered what had happened between them. "Who's George Douglass-Marten? And Dr. Chatto?"

"They're from the Museum. I work with them."

Brian nodded. "You've made some friends here, I guess."

I had gotten back into the bed and pulled the covers up over my inadequate hospital gown. "You have, too." I watched Brian's face flush red; he turned away and looked out the window, but even the back of his neck went scarlet. I made a heroic effort not to enjoy his discomposure. I'm proud to report that I failed.

After an uneasy moment, I asked, "Did you find the Vauxhall?"

"Yes," he said, turning around and looking at me again. "I've got it in the car park below."

"So you're taking me back to Betony Lodge?"

Brian nodded. "For a while. It'll take me a few days to sort things out, but we'll be back home—real home, not England—in a few weeks."

I stared at him. "What do you mean?"

"Kerys, I thought you understood. I'm taking you back to the States. You've had a close call. *We've* had a close call, as a couple. But if we work on things, we can fix them. I know we can."

I was about to answer him, but just as I opened my mouth to begin, a nurse aide came in with one of those cloth shopping bags. She walked up to my bed and handed it to me. "I told a chap down the hall that I'd give this to you. He didn't want to come in himself, just told me to give you this."

I thanked her, and reached into the bag. My fingers closed over a book, and I sighed with pleasure, as if I had just eased myself into a warm bath. When I pulled out *My*

Time at a Lunatic Asylum, I knew that it was Tom Hardie who had brought it for me.

"What's that?" Brian had walked over to my bed and was craning his neck to look at the book. Instinctively, I put it back into the bag.

"Nothing important," I said. "Just a book. Get the car ready, Brian. I'm ready to go back home. To Betony Lodge."

Chapter Twenty-Four

Deal, then, her groping skill no scorn, no note
of malediction;
Not long on thee will press the hand that hurts
the lives it loves;
And while she plods dead-reckoning on, darkness
of affliction,
Assist her where thy creaturely dependence can
or may,
For thou art of her clay.

--Thomas Hardy, "The Lacking Sense"

I still find it sad that, even in the final days of my relationship with Brian, I could not tell him about Cecilia Davis's book. Apparently I had missed my one opportunity to do so, and it was not possible for me to rewind events and emotions to rectify this. However, I was able to explain to him, quite clearly and on several occasions, how necessary it was that he take his possessions and leave me to live by myself in Betony Lodge.

"I don't understand," he said, the very last time we broached the subject. We were back in the flat, and I was sitting on the couch. "I've said I was sorry. I've promised I'd never do anything like that again." He looked at me from across the room, where he was making us some tea. "You know I really do love you, Kerys. It was just a fling. Men have flings. Some women have flings, too."

I looked up from *My Time at Lunatic Asylum*. "I

guess they do," I said, not really interested in the conversation.

"I mean," he said, staring at me as he poured the tea into our mugs, "I could easily ask you what kind of a 'friendship' you had with that Tom Hardie guy, couldn't I?"

"You could," I said. "But you won't."

He brought the mugs over to the couch, almost tripping over Diggory in transit. The kitten squealed and ran off to hide under the bed. "I'm not so sure I won't, Kerys. He was awfully combative the night you…the night you disappeared. I think he might be more interested in you than you realize."

I sighed and took the cup of tea from Brian. "You know, Brian, there are many more ways to relate to people beyond the mere physical."

"Yes, but the physical is the easiest and the most common way of relating to other people. Freud said that, I think."

"I'm not so sure he did. But even if he did say it, it's irrelevant. It has nothing to do with you and me. Tom Hardie has nothing to do with you and me. All that matters is that we made a mistake. We rushed things. We never should have gotten married. Maybe it was easier to do it that way, but that doesn't mean it was right. And as it turns out, I know now that it was wrong."

Brian started to argue, but I didn't want to listen any more. He'd been arguing with me about this for the last two days, ever since I'd come home from the hospital, when I insisted he sleep on the couch while I took the bedroom. He simply didn't seem to understand that I was done—finished with him, with us.

Not willing to continue the conversation, I set aside my book, took my coat from the hook, and left the flat. I went down the stairs and headed out the back door into the garden. I needed some fresh air; I needed to feel connected to Betony Lodge. Or rather—I might as well say it—to Warrinder House and the people who had once lived in it.

I saw now that their lives had become more real to me than my own. I wanted to be having tea with Cecilia Davis or Dr. Bellemeade, not with Brian. I wanted to console the patients of Warrinder House, to bring out their stories, to make up for the evil things that had been done to them. I felt like a character from one of those time-travel stories; if only I believed enough, I would somehow be transported back to the 1840s and meet one of the patients, Mrs. Davis herself, perhaps, out in the back gardens. I stood there and closed my eyes for a moment, wishing for a miracle.

Instead, I felt the wind pick up and a few drops of rain plinking at the crown of my head. I walked through the grounds and up to the trees that were encroaching on the property. Even then, I didn't stop; I went well into the forest, making my way over leaves and moss, climbing uphill through the brush and beyond the scrubby outlying trees, into the darkness of the mature wood. If there was a path, I couldn't find it, yet I went on, because I was determined to get to the top of the tree-covered hill that morning so that I could look down upon Betony Lodge and survey its grounds.

It was a good twenty minutes before I reached the

peak of the hill; I'd had to rest on the way, leaning against the rugged bole of an oak whose solidity buoyed my spirits. At last I made it to the crest of the hill, just as the shower stopped and the sun emerged from the clouds. I turned around and looked back towards the way I'd come.

Below me and to my left lay Betony Lodge, like a house in one of those miniature models of towns that retirees spend their final years making. The roofline was clearly visible, and I thought about those thirty minutes I had spent on it with Ethan. The boy was gone now; Leanne and Gary had decided to move away, into Lyme, hoping to avoid any more incidents. I couldn't help but think they were simply trying to separate me from Ethan.

Out in the distance, I could see the Channel, a wide, flat ribbon stretching across the horizon, framing the woodlands and the town of Lyme Regis with a comforting border. I could not see Lyme itself; the town was hidden beneath the curve of the hill I was standing on. I wondered whether Mrs. Davis had ever climbed up here and looked down upon the house that had become her prison. I hoped she had, because from this perspective, all lives looked small and inconsequential, my own most of all. And that made all the pain easier to bear, somehow.

I jumped when I heard his voice, even though I had been expecting it all along.

"Hello, Kerys." Tom Hardie was walking along the ridgeline, his metal detector on his shoulder. "I wanted to call and see how you were doing, but it seemed too...complicated." He stopped walking when he approached me and set the end of the detector on the ground, leaning the handle against a tree trunk.

"Thanks, Tom," I said. "I'm doing fine." We both turned and looked out at the ocean for a moment, and then I added, "Thank you for thinking to bring me the book. It was very kind of you."

"You're welcome," said Tom. "Here—take these things as well. You might be needing them." He handed me my cell phone, as well as Mrs. Davis's locket.

"You took it from my flat?" He dropped the locket into my palm and my fingers closed tight around it. I said nothing about my cell phone, and I was grateful that Tom didn't, either.

"I wanted to make sure it stayed safe. After all, I had no idea that Brian chap really was your...."

He hesitated, and I finished the sentence for him. "Husband. Well, we're all entitled to make one mistake in life, aren't we?" I turned back to look at the Channel. "Anyway, he won't be for long. But thanks for taking care of the locket. It's very important to me."

"I know," said Tom. We both stood there for a few minutes, saying nothing, just looking out at the sea beneath us. Finally, Tom picked up his metal detector and put it on his shoulder. "Look, Kerys, when you get everything sorted, if you want to go detecting again, or if you just want to compare notes, give me a call." As soon as he said that, I knew he wouldn't pester me with phone calls and invitations, that he was content to wait until I was ready to call him. And I was grateful for such true-hearted patience.

"Thanks, Tom," I said. "I will."

The sun went back behind a cloud, and as the wind picked up and the rain began to fall again, we parted, I to go back down the hill towards Betony Lodge, and Tom back through the forest, retracing his path.

Chapter Twenty-Five

"Heart-halt and spirit-lame
  City-opprest,
Unto this wood I came
  As to a nest;
Dreaming that sylvan peace
Offered the harrowed ease—
Nature a soft release,
  From men's unrest."
      --Thomas Hardy, "In a Wood"

That's how I ended up here, in Betony Lodge,
living by myself in a house that is big enough for three
families. I don't mind the solitude; I rather enjoy it. The
construction going on in the large flat downstairs, the one
that Ethan kept entering, doesn't bother me, either;
constant noise might upset some tenants, but I'm used to
noises, after all, and when I let myself into the flat, after
the workmen and women have left, I am fascinated by the
way I can see Warrinder House emerge from the tasteless
modern decor that has covered it for so many years. It's
liberating to watch, and I go down there pretty much every
evening to see what else has been set free, released from
the tawdry improvements of the twentieth century.

   While I miss Ethan, it is a relief not to have to run
interference between him and his parents. His sensibilities
were too finely wrought, I think, to live in a place such as
this, and whenever I see him in Lyme, as I sometimes do
when I am shopping or when I have stopped to meet Tom
for a pint at the Angry Badger, he seems a normal little

boy, happy to scurry across the playground, chasing after balls and playing tag with the other children.

As for Brian, I fully expect him to marry Bronwyn as soon as our divorce is final. England—or Wales, rather—has been very good to him, allowing him to make a splash in its literary world, and it comes as no surprise that he wants to stay there. Several months ago, I saw his picture in the *Times Literary Supplement*; it was taken at one of his poetry readings. Bronwyn was standing next to him, their arms around each other's waists, and they were smiling into the camera. The bulge showing beneath Bronwyn's tight sweater suggested that Brian will soon be adding a child to his list of accomplishments.

As for me, I'm finishing my research on Thomas Hardy, and although my fellowship will soon run out, I signed an additional year's lease at Betony Lodge. Like Brian, I'm in no hurry to return to the States. I have edited Cecilia Davis's book, and next year it will be re-issued, with my introduction; after I presented a paper on it at a conference, a well-known publisher approached me with a contract. The "discovery" of the book, as well as the doll, was handled quite ingeniously by Tom, who claimed he had unearthed it at a car boot sale ("garage sale" to Yanks). The Lyme Regis Library never inquired after the book, and I still have the original volume, although I plan to donate it to the Hardy Museum when my edition is in print—that is, if I find that I can part with it. Tom keeps the doll that Ethan gave me on a shelf in his workroom, he tells me.

I have decided that I will stay here, in Betony Lodge, as long as possible. After all, here I have the beginnings of a professional life that is so much richer than it would have been in the States. Besides, I like it here; Lyme Regis is a jewel of a town, and George Marten-Douglass was right when he said that Dorset was full of wonderful sights. Durdle Door, impressive as it was at night, is simply magnificent by day, and I never tire of the other places on his list.

Above all, the woods behind Betony Lodge are delightful to roam, and I am learning my way through them, discovering old footpaths that lead up onto the heath and some that lead down to the town below. I have even found the path that Tom Hardie uses to come here, and one morning not so long ago I surprised him by showing up at his house, a small cottage at the end of a little-used lane.

Tom and I are good friends now, close friends. Will it develop into anything more? I don't know. He's twice my age, and I suspect that that point, as well as the fact that I am a scholar and belong to a world in which he has no part, is an impediment for him, as it is for me. But, as I said, we are friends, and I am happy if that's all we remain. Good friends are so much harder to find than lovers, after all.

And as for Cecilia Davis, I will say, since it is unlikely that anyone I know will ever read this account, that I still hear her from time to time, but thankfully there are no more sobs or moans. Sometimes I even hear laughter, girlish giggles that make me smile at some unheard joke; but most of the time, I am aware of her only because of a pervasive sense that there is someone else here with Diggory and me.

I am never lonely at Betony Lodge, because I know that, like the thicket of trees rising behind the house, a living forest clinging to its steep slope within sight of the slate-blue sea, I belong here. Just like the small animals that scurry through the brush, chittering and barking as they scurry up to their nests in the weathered oaks, I have become a part of this place. Often, sitting on the hill behind my house, I watch the birds that light upon its roof, thinking I am like them; they stay for hours, singing, though free to fly off in any direction. What a gift to have discovered peace in this house and its environs, comfortably nestled in the wilderness of my own mind! For the first time in many months—perhaps the first time in my entire life—I am happy, because here at Betony Lodge, I have found my home.

If you have enjoyed *Betony Lodge*, you may also enjoy reading the first book of the ***Asylum*** series, *Effie Marten*—available as a Kindle book and in paperback from Amazon.

83202156R00164

Made in the USA
Columbia, SC
09 December 2017